"You were going to instruct me?" Greg questioned.

Didn't the woman have an ounce of conscience? he wondered. If she leaned any closer, he'd need to be a saint to resist the temptation of her lips.

"You don't know how to..." *Kiss.* The word almost slipped out. Flustered, Catherine looked down at her dangling foot. "The arch. You begin wrapping around the arch."

The beaten egg white on the rag was cold. His hands hot in comparison. Catherine blamed these sensations for the breathless quality of her voice.

"Now wrap it once around the ankle, then again over the arch and back again. Not too loose. No, no, that's much too tight."

"Make up your mind!" he snapped. Greg couldn't blame her. It was all his fault. And it had nothing to do with being in her bedroom; he'd viewed his share. It wasn't even the sight of her dimpled knee, or shapely calf, or dainty toes that made him testy. It could be blamed on his unwillingness to hurt her and the simple knowledge that touching her played havoc with his heart rate.

Dear Reader,

Multi-award-winning author Theresa Michaels has long been a favorite of our readers, and if the response to the first book in her new series is any indication, her trilogy of Westerns about three widows who are best friends is going to be a wonderful success. In this month's title, *The Merry Widows—Catherine,* a city banker forced to spend a year recuperating in the country goes head-to-head with a practical country widow and learns that some of life's greatest pleasures are the simple ones.

Corruption, jealousy and the shadow of barrenness threaten the love of a beautiful Saxon woman who has a year to produce an heir, or be separated forever from the knight who holds her heart, in Shari Anton's stirring medieval tale, *By King's Decree.* And in *Devlin,* by author Erin Yorke, an Irish rebel and an Englishwoman whose life he saved must battle distrust and betrayal before finding the happiness they both deserve.

Deborah Simmons also returns this month with *The de Burgh Bride,* the sequel to her steamy adventure, *Taming the Wolf.* This book is the story of the scholarly de Burgh brother, Geoffrey, who has drawn the short straw and must marry the "wicked" daughter of a vanquished enemy, a woman who reportedly murdered her first husband in the marriage bed!

Whatever your tastes in reading, we hope you enjoy all four books this month. Keep an eye out for them, wherever Harlequin Historicals® are sold.

Sincerely,

Tracy Farrell
Senior Editor

THE MERRY WIDOWS

Catherine

THERESA MICHAELS

Harlequin Books

TORONTO • NEW YORK • LONDON
AMSTERDAM • PARIS • SYDNEY • HAMBURG
STOCKHOLM • ATHENS • TOKYO • MILAN
MADRID • WARSAW • BUDAPEST • AUCKLAND

ISBN 0-373-29000-4

THE MERRY WIDOWS—CATHERINE

Copyright © 1998 by Theresa DiBenedetto

Books by Theresa Michaels

Harlequin Historicals

A Corner of Heaven #104
Gifts of Love #145
Fire and Sword #243
Once a Maverick #276
Once an Outlaw #296
Once a Lawman #316
†*The Merry Widows—Mary* #372
†*The Merry Widows—Catherine* #400

Harlequin Books

Renegades 1996
"Apache Fire"

*The Kincaid Trilogy
†The Merry Widows

THERESA MICHAELS

is a former New Yorker who resides in south Florida with her husband and daughter—the last of eight children—and three "rescued" cats. Her avid interest in history and her belief in the power of love are combined in her writing. She has received the *Romantic Times* Reviewers' Choice Award for Best Civil War Romance, the National Readers' Choice Award for Best Series Historical and the B. Dalton Bookseller Award for Bestselling Series Historical. When not writing, she enjoys traveling, adding to her collection of Victorian perfume bottles and searching for the elf to master her computer.

For all my readers.

Chapter One

❧❧❧

He figured he was paying for past sins, large and small, maybe even some unknown that he had never dared acknowledge.

This was the latest reason Gregory Mayfield added to the mental list he composed as cause for his present torment, and to keep his sanity.

Others already explored and listed involved his younger sister Suzanne. Those reasons had definite cause and effect, others were shimmering so faintly that only the spider spinning the web was aware of the connection.

Under the guise of sisterly love, Suzanne, charming minx and dearest to him of all, was certainly capable of offering him torture along with a possible cure.

And in that hope he was suffering through his third day of travel with one Mrs. Horace Pettigrew.

If he had Suzanne within reach, he would disregard his long-held friendship with her husband, and Suzanne's excellent mothering of the most delightful brood of children, and take serious steps to send his sister on to a greater reward.

Most likely, Suzanne would come back and haunt him.

Another dip in the road, another bone-jarring jolt of the stage traveling at breakneck speed toward the town of Hillsboro. Mrs. Pettigrew began another series of cooing noises.

His fellow passenger, so generously endowed that she required a seat to herself, coaxed her Blenheim spaniel to have another bonbon to calm his tummy.

Gregory spared a glance at his seatmate, a drummer who had tried selling him one of his Colt pistol samples when he discovered that Gregory didn't own a gun. The man snored in his corner, owing to the empty flask still gripped in one hand.

"Won't you have a bonbon, Mr. Mayfield?"

Gregory swallowed hard as his gaze returned to Mrs. Pettigrew. Her coy voice ruffled his nerve ends. He sympathized with the little dog being fed more candy. But not verbally. He had learned his lesson on that score.

"Thank you, but I must refuse." He watched the drooping sway of the feathered profusion extended from her hat. Fat sausage curls framed her face. Gregory couldn't help but liken her curls to the dog's long ears.

The air inside the stage was stifling. Undoubtedly, it was cooler outside. Mrs. Pettigrew insisted the leather coverings be rolled down and tied in place over the windows once they got under way. She proclaimed there was no view worth mentioning on this stretch of road in the New Mexico Territory. Gregory had to take her word. He had never been west of the Mississippi.

Any gentleman worthy of the name would have given in as graciously as he had done. But he longed for a cooling breeze as the drummer was not prone to frequent bathing. And when he added the fumes of the empty flask to the dog's excited, damp little accidents concealed in the ponderous folds of his mistress's gown, it was sheer bravado that he hadn't lost the contents of his stomach.

As if directed by his thought, the stage's violent rocking sent his stomach churning.

It was a pity he couldn't find comfort in the driver's claim that the stage line had not lost a passenger all week. He shuddered to think what the prior records would reveal.

He had truly come to a sorry pass when such mundane thoughts occupied his time. He liked to blame all the changes he had undergone on his illnesses of the past few months, and often did when questioned. But he admitted to himself that the vague restlessness and boredom had set in long before he had been laid low. It made no sense no matter how many times he examined his feelings.

He liked his ordered life. Routine and organization in all things led to a man's contentment.

Or so he had believed. What had gone wrong? When had he begun adding his own silent questions to those of his sister's about the life he had made for himself? Why was he no longer happy?

The jolting sway of the stage as it followed a sharp dip in the road made him close his eyes. Just in time, too. He could see Mrs. Pettigrew getting ready another of her random remarks, which would lead to another round of prying questions. Lord, spare him from matchmaking mamas.

His fortune, amassed through shrewd investments, made him a prime target for those marriage-minded individuals who longed for company in their misery. He received enough invitations from New York's blue book to keep four men entertained. But he no longer accepted invitations to weekend house parties. Twice he had found unwanted bedmates waiting in his room. One, an attractive widow who made no secret that her husband gambled away her fortune, and the other, a young woman barely out of the schoolroom. He had immediately retreated, found his host for a nightcap and suggested a game of billiards with high enough stakes to while away the night. No one was going to trap him into marriage.

His illness ended the business arrangement with his latest mistress, one in a long string of discreet relationships. Emotional entanglements were not for him. He'd watched one too many friends set aside dreams of the great feats they were going to accomplish, once they had been dragged to the altar. There were times when he wished that his parents or his aunt and uncle were alive, but never when he saw the manipulations those relatives used to enlarge fortune and family.

His sister truly had no idea how lucky she was to have made a love match with an eminently suitable man.

And, as he had assured her time and again, eventually he would marry. But never to someone with Suzanne's independent nature. She led her husband a merry dance with her involvements in arenas women had no place being.

Yet he couldn't abide an insipid miss who couldn't string two thoughts together, much less speak them without consulting her mother.

Other men envied him. They sought his advice on matters of business as well as those of a more delicate nature. They especially admired his adroit evasion of the matchmakers, including his sister. He hadn't met a woman yet who made him desire her company for more than a few hours, outside of bed, that is.

Suzanne, from her privileged place as his only living blood relative—her family aside—declared him a cynic whose stubbornness would be his ruination.

She wished him happy, and to her that meant marriage. The woman, much as he loved her, was an infernal thorn in his side.

Gossip cloaked as conversation bored him. He didn't care who was seen in the company of whom, and why it mattered. He didn't care to know why the merchant princes—of stockyard, railroad and mining fame—were buying impoverished British titles, and the men who claimed them, for their debutante daughters. Nor did it interest him to know—a fact that Suzanne found deplorable—that more young women were turned out of Miss Bidwell's Finishing School to become brides in their first social season.

Nonsense. The lot of it. He made no secret that a woman quickly lost her appeal, no matter how lovely she was, if beauty and breeding were all she had to offer.

What roused his hunting instinct was the challenge of putting together a successful business deal against odds that were nigh on impossible. Suzanne, with sisterly concern, claimed he was obsessed with making money, and that obsession would likely kill him.

Pride stopped him from admitting that she might be right. It was a painful admission to make, that having faced death's door, he now found even his greatest joy had begun to pall.

The stress of his thoughts brought back the nameless

dissatisfaction to a greater degree. He pressed one hand against his midsection as if he could contain the knife-like burning pangs setting fire to his stomach.

"Mr. Mayfield? You've grown quite pale." Mrs. Pettigrew leaned forward to touch his arm.

Gregory opened his eyes. He felt beads of sweat on his forehead and quickly used the handkerchief from his inner jacket pocket to wipe his face.

"Won't you have one of our bonbons?" she asked in a solicitous manner. "Posie won't mind sharing. You can see how calm they have kept my little darling."

Gregory refused. Politely, firmly, and then hoped the woman wouldn't pursue another inane conversation about her pet.

Alas, his hope was crushed as he was once more treated to the history of the spaniel's breeding. It was a measure of the good manners instilled at an early age and reinforced by society that he managed to maintain his civility. He nodded, not really paying attention, for he had no choice. Well, that wasn't quite true, he reminded himself. He could ride outside on the driver's seat.

And as she talked, Mrs. Pettigrew continued to unwrap another candy, pinched off a bit and fed it to the dog, then plopped the balance into her mouth. All was done with accompanying cooing noises.

With the windows blocked there was no place for him to look but the floor. Someday, his sister would pay for this.

Gregory slipped his gold pocket watch from his vest pocket just as Mrs. Pettigrew lifted the watch pinned to her ample breast.

"Won't be much longer now, Mr. Mayfield. Are you

being met? If not, my daughter's carriage will convey you to your destination.''

"No need to concern yourself. I'm quite sure there will be someone there to meet the stage." It was a necessary lie. He never offended women if he could help himself. Even bores like Mrs. Pettigrew. But he had no intention of continuing any association once they arrived in Hillsboro.

Suzanne had made all the arrangements with an old school friend she had kept in touch with. His sister promised he would have peace and, most of all, privacy to regain his health. Avoiding any future contact with Mrs. Pettigrew was the first step toward that goal. He folded his hands across his stomach and closed his eyes.

Two bouts of pneumonia had taken their toll on him. But it wasn't until Suzanne found out about the increased stomach ailments no matter what he ate that she went to war. After numerous arguments—himself on one side, his sister, her husband and learned physicians on the other—Suzanne threatened to keep him from seeing the children he adored. She gave him a browbeating worthy of the veriest shrew. Then, she turned and pleaded that she feared he would meet an untimely end on his present path.

He had had to give in.

Gregory hoped the widow Hill, soon to provide his bed and board, was the opposite of Mrs. Pettigrew.

The first loud crack made him attribute the sound to the driver's whip. The rolling rumbles that followed brought a sage announcement from Mrs. Pettigrew.

"Just a cloudburst, Mr. Mayfield. Our spring weather, don't you know. The sun will be out before you know it.'' She confirmed this with a peek behind the leather shade.

Rain struck immediately, proving the woman right. She winked at him behind her spectacles. The dog whimpered. She drew her shawl around the pug-nosed pet, whispering that the storm would pass quickly.

Gregory wasn't so sure. The rain sounded more like hail striking the trunks and baggage piled on top of the stage. The drummer next to him stirred, emitted a loud snore, then relaxed back in slumber. The forceful drumming noise thankfully obliterated Mrs. Pettigrew's voice.

The mere thought of having the stage mired in mud with him confined for a longer period of time with this woman and pet made him inwardly shudder. He was no coward, but he wondered if he could walk the rest of the way. And this, despite the threat of another bout of pneumonia. His fingers tightened on the sterling silver knob of his walking stick.

Surely the fates would not be so cruel.

As if in answer, the stage lurched to one side of the road. He prayed harder for journey's end. A quick end, he amended as candy was once more offered to cure his travel sickness.

The stage appeared to take a turn in the road on two wheels. Another lurch nearly unseated him. The woman's basket, residing on the seat beside her, spilled its contents on the floor. A thick, dried sausage fell on his foot. Jars went rolling. The dog's yips were added to Mrs. Pettigrew's mixture of apology and fear that her goody basket was ruined.

Just as Gregory reached for a jar beneath his seat, a crack sounded. He was thrown forward. He saved himself from landing on the woman's lap by bracing his hands against the seat. When he tried to right himself, he found the stage rocking to a stop. The floor was now tilted.

Mrs. Pettigrew's alarmed cries were more than he could stand. He bolted outside and promptly got soaked.

The driver, Reggie Humbolt, glared at him. "I'll have that backward by-blow of Charlie's fired for this. Look what he's done."

Gregory glanced from the man's pointing finger to the wheel. It wasn't quite off, but hanging by a hair.

"Can you fix it?"

"Don't see why we can't. You tell Mrs. Pettigrew to sit tight and rouse that drummer."

"I heard you, Mr. Humbolt. You can be assured I will sit right here. I charge you to hurry. Poor Posie is a nervous wreck with your reckless driving."

"Wasn't my driving, ma'am. Was Charlie's boy that didn't do as he was told. Warned him that wheel seemed loose. Told him to check it. I might be old, ma'am, but I ain't blind. Know when something needs doin'."

Gregory wiped the water dripping down his face and leaned against the door. "Mrs. Pettigrew, might I impose on you to wake the gentleman?"

"He's drunk. Didn't turn a hair when we stopped."

"Please try. I believe we'll need his help." He was thankful that his daily bouts of fencing kept him in good physical shape. And he discovered that beneath Mrs. Pettigrew's breast, there beat the heart of a shrew. She prodded the drummer with the tip of her parasol, calling curses upon his head, invoking him to wake up and help his betters or suffer deserved persecution at the hands of the newly formed Hillsboro temperance league.

The man mumbled, curled to his side and snored.

"Worthless," the woman announced.

And that ended that.

Reggie removed a short, stout log from beneath the stage, then a shovel. "We'll get this fixed in a shake of a calf's tail. You wedge the shovel beneath the wheel while I brace it up. We'll knock it back in place and be on our way."

"Sounds simple enough." Gregory harbored doubts, but he was willing to try. Rain soaked his clothing until it clung to his skin. He followed Reggie's orders, but the man had no idea that Gregory had never used a shovel. The mud made it easy to position the shovel beneath the wheel, but each time he exerted his weight, he sank into the mud. Martin, his valet, would cringe to see his half boots and vocally despair of ever setting them to rights. It was the least of his problems.

Sitting in a stagecoach for three days had not kept his muscles limber despite the continuous jolts and swaying. The strain of his effort to follow Reggie's gruff orders showed with immediate aches and a sweat. Chilled to the bone, he swore as rain collected in his hat brim, and each time he bent his head, water dripped down to blind him.

Gregory lost track of time. Finally, Reggie motioned him aside and pounded the wheel back onto the axle with his stout board. Shaking from his labor and the lingering weakness of his illness, Gregory had to make several attempts before he entered the stage.

Mrs. Pettigrew unselfishly offered him her shawl as he regained his seat. He refused, and thanked her for the kind offer.

He needed a blanket. A thick wool one. And a down-filled comforter. Woolen socks and his cashmere robe. A fire. A hot bath, and Martin bringing him a stein of hot buttered rum.

And quiet. Blessedly peaceful quiet.

Not, he thought, necessarily in that order. But all would be most welcome. He couldn't have any of the material things his wealth afforded to comfort him. He couldn't even have relief from the woman's infernal fussing.

So he sat, dripping water and plastered with mud, squishing in his corner of the seat as Reggie sent the horses racing along.

There was nothing whatsoever he could do about the matter. There was really no point now in teasing his mind with the horrors his rash decision might have in store for him.

But his thoughts turned to his coming meeting with the widow Hill. Lord, grant this one wish. Let the woman be kind and compassionate, and have an obedient streak the width of Mrs. Pettigrew's bustle.

"And mute," he muttered as the solicitous woman prosed on about the ailments one could take from a chill.

Definitely mute. Gregory glanced balefully at the unconscious figure of the snoring drummer, wriggled downward in his seat and closed his eyes.

The Lord and fate would never be so cruel as to deny him his wish.

Chapter Two

Catherine Rose Hill in twenty-two years had never outgrown her love for surprises. She believed that to be true until today. And as her income-producing flock of chickens had grown over this past year, she had developed a tendency to name her days after the various ways to cook eggs.

Some days were as soft as a three-minute egg, a few were hard-boiled, some deviled, others poached. Here and there were scrambled days, others perfect sunny-side up ones—which Catherine loved best of all. Then came over-easy days, a second favorite. Of course, there were the rare rotten ones.

This lovely April day of 1882 had brought to her home in Hillsboro in the New Mexico Territory a surprise. One Gregory Michael Mayfield the third, rolled in a rotten, scrambled, bedeviled omelette.

Her paying houseguest—and from the amount of luggage in the Bott's Livery buckboard, it could be no one else—had arrived three weeks early.

Catherine, perched in the upper branches of a newly budded cottonwood tree, wondered if she had made a terrible mistake in agreeing with her friend's madcap scheme to save her brother from himself.

In the next moment she reversed her thinking. It was uncharitable to doubt her friend's motives as anything but sincere. The man had been ill, was in need of rest.

A more practical side of her nature reminded her of the fact that she had already spent his money. She didn't have the funds to replace what he'd paid, and couldn't back out of the arrangement she had made with his sister.

Friends did not desert each other when in need. And Suzanne, despite the miles and years that separated them, was a good friend.

Still, Catherine hesitated to make her presence known to him.

There was something odd about his appearance as he climbed down from the buckboard and approached the front of the house. Suzanne had warned her that her brother was a stickler for social niceties. He'd be appalled if she called out to him while up the tree.

But Catherine's hard-won independence and all it entailed reasserted itself. She no longer depended upon anyone to order her days or make decisions for her. Those restrictive days had ended with her husband's death. She could handle one male boarder for a short time. Only a month. If all went well with her friend Mary's birthing, then Sarah, a widow like herself and owner of the house, would return before the end of Mr. Mayfield's stay.

Then again, Sarah had been vague about when she would return.

Catherine pressed back against the crook of the tree. If asked at this moment, she couldn't have explained why she continued her hidden observation of the perplexed male who peered into the parlor window.

But he was closer now. A black brimmed hat hid his face. She realized the brim drooped. Some new fashion from New York, no doubt.

He stepped to the edge of the porch. Catherine looked straight down at him. The impeccably tailored gray suit clung to his wiry build. There was something wrong with the way he looked, but she couldn't define it. She wished she remembered more of Gregory Mayfield as he had been, to better judge the man he had become.

But impressions made on a six-year-old mind of a young man sent off to military school were at best vague. Gregory, at fourteen, had had little time for either his sister or her friends.

Enough musing! She had to get down with the kitten she had climbed the tree to rescue without Mr. Mayfield seeing her. Easier thought than done.

If Lord Romeo behaved as an adult cat should, he would be the one caught out on a limb.

The tabby kitten resisted her coaxing. Catherine braced herself. She lifted the kitten and tucked it between her shirt and camisole. Freeing a bit more of her shirt from her pants made a pocket.

"Poor baby," she whispered, wincing as the kitten's tiny claws, sharp as needles, pierced her skin. "We'll both owe Lord Romeo for this one."

The weighty, battle-scarred tom with orange-marmalade and new-cream-colored stripes felt it was beneath his dignity to climb trees for any reason. But then, Lord Romeo had other uncatlike traits she tried not to dwell upon.

The sudden pounding on the front door warned her

of her guest's impatience. And Suzanne would not appreciate the welcome, or rather the lack of one, that Catherine offered her brother. Not after the trouble Suzanne had gone to getting her brother to agree to this trip.

But why did the man have to arrive so early!

Catherine felt for the branch below with one foot. When her footing was secure, she stretched once more for a lower limb. Her hands scraped against the bark of the tree as she slid a little. She tried to ignore the mewling of the frightened kitten, but she couldn't ignore the claws digging into her tender skin.

She couldn't press tight to the trunk or she would crush the kitten. Her arms were stretched high above her head, her long legs stretched below as she sought firm purchase on another limb.

Just as her foot pressed against the solid branch, the kitten wiggled its way to her side. Catherine released the branch with one hand to hold the kitten still while she was placing her other foot on the limb below.

She had never mastered the art of tree climbing. Her parents did not believe in allowing her to learn boyish skills. Marriage to Louis offered neither the chance nor the desire to indulge in a childish joy.

She was trying to hurry. The kitten moved once again, this time clawing its way up until the tiny head with ears laid back popped out of her shirt. She was startled. But her move to push the kitten beneath her shirt cost her her balance.

Her hand failed to grab hold. Her feet slipped from the branch and down she went.

Her ankle wrenched beneath her as she twisted to land on her back. She flung her hands over her face to protect herself as the kitten clawed, then scampered over her head before bolting toward the barn. Lord Romeo gave chase.

Catherine hurt in so many places that she didn't know which one to think of first. Squeezing her eyes shut and hiding beneath the cover of her hands was only momentary relief. She suddenly sensed a male presence close by.

She'd thought she was at a disadvantage only minutes before, but now she was dismayed to find herself sprawled on the new spring grass at the feet of the man.

A quick peek showed muddy boots. Where could he have gotten mud on his boots? There had been no rain this week.

Hiding was ridiculous. She was not a coward, despite the overprotective upbringing and marriage she'd endured. She flung her arms to her sides and opened her eyes. She stared at him. He looked as if someone had dunked him in a horse trough. Either that, or this man went swimming with his suit on.

But hope was not dead. She smiled. "Please tell me you're lost and stopped to ask directions."

"Only if you'll tell me you're not the widow Hill," Gregory countered.

"Oh dear," she muttered. That crushed the hope she harbored. He was Suzanne's brother. The way he leaned over her made her attempt to rise awkward.

Racked with a chill, Gregory straightened. He eyed the woman sprawled at his feet with a sense of doom. "So, am I graced with the...er...presence of Mrs. Hill? Or have you just dropped in to add misery to an already horrendous day?"

Stuffed shirt! "Ah, you're one of those," she muttered, letting her impulsive nature rule her tongue.

He stepped back. "I beg your forgiveness not to pursue that remark."

Catherine's smile disappeared. The sarcastic bite of his voice left no room to find humor in this. She struggled to remember charity was a virtue. The man had been seriously ill, he had been traveling for days. They couldn't have all been sunny ones, either, to judge from his damp clothes. She tilted her head back to look at his face.

Suzanne's description of her brother left a great deal to be desired...like the truth. There was a definite hitch in her breathing. She knew it was rude to keep staring at him, but couldn't stop herself from doing it.

She attempted to reconcile the man eyeing her with distaste with the boy she vaguely remembered from childhood.

The two remained separate.

He was not a handsome man. Not that she set a great store on a man's looks. Not anymore. Gregory Michael Mayfield III had pride stamped on his features in a lean and predatory face saved from ruthlessness by the natural seductive curve of his lips. Intensely male features. Strong. And this despite the illness that had left him pale.

Dark brown hair, neatly trimmed to collar length, appeared thick. His sideburns swept his lean cheeks. His eyes were a green so dark they almost appeared black, but were saved by a scattering of gold flecks. At least she thought they were gold flecks. It could have been a trick of sun and shadow.

A poet's face with a warrior's eyes.

His brows nearly met over a straight, thin nose as his frown deepened while she continued staring up at him. Rarely at a loss for words, Catherine couldn't think of one to say. The man and her position defeated her. What had happened to the backbone she had been firming from the first months of her widowed state? Likely it was crushed beneath her or squished beneath the man's boots.

She glanced at his hands, extended to help her up. He wore driving gloves. Finely tanned ones, too. Louis disdained wearing them. He had been proud of his hardworking, callused hands. She suddenly remembered that Mr. Mayfield was a man who dealt with enormous sums of money, while her savings amounted to one hundred and sixty-three dollars and thirteen cents. But while Mr. Mayfield had amassed a fortune that cost him his health, she had nothing to be ashamed of. She had worked hard for the first time in her life to earn every cent she had saved.

"Far be it from me to rush a lady," Greg said with every attempt to keep irritation from his voice, "but I must insist that you show me to my room."

"So sorry to keep you waiting," she snapped. But as Catherine reached for his extended hand, Lord Romeo returned to protect her. She rolled to her side, her glaring look a silent communication that her cat should stay put. She waved Greg off when she saw Lord Romeo was not going to obey her.

The massive tom, marmalade hair bristling, one ear pressed flat to his head, the other—torn in a long-ago fight—dropped to one side, giving him a quizzical look, wiggled his body into an attack crouch. Battered appearance aside, the cat—as most animals discovered—was a fierce opponent.

"No! Don't!" Catherine ordered the cat, and to Greg said, "Get back."

With a hissing growl the cat lunged for Greg's hand.

Greg, his expression one of disbelief, barely managed to snatch his hand up and away in time.

First the bonbon-eating Posie, now this mangled-looking creature. Outside of enough! His only association with cats brought the opinion they were placid, downright lazy creatures content to sit and stare out a window for hours. Or else they rubbed against one's black evening trousers, leaving behind copious amounts of hair that were an embarrassment and the despair of his valet.

"Don't touch the cat," she warned. Then made cooing noises to coax Lord Romeo to her.

Greg ignored her, his gaze riveted on the animal.

Lord Romeo, too, ignored her pleas, intent on the man.

Catherine struggled to her knees, but she couldn't put weight on her ankle. If she hadn't been aware of the damage the cat would do, she would find him comical. A peek revealed the man's fascination.

Lord Romeo, massive body arched, performed a stiff-legged dance that brought him behind Greg, then to the other side. To keep the animal in view, Greg had to twist his upper body. Between the continuous growls and the strange hopping dance, he thought the cat was issuing some sort of challenge to him. But he was afraid that the cat would hurt the widow. He braced himself to make a grab for the cat the moment it came closer.

The growls lowered in volume but were all the more threatening. Truly a dangerous creature. Raucous squawks distracted him. He rubbed his eyes, uncertain that it was a flock of chickens advancing on them. The cat jumped in anxiety, or perhaps, Greg thought, he was projecting his own feeling on the cat.

Greg spread his legs to evenly distribute his weight. He lunged for the cat and slid on the lush new spring grass. He went down with a thump. His hat sailed off toward the converging hens.

"I've come to a lunatic's house." He shook his head, shocked to find himself sprawled on the ground. Enough—this day was truly enough. But he didn't act quickly enough to stop the attacking cat. Three thin scratches appeared on his wrist between the edge of his glove and the cuff of his jacket. He yanked his hand back and tucked it in his pocket. Visions of lawyers and court danced in his thoughts.

Lord Romeo continued his war dance.

Catherine crawled over to Greg and shooed the cat away. The cat was not in an obedient mood. Or, it could be, she thought, striving to find some explanation for his most unexplainable behavior, that the cat couldn't hear her over the loud squawks of Miss Lily and the new flock of guinea hens.

She was thrilled that Mr. Mayfield hadn't drawn a weapon. Louis would have shot Lord Romeo, then turned the gun on the hens. Miss Lily, her first hen, and the cat's cohort in more mischief than she wanted to think about now, had her feathers ruffled. Catherine didn't know where to direct her attention. Lord Romeo required forceful discouragement. She had no sooner shooed him away, when she had to wave off the hen. Handicapped by the pain in her ankle, she couldn't move as fast as she needed to.

Miss Lily—as she repeatedly had done in the past—eluded her reach. It was one reason why the old hen had never made it to the stew pot. Louis would have mocked her making a pet of the hen, but then

Louis was no longer around to declare that animals were never meant to be pets.

Breathing hard from her exertions, Catherine gave up all effort to deter the animals. She flung herself over Greg's body.

"Enough!" she yelled. "There's no danger from him. Get back! Go on, you silly creatures, go!"

It took her a few minutes before she brought order. Miss Lily, cackling as she rounded up the smaller guinea hens, herded them away a short distance, where they proceeded to investigate the foreign presence of Greg's battered hat. Lord Romeo resumed his attack crouch, his tail whipping from side to side, as he waited for an opening.

"Don't you dare move on him, my Lord Romeo." Catherine waited a few seconds, then rolled off Greg. As the realization that she had lain upon a perfect stranger hit her, heat rose to her face. She lay on her back, afraid to look at him. "I'm sorry," she whispered. "I hope you will forgive them and me. They've never done this, you know. I can't explain it."

Greg had to turn to wipe the grass and earth from his mouth and nose. He eyed the cat, then turned to the widow. She ought to be locked up as a public nuisance for wearing pants that left nothing to a man's imagination. But she repeated her apology and he had to respond.

"Are you suggesting this was a random attack? Of course, you are. It could be nothing else. Suzanne's schemes tend to involve me in the most absurd circumstances. But think nothing of it. Just more of the friendly western hospitality I was warned to expect. Truly, madam, you need not have gone to such trouble.

All I wanted was to be shown to my room. I've had a most trying day.

"Perhaps my sister didn't mention the reason for my visit? What's that?" he went on quickly, too quickly for Catherine to speak. "You don't remember reading that particular bit of correspondence? Well, allow me, madam, to remind you. I required peace and privacy." His voice rose on the last as he noticed the anxious blue eyes that watched him from beneath the tangle of blond hair.

Catherine saw that there were gold flecks in his deep green eyes. She fought the feminine awareness alerted by his mellow tone of voice. But his sarcasm had to be acknowledged. She angled her head to the side. "You are very angry."

"Madam, you aren't even close to knowing what I am feeling at this moment."

"You're right to be furious. If the kittens hadn't—"

"Kittens? Do you mean to tell me there are more of that creature's breed about?"

"A new litter," she murmured. *Oh dear, he hates cats. How can I set things right?*

"Say no more. I'm leaving."

"But you can't!"

"*Can't*, Mrs. Hill? Watch me."

Chapter Three

Greg arrested his move to rise as he looked, really looked at the widow. A tendril of hair curled over her smudged cheek. Blond hair shaded from newly churned butter to the gold coins in his pocket. Dewy fresh skin begged a touch.

He studied her profile, her chin a sharp line saved by the generous curve of her mouth. Her nose had the suggestion of an upward tilt at the tip, giving her a saucy look. He watched the long sweep of her pale lashes as she closed her eyes. The widow appeared provocatively tumbled and he caught himself leaning toward her. He jerked his head back, closed his eyes briefly and wondered what he was doing.

When he opened his eyes, he saw that the cat had edged closer. "That animal has moved. Is it safe to get up?" He wished the words unsaid. He had been humiliated enough. But the cat stared at him with the intense curiosity peculiar to cats. The look unsettled him.

Catherine longed to laugh to release the tense air, but something warned her not to do it. She knew he had studied her, and couldn't help wondering what he thought. A year ago she would have been mortified to find herself lying in the grass with a perfect stranger. Especially one whose nearness sharpened her senses. That was a complication she could do without. Her widowed state was allowing her to savor the freedom from anyone's dictates for the first time in her life. As much as she missed the intimacy of marriage, she had no intention of allowing a man to rule her life again.

She rolled away from Greg to glare at Lord Romeo. He sat staring at them, licking the fur of his forepaw. "It's safe enough. He's very protective, but I swear he's never attacked anyone."

"If you believe I'm honored, you are mistaken."

Catherine bit her lip. She had to repair the damage. The cat paid no attention to another warning look as he lay on his side grooming his paw. She stood quickly, wincing as she put weight on her ankle. But it was a minor pain compared to the one coming to his feet at her side. She had to get him to reconsider his decision to leave. Suzanne would never forgive her if she failed in her friend's directives. And there was her own pride, too.

Ridiculous as it made Greg feel to be wary of a creature smaller than himself, he stood with his gaze locked on the cat's whipping tail. The fact registered that the battle-scarred animal resembled the wild bobcats that populated the forested areas near the Hudson River in New York, where several of his friends built their summer residences. A quick look showed the lovely young widow deep in thought.

He felt embarrassed. He had handled this badly, but considering only this day, his patience had been sorely tried. What else he could have done he didn't know. His sister meant well, thinking he would find comfort returning to the land of their birth. It was obvious that his sister had no idea of the woman's pets. Obvious, too, that she had been mistaken in her belief that widowhood added some maturity to lovely women.

He brushed off his clothes. The suit was completely ruined with the addition of grass stains. He wouldn't miss the cost of a new suit, but that was beside the point. The fact remained that he had made a decision to leave and leave he would. Lord only knew what else waited for him. On second thought, Suzanne's devious turn of mind probably did, too.

"I'll pay for a new suit," Catherine offered. *Please let him say no.* He'd never miss the money while she'd use her savings to buy his buttons.

"Think nothing of it. I couldn't accept. But you are kind to offer." Greg had no one but himself to blame for agreeing to his sister's harebrained scheme, even if she forced him into a bet with the best of intentions. His wrist stung from the scratches. He drew his cuff down to cover them. The last time he had been marked was for the most pleasurable of reasons, a brief affair with a statuesque German beauty whose appetite for men and her music proved too volatile for him. Assessing his condition, he decided he was lucky to still be standing.

"About your leaving…" Catherine began.

"There is no 'about' concerning it."

"I can't return your money."

"Have I asked you to do so?" He stared down at the scraped leather of his boots. A disgrace. He would pay a year's wages to have Martin with him.

"No. You haven't. But I want you to know that I am stuck with a cow. Purchased on your behalf."

Well, she had gotten his attention! He turned to look

at her with an expression on his face that proved her assessment. Poet's face, warrior's eyes.

"My dear Mrs. Hill, have I inquired as to how you spent the money I paid for a month's stay?"

"No. But—"

"Please," he requested in a very soft voice, "do not trouble yourself over the money. Consider it a gift."

Catherine straightened, ignoring the pain in her ankle. She bristled at his dismissive tone. She had never had a man remind her so much of her deceased husband. But when she replied, her voice was cool and very controlled.

"You have made an error, Mr. Mayfield. I don't accept gifts from strange men. I don't accept money from any man. You paid for a month's room and board. That's what you'll get. Because you are my friend's brother. I should hate to write her that you quit before you began."

Just like every woman he had known—mention money and even the meekest mouse discovered a fighting spirit. But then he realized she didn't want the money as a gift. And she had a point.

And the bet, he added to himself. He had too much at stake to risk losing the bet between himself and his sister.

"If you'd be so kind as to show me my room, I won't trouble you further."

Catherine shook her head, a rueful smile on her lips.

"Don't tell me. That is a problem. But of course, that's exactly what you'll tell me."

"It's not ready. You're three weeks early." She was unsure what to make of him. Anger would be nice. She could deal with anger. A little pain, maybe embarrassment, those she could soothe. The good Lord knew she

had plenty of practice during her marriage in dealing with both her husband and his cantankerous father. But she was uncertain how to deal with this cool resignation.

"Perhaps Suzanne didn't make it clear that we don't take in boarders. This is a favor to your sister," she stressed, needing to make the fact clear that it was her decision. "Truth to tell, I hadn't given your arrival any thought in the bustle of getting Sarah ready for her trip."

"Sarah?"

"The widow who owns the house. We were three widows living here together. Then Mary married last year. Sarah has gone to stay with her for her lying-in."

"Then you're here—"

"Alone," she finished for him. "Me and the chickens. And Lord Romeo. You can rest in the parlor while I make up your bed. That is, if you've reconsidered your decision to leave?"

"I've reconsidered." *As if I have a choice.*

"Come along then."

Greg cast a look of regret at his hat. One of the hens was nesting in it.

Catherine turned and saw what he was staring at. "Oh, Miss Lily, how could you?"

"Miss Lily? And that animal?" he asked, pointing at the cat.

"Lord Romeo," she answered in a choked voice.

He shot her a forbidding glance. "There must be a story behind those names. Lord Romeo, indeed."

"It's true. He has an amorous nature. Miss Lily's temperament is match for a housekeeper my father hired when I was little." His look showed what he thought of her explanation. She placed her hand on his forearm, gently directing him to the front door. The man seemed bent on goading her. She had apologized, she had offered to pay for his ruined suit and hat, all the while she wished she could send him packing. *The money, Catherine, please remember the money and your friendship with Suzanne.*

The reminder was enough to bring a bright, false smile to her lips. She would not allow him to intimidate her. With the help of Mary and Sarah she had learned how capable she was to handle her own affairs. They would be proud, as she herself was, that she had not dissolved into tears. Really, the man looked at her as if she were some strange, unknown creature he wasn't sure what to do with.

"I assume there is someone to help with my luggage."

Catherine showed more teeth. "No one here but me. I thought I made that clear. But don't let it worry you, Mr. Mayfield. I'll manage it all." Brave words when she could hardly put weight on one ankle, not to mention the aches and twinges that made every step an effort. "You will find that the West breeds hardy women," she found herself adding. "Independent, self-sufficient ones."

Greg looked from the pile of luggage in the buckboard to the widow. He was a man who believed that everyone and everything had a place. The lovely young Mrs. Hill did not appear strong enough to lift one piece of his baggage, much less all of it. The woman obviously needed to wed. There were some things better attended to by a man. But until one came along, he was the only available male in sight.

Traveling without the services of his valet was one more condition of his sister's bet. This journey was the first time he had been inconvenienced with the concern of handling his own luggage. But he was learning.

Organization was the key.

"If you'll see to making my room ready, Mrs. Hill, I will tend to unloading the luggage."

Catherine stopped. She considered her forgiving nature a weakness when dealing with men, and one she hoped to curb, but his tone of voice made her wish she could breathe fire to singe the condescending male where he sat. He might as well have patted her hand and said, "There, there, little woman, don't fret. I am a man. I am strong. I am here."

It was the most irritating, male tone of voice that spelled out to the much smaller, weaker female she had better leave such a task to him—the man.

Catherine had absolutely no sense of humor when dealing with this attitude. It didn't help him one bit that he was already reminding her of Louis. She could hear echoes of Louis's voice proclaiming that she was far too delicate, too soft, too weak, too…female to do half of what she wanted to do. She couldn't order the house, they had a housekeeper to do that. And maids, and a driver for her to go buy something pretty for herself. Louis believed she could shop day after day and enjoy it. One time she had strolled down to the corrals, where the men were breaking in horses. They had been married less than a month and she chafed at the restrictions imposed by him and his father. Louis was furious when he saw her and hustled her back to the house. She had no business being there, and none to be outside without a parasol to protect her skin.

Catherine shivered as she left the past behind. She had to take a deep breath and release it before she trusted herself to face Gregory Mayfield. Her hands curled at her sides. Her back was straight and her chin angled in what could only be described as a challenge.

"Mr. Mayfield, we have begun on an...awkward note. But allow me to make one thing very clear to you. You are the guest here. You do not work. You rest. Enjoy the country. Eat what I cook. Sleep when you will, but never, ever tell me that I can't do something. Now, sir, the parlor's on your left as you go inside. Have a seat and wait for me there."

Awkward note? Was that what she called it? Greg found her term an understatement, to say the least, while her brisk, commanding tone set his neck hair on end. No woman—with the exception of his younger sister—had ever spoken to him in that tone of voice and gotten away without a tongue-lashing in the same vein.

He gritted his teeth, cautioning himself not to over-react. He glanced at the sorry nag hitched to the buck-board and thought of his own team of perfectly matched bays. Bet or no bet, this situation was going to be rectified quickly. On his terms.

"One moment, Mrs. Hill. It has struck me that you are putting your reputation at risk by insisting I stay without benefit of another woman in the house."

"Do you think we are living in the Dark Ages, sir. I am a widow. You may as well know the townspeople call us the merry widows. I assure you nothing I do would give cause to any gossip. There will be no im-proprieties. Set your troubled mind at rest." It wasn't exactly a lie that tripped easily off her tongue. She was attracted, but his attitude put a stop to that.

Greg looked at her. She was goading him. He was sure of that. If he had thought of a provocative tumble before, she was simply provocative now. How dare she stand there so calm? From her scuffed boots to the masculine-cut trousers tucked into them, trousers that bagged at her hips but defined her slender waist with the aid of a rough, tanned strip of leather, to the narrow blue-and-white farmer's shirt with its banded collar— to say nothing of the three buttons opened at the neck—there was nothing about the woman to demand and hold a man's attention.

Yet Greg found himself attracted to her.

The thought was startling. He had known his share of beautiful women. And he had never noticed a woman whose natural beauty needed no artifice. One who not only appeared to take that beauty for granted but, more important to him, disdained it as a useful tool to get her own way. He could not accuse the widow of flirting with him.

Fascinating.

His gaze returned to her face as she stood by the front door waiting for him to enter the house. Her dainty features were framed by tousled blond hair. His usual arrogant manner used to dismiss underlings in the past was held in check when her direct gaze met his.

Catherine stood there, refusing to look away. She chided herself for lying to him. Well, a little white lie. *No improprieties?* She had to get over worrying what everyone thought of her. She had been ruled by parents and later Louis with those words. Of course, she had no intention of dragging him off to bed as his question seemed to indicate. Despite their beginning she did find him attractive. She had often lamented to Mary and to Sarah that she missed sharing Louis's bed. She was young, she had wants, and she refused to deny them. But it was one of the few regrets she had about being a widow. She firmed her resolve not to back down and continued to stare at him.

Greg had seen eyes every bit as blue layered with steel over a poker table, but always on the face of a man. Almost instantly he reconsidered that. He was seeing the same militant look of his sister and other women in the newly formed Ladies Liberation League. He was tempted to ask the widow if she was a member but stopped himself.

By all that is holy, what have I gotten myself into? He couldn't answer his own question. She motioned to the open door. He swallowed. Hard.

A familiar burning sensation rose from his stomach and set the center of his chest on fire. He stepped inside. It was useless to curse the illness that made anger and argument so painful. He stood within the cool, shadowed hallway. The very disorder that made meals an event to dread was bad enough. Coming as it did on the heels of the inflammation of the lungs that had kept him bedridden for almost two months was the reason he was here.

Rest. Peace. Privacy.

His minx of a sister took full advantage of the physicians' warnings to make serious changes in his life or he'd end by killing himself. This trip was to help cure what ailed him.

Fresh country air, good wholesome food, no worries. No business to tend, no sleepless nights, no…ah, he couldn't go on. A pipe dream to achieve.

And now he had the strong-willed widow to contend with on a daily basis.

Where was the justice?

He couldn't forget Suzanne's plan to help her widowed friend, who had refused all monetary assistance.

He knew little of the circumstances that had brought Mrs. Hill to live with two widowed cousins in the same straits.

Catherine, he recalled Suzanne warning him, had a great deal of pride.

Having been recently force-fed a dose, Greg scowled as he strode into the parlor. There he stopped short. His gaze went to the comfortable-looking wing chair set in front of the windows. Beside it stood a side table and lamp.

"Inviting," he murmured.

He slowly turned. The room appeared sparsely furnished. Not at all what he expected to find in a house filled with women.

Where was the infernal feminine clutter so dear to women's hearts and despaired of by men forced to navigate such rooms?

A pottery vase, a few candlesticks and a clock decorated the mantel. A cut-glass decanter and glasses on a silver tray rested on the library table behind the settee.

Greg smiled. He would be comfortable in this room.

He walked to the windows. A twitch of the lace curtain revealed the lovely widow struggling to lift one of his bags.

He wondered if Mrs. Hill enjoyed tasting her pride. He'd be damned if she was going to stop him from helping her.

And for the first time, in much too long a time, he found himself looking forward to the next go-around with the widow.

Chapter Four

Greg stripped off his gloves, then removed his ruined jacket. He pulled off his string tie and tossed his clothes on the side chair angled toward the settee. His shirt-sleeves were rolled up with lopsided results, for his labors of the past twelve years involved using a keen mind to make money, not caring for his own clothes. Just as he reached the doorway, he paused. As his anticipation rose at the thought of confronting the enticing widow once more, the burning sensation in his stomach subsided.

He didn't even consider that Suzanne might have been right about the changes he needed.

Catherine paused in her effort to push one of the smaller trunks to the edge of the buckboard. She watched Greg's lithe stride as he crossed the porch toward her. She saw his glance at the three smaller monogrammed leather bags she had already unloaded. "No heavier than the feed sacks I haul for the animals," she said.

"You're stronger than you appear."

"Yes, I am. Don't make the mistake most men do and let appearances fool you."

"Then you must do the same," he replied.

While he carried the bags inside, Catherine took the words to heart. He had lived in eastern society for the past sixteen years. A gentleman to the core, a stickler for the rules that governed polite society. Yet he had removed his tie and jacket, rolled up his shirtsleeves and come to help her. Suzanne, she thought, had a lot to answer for.

She wiped the sweat from her brow. He presented a distraction she had no time or inclination to indulge. Living alone with him in the house for several weeks was going to prove a test of will. She didn't like the physical attraction she felt for him. He returned to take the third bag inside. His dark brown hair was mussed as if he had run his fingers through it. One lock fell over his brow, giving him a rakish look. She glanced at his pale forearms, lightly dusted with hair, and the long, tapered fingers. She was staring at the spot he'd been at for only a few moments, struggling to understand the shimmer of warmth unfurling inside her.

"Mrs. Hill? Mrs. Hill?"

She was startled to find him leaning against the buckboard, staring up at her.

"I owe you an apology, Mrs. Hill. I have arrived early and inconvenienced you. I suggest we start over. You will allow me to help as an expression of my sincerity."

His smile did not calm her insides. His apology was another surprise. It wasn't his formal tone that made her hesitate, but Suzanne's warning that her brother had an obsession to be in control at all times.

That would make for some interesting bed sport. If her insides were warm, her cheeks felt hot. What had she been thinking? Foolish thoughts, no more. But control of situations was a problem for her. First with her parents, then in marriage, she had never been allowed to decide what to do with her time, with her life.

Nearly eighteen months of independence and she still found it a potent brew to drink each day. She had grown fiercely protective of her rights as she perceived them. Catherine felt a little guilty, for Louis had not been a cruel man, just typical for the time. She mourned his death at a young age, and in her own way. It was a terrible thing to discover that passion was a poor substitute for deep, abiding love. And she wouldn't lie to herself. She had deeply resented, almost hated the daily command performance of how she had spent her day. Woe to her if all had not been to his exacting plan of what was right and proper. His death had set free an imp of mischief that allowed no such restrictions.

"Is there something wrong?" Greg asked. "Have I said something to offend you?"

With a slight shudder, Catherine shrugged off the past. It was petty to argue with the man after he had apologized. Obviously he could be reasoned with, and it certainly didn't hurt that she found him attractive. She curbed those thoughts. He was here to get well, not to ease her longings.

Greg, not noted for his patience, began to be irked with her continued silence. What did the woman want from him? An apology on bended knee? Groveling at her feet?

"Madam, have I somehow created a difficult problem? Either you accept my apology or not."

"Sorry," she murmured. "I am sorry. I'm afraid I was woolgathering."

"Do you know," he said, tilting his head to one side, "I'm inclined to believe you."

Catherine was uncertain if he was provoking her or stating the truth. "Do believe me. I never lie. Well," she corrected herself, "hardly ever."

"Not about important matters," he observed.

She shied from replying. She didn't know one woman, herself included, who cared to be read so easily, or so quickly, by any man, even if what he said was true. She found that the day suddenly seemed warmer under his direct gaze. A most irksome habit of his.

"We'd better finish unloading your luggage," she suggested.

Ah, I've hit a nerve with that one, he thought. But he let it pass without comment, tucking the knowledge away. It only made his curiosity about her intensify.

"And my apology is accepted?"

"Accepted."

"Then may I suggest—"

"I knew it." Catherine pushed aside her loose hair. "Give a man an egg and he'll want an even dozen."

"I'm sure there is some country wisdom in your remark, but it escapes me." Greg put his hands on either side of the small trunk that Catherine had been wrestling with and dragged it closer.

"What are you doing, Mr. Mayfield?"

"Taking the trunk off."

"I can see that for myself," she returned with a touch of asperity. "I meant to know how you intend to take it off."

"Watch. And perhaps lend me a hand." Greg bent beneath the edge of the trunk. "Push it toward me, if you please,'' he ordered. When the trunk's weight was centered on his shoulder, he started to rise.

"Careful now," Catherine warned. "Don't strain yourself. I don't think this is a good idea. That trunk is heavy. Suzanne would never forgive me if you hurt your back."

Greg straightened, gripping the trunk with both arms. "Your advice, madam, is noted." Damn, but the woman was right. The trunk was heavy, and he was no dockworker with the brawn to lug it about. Pride refused to allow him to admit that she was right.

Catherine watched him stagger beneath his burden as he held on and maintained his balance. Twice she thought he would fall, and twice bit her lip rather than call out. He wouldn't appreciate her cautioning him again. She took matters into her own hands. She removed the coarsely woven lap robe from beneath the buckboard's seat. She was careful about putting weight on her throbbing ankle as she climbed down, spread the material on the ground, then climbed back into the buckboard.

A loud thump came from the house. She waited with bated breath for some indication that he was all right.

Silence.

She was torn. Should she stay or go see if he was hurt? He was a prickly sort, and she had no desire to provoke. On the other hand, she had a responsibility to make sure he didn't injure himself.

As she leaned forward to climb down again, Greg strolled out of the house. He brushed his hands one against the other in a self-satisfied manner.

"Ready for the next one?"

"Yes, but this time we'll do it my way. Less effort, you'll agree." She pushed off another trunk before he could open his mouth. "Now, you take those two ends, and I'll grab hold of these. We'll drag it up inside."

Three trips later and an exhausted duo surveyed the trunks in the hall.

Catherine spied her cat sneaking up the stairs. She had no doubt he was going to Mary's old room, the one where she had already put Mr. Mayfield's luggage. With her guest now settled in the parlor with his trunks of books, one of the few pleasures Suzanne allowed him, Catherine then wasted no time in mounting the stairs. The throbbing in her ankle reached an unbearable level, but she had to forestall the cat's mischief.

Lord Romeo surprised her. He sat in the middle of the bare mattress grooming himself. She might have been another piece of furniture for all the attention he paid her.

"You and I are going to have a talk," she warned the cat. "Off you go." She reached over the bed to lift him up and set him on the dresser. "There's a new house rule for you. This is the last time you come into this room until our guest is gone." With a rumbling purr, the cat licked her hand. She scratched behind his ears and was rewarded with another lick. He raised his head, a sure indication that he wanted his neck stroked. Catherine obliged.

"He doesn't like cats so you see the sense of forbidding you his room. I'll make sure he keeps temptation out of your way by closing his door at night."

Lord Romeo ceased purring.

Catherine left him to take what she needed from the linen closet. She returned to make up the bed. "I know you like to sleep in here. But you'll obey me this time or I'll banish you to the barn. Think about that if you've got mischief in mind. All those kittens climbing over you, demanding to play while you'd like to sleep. Let's not forget Hector. That rooster doesn't like you, even if Miss Lily does.''

She tucked the ends of the sheet beneath the mattress and glanced at the cat. He sat on the dresser with his forepaws tucked beneath his body, eyes slitted.

''If you're very good, you'll have salted fish every day that Mr. Mayfield's here. I'll promise extra cuddling, too.''

''That animal hasn't the sense to appreciate your bribes,'' Greg said from where he stood in the doorway.

Catherine was too startled to hear the wishful note in his voice. And she took exception to his belittling Lord Romeo's intelligence. ''He understands. Don't doubt that. See how his tail is whipping from side to side. He knows you dislike him. Cats, Mr. Mayfield, are sensitive to the people they come in contact with. If they have an aggressive nature, they will provoke someone who doesn't like them. Trust me to be telling you the truth.'' She spread the quilt and plumped the pillow. ''There, all ready for you.''

''I usually sleep with three pillows.'' *When I sleep alone.* But he didn't add the last, for he had a feeling the dainty-looking widow had an aggressive nature to match her cat's.

''Three?''

''I like my comfort. If you don't have—''

''Oh, I can provide all the comforts of home. I'll just be a minute.'' Catherine willed herself not to limp as he stepped aside to let her pass into the hall. She had the strange sensation of being watched and judged. Lord, if he turned out to be anything like Louis, she

Otherwise languid glances and other not-so-subtle invitations would not come his way.

If he could only put a name to this vague discontent, he could do something to correct it. His gaze fell on the washstand, in particular the water pitcher. He could do with a wash and a shave. Empty, he discovered a moment later. But what a perfect excuse to rejoin the lovely widow. He didn't understand why he was drawn to her when he wasn't even sure he liked her. She certainly held no resemblance to any woman who had attracted him in the past.

There was just that indefinable something that intrigued him.

Greg's entrance into the large, sunny kitchen was abruptly halted. The widow was bent over the open oven. Her perfectly shaped derriere was outlined by the taut pull of her trousers. Had the woman no shame? But it made for an arresting, and arousing, sight. He leaned against the door frame, water pitcher dangling from one hand, while he admired the view. His sudden lusty thoughts didn't raise a speck of guilt.

Catherine, unaware of his presence, poked the tops of the biscuits she had baking. The teakettle whistled, adding its steam to that of the boiling pot where eggshells clacked against one another as they cooked to the hard-boiled stage. She intended to serve her guest coddled eggs, but she was hungry, too, and hated runny eggs.

Mary and Sarah teased her that, no matter what troubled her, she never missed a meal. She smiled thinking about it, and how lucky she was not to resemble Caroline Arquette, a widow who owned the town's café. Caroline swore that she had an image to maintain as both the owner and cook, and as a Frenchwoman by marriage. Catherine pushed the tray back and closed the oven door.

She snitched a pinch of gingerbread Caroline had traded for two dozen eggs only this morning. Licking her lips so not to miss one crumb of the spicy cake, she caught herself wondering how Greg's lips would taste. She imagined his face, honing in on his eyes. Definitely spicy, she decided.

Suzanne's mention in one letter that her brother was refusing all effort to seriously look around for a wife popped into her mind. She didn't know why that idle bit of information or the fact that he no longer had a mistress in keeping mattered to her. She had her own problems with a few local men, especially with Hillsboro growing rapidly this year, who attempted to court her. She discouraged them all. It was far too soon to think about marrying again.

She had made a terrible mistake with Louis. She thought passion was love. It was not, and it was not enough to build upon. She had never looked beyond the whirlwind courtship to the endless days of being no more than a china doll to adorn his arm when he chose, grace his house and behave like an empty-headed doll who had no thoughts of her own, no dreams, no desires beyond pleasing him. No, there would be no marriage for some time.

And she knew from the kisses she had sampled, it would not be anytime soon. She wanted a love like the kind Mary and Rafe shared. One had only to look at them to see it.

She pinched off another corner of the gingerbread and savored it. Soft and spiced. She was sure that was how Greg would kiss a woman.

"Do you share?" Greg asked when he had tortured

himself long enough with the bewitching sight she made.

"What?" she replied absently.

"Do you share?" he repeated, his senses fully engaged. Envy for the disappearing cake made him aware of how easily she aroused him.

"What are you doing here?" Catherine spun to face him.

"I merely asked if you would share a taste of whatever put that dreamy look on your face?"

Heat flooded her cheeks. *If only you knew, you'd run as far and as fast as you could.* "Spice." Her voice squeaked. She cleared her throat. His amused expression combined with her guilty thoughts demanded a correction. "I mean, it's freshly baked gingerbread."

"Ah." He kept his disappointment hidden. A more suggestive answer would have him across the room to taste those lips. But there was no guile in her gaze. "Memories of childhood. I don't think I've tasted gingerbread since then."

"Your mother's. Suzanne and I would hang around the kitchen and pester her for the first piece. She would scold us and say it was too hot—"

"And the cake would crumble if she cut it."

"And burn our fingers."

"And Papa always got the first piece." Greg looked away as she apologized. "No. It was a good memory of them. Their deaths were an accident. I'm only sorry that I wasn't here for Suzanne. She was only sixteen, far too young to have her world ripped apart."

"Your aunt came so quickly to take her away. We wanted, that is, my father offered to have her stay with us. But your aunt thought she needed new surroundings."

Her voice trailed off to a whisper. She struggled with tears. Talking about his parents' deaths only made her remember her own father's. She, like Mary, had also lost her mother early, and later her father, and then she had Mary and Sarah to comfort her.

"Now I'm the one who is sorry this talk has saddened you." Greg thought of her loyalty and her compassion despite her young age. Her letters were a lifeline to Suzanne those first years away from the only home she had known. He had been serving out his enlistment in Europe, too far away to be a comfort. For a brief moment he held a faint image of four little girls sitting beneath the ancient oak by the back door of his home. He had been invited to their afternoon tea party with dolls and giggles and offers to share their bounty. He recalled big blue eyes and long blond braids.

He tried to hold the image, to see the memory of the lovely young woman before him in greater detail, but it disappeared. "Why wouldn't you allow Suzanne to help you when your husband died? She wanted you to come and live—"

"With her?" Catherine finished for him. "It was like your sister, kind and generous, but I couldn't accept."

He noted a slight trembling about her mouth and chin. That chin—spelling stubborn—made his spirited widow appear vulnerable. He started toward her when she lifted a hand to stop him.

"I couldn't accept because I won't live on anyone's charity. I tried to explain to her, but she didn't understand."

"Pride—"

"Yes. I have a great deal of pride. Here with Sarah I have a home where I can earn my own way. It means more to me than having some man control my purse strings."

"Men handle money better than women."

"So a man would say." A light of battle gleamed in her eyes. "I suppose you're of the opinion that marriage is a woman's only salvation. Ha! Life is unfair to females. Men are all alike. They grow toward freedom while women grow into captivity. That's my opinion of marriage."

In any other woman he wouldn't have believed she was telling him the truth. But he believed Catherine Hill. He found he admired her for making her own way when marriage offers would have poured in once her period of mourning was over, especially if she had gone to live with Suzanne. And knowing his brother-in-law as he did, there would have been no question of her paying for her keep or the fripperies so dear to a woman's heart. Dear to the women he knew, at any rate. That included his sister, if his brother-in-law's moans over her monthly bills were to be believed.

Greg ran an appreciative eye over the widow's masculine clothing. He wouldn't mind seeing that graceful, slim body dressed in the latest Paris fashions. She objected to marriage, but was she open to an offer of carte blanche?

"Was there something you wanted? I assume you didn't take your prescribed rest."

"Water?" He held up the forgotten china pitcher.

"Hot?"

"Yes, as a matter of fact I am." Greg had never, ever blushed in his life, but he could feel heat rush to his face as he realized what he had said.

Catherine wisely didn't respond. But she took him at his word. "There's the pump." She waved toward the dry sink. "Help yourself. Sarah had that installed a few weeks ago. Before that we had to draw water from the well out back. If you find that too cold, there's always water heating on the stove."

Rusty, old man. Illness had robbed him of the ability to bait her into a dance of double entendre. Pity, it would liven up the days. And the nights... He left that thought.

Catherine kept her attention on the pot of cold hominy as she poured in the hot water a little at a time. Usually she fried the leftover hulled corn that served as a hearty breakfast, but Greg couldn't eat fried foods. Done for the moment, she looked over at him. He stood with a bewildered expression as he stared at the pump.

"If you pump the handle, the water comes out of the spout."

"Right."

"Mr. Mayfield, you did say you wanted water."

"Yes. I've been studying this. It would be easier hauling water from the well. I haven't used a pump."

"Never used a pump?"

"True. I've a full staff at home. Martin, my valet, usually tends to my needs."

"How does your staff get water?"

"No need for disbelief. I haven't the faintest idea. Upstairs, there are bathrooms. I imagine there is some similar arrangement for the staff below stairs. As for the kitchen, Mrs. Hill," he noted with a swift look around the large, sunny room, "I've never found the washing of dishes and pots to be of vital concern to my comfort."

She was sure that last remark was meant to put her in her place. All it did was bring a militant gleam to her eyes. "I can assure you, Mr. Mayfield, its absence would indeed be of vital concern if you found yourself without a clean dish to eat from.''

"And I assure you, Mrs. Hill, my staff is far too well trained and well paid to allow that to happen.''

Catherine gritted her teeth. Suzanne had been right. He was obstinate. "Here, we have you and me, the hand pump, the outhouse and the chamber pot.''

But her muttered words were lost as he vigorously applied himself. He pumped and water gushed out.

Unfortunately, he had forgotten to put the pitcher under the spout. Water splashed all over as he continued to pump harder while maneuvering the pitcher in place.

Catherine forced herself to remain where she was. Temptation loomed to show him the proper way, but she fought its lure, despite the mess he was making on the floor. She couldn't spoil that look of boyish delight.

She also couldn't help but wonder what other surprises he had in store for her. Obviously, she had taken a great deal for granted when she agreed to his staying. She knew she had to cook for him, do his laundry and oversee his avoidance of anything to do with business. She had never expected to show him a basic skill like pumping water. Was this the way she would help him change the way he lived?

She wasn't sure she had the patience. But her charitable nature reasserted itself. He would likely judge her inept at earning a good profit with her egg business.

He turned to look at her, dripping pitcher in hand.

Catherine boldly ran an appreciative eye over him. Her impish grin invited his in return. "You have the makings of a first-rate kitchen helper.''

Pleasure from her approval spread inside him. No matter that it was a simple, almost ridiculous thing to would not survive the next few weeks. But Louis had never ruffled her nerve ends with his nearness.

Greg strolled into his room and with considerable apprehension approached the cat. "The widow credits you with intelligence. I propose we have a truce. You keep out of my way, and I'll do my best not to annoy you." He felt foolish talking to the cat, who sat with its tail wrapped around its hindquarters. He almost believed the widow when the cat turned its head and regarded him with great green eyes that held a faintly annoyed look, as though Greg had no business discussing matters best left to his mistress.

There was a small porcelain bowl filled with dried flowers on the corner of the dresser. A faint, pleasing scent rose from it. Greg kept his eye on the cat's tail. There came a rustle and footsteps from the hall. The cat sprang from the dresser and shot across the room. The animal's lunge pushed the bowl to the edge of the dresser. It teetered there.

Greg grabbed for it. He caught the bowl, but not the contents. Still, he attempted to snatch the dried flowers from the air. His stomach slammed into the sharp point of the dresser. He swore as pain spread, but he clutched the bowl to him.

"Are you so stubborn a man, Mr. Mayfield? Must you provoke my cat after I warned you?"

He faced her. She had an armful of pillows and a candlestick dangling from one hand. Her head was tilted to one side. There was something regal about her as she met his gaze with a faintly scornful look. Perhaps it was because of the way her brows arched, or the disdainful droop of her lovely lips. Pity about her mouth, it was made for kissing. He shook his head.

What put that thought in mind? He wanted no militant miss in his life. Not even temporarily.

"I did not provoke that creature. I merely tried to save your bowl from breaking. You seem to have enough to do without picking up shards of porcelain."

Catherine stared pointedly at the potpourri scattered over the hardwood floor. She nodded. "Yes, I can see how you've saved me additional work."

Greg felt his face grow hot. "I made the attempt. I did keep the bowl from breaking," he observed icily.

"Yes, you did." Catherine crossed to the bed and dumped the extra pillows on it. She set the candlestick on the bedside table. "You must be exhausted. Have a rest. I'll call you when I'm ready to serve your meal."

Poison, most likely, he thought. Greg listened to the door close behind her. Confound that woman! And confound her damn cat! Provoking creatures. A light tap on the door stopped him from ruminating further.

"Yes, what is it?"

"May I open the door?" Catherine asked.

"It's your house, madam."

Oh dear, he's back to calling me madam. As if this were a brothel. But then she was reminded that when Mary's husband, Rafe, had come seeking aid for his wounded daughter, he thought the merry widows ran a brothel. But really, *madam?* Cranky male. She opened the door a crack. He had not moved from his place in front of the dresser.

"I'm the one who apologizes this time. Thank you for saving the bowl from breaking. Forgive me?"

Contrary woman! Using that syrup-laden voice to disarm his anger while she was likely making faces at him behind the protection of the door.

"We'll begin anew, Mrs. Hill. Again. One of these

times, I'm sure we'll get it right. And now, if you will allow me, I'll do as you suggested and rest. It's been a most trying day. Unfortunately, it isn't over.''

A nicely delivered snub! Catherine was tempted to stick her tongue out where he couldn't see her do it, but withheld that childish gesture. ''As you wish, Mr. Mayfield,'' she murmured, and closed the door. It was a pity, she mused as she limped down the hall, that men didn't have visible feathers. She would love to see Mr. Mayfield with his all at sixes and sevens. Provoking male creature!

She could fix his tail feathers. She could prepare a meal according to the strictest dictates of Suzanne's instructions from the man's physician. The man needed coddling. She'd give him coddling. Charity and compassion, a nagging little voice warned.

''Yes, and they begin at home. Start as you mean to go,'' she reminded herself.

Using the banister to brace her body, she hopped her way down the stairs. Her ankle wanted tending, but that she'd forgo until after evening chores.

All thought of curbing her impulsive nature fled.

There was something about her houseguest that tickled the devil in her. She was going to enjoy matching wits with the man.

And she had the strangest sensation that Gregory Mayfield felt the same.

Chapter Five

For the first time in days, Greg had what he wanted. Peace and privacy. Then why, by all that was holy, was he pacing his room? Having a solid floor beneath his feet should please him no end. The cessation of the rocking motion of the stagecoach, the lack of incessant conversation and the absence of his drunken, snoring seatmate all should be reason to celebrate.

Then why was he restless?

The bed, with its soft feathered mattress and clean-smelling linens, invited him to rest. The pillow held the indentation of his head where he had lain for a few minutes.

Still, he paced.

Moving the lace curtain aside, he stared out the window. The view of towering treetops and mountain peaks transferred itself into his thoughts as lumber to be milled to meet the growing demand of the men building shoddy housing for the immigrants flooding the eastern shore in search of a better life, a richer one, too, and to feed the demand for grand estates of newly made millionaires.

Mining the forbidding-looking mountains provided

riches to be transformed to adorn the bodies and the homes of the wealthy.

Money. He couldn't even remember when the game of amassing a fortune to provide for Suzanne's future, as well as his own, had become an obsession. His sister called it that. He couldn't admit to her that she was right. Greg turned away in disgust.

But old habits died hard. He looked at his watch. If he were still in New York, he'd be at his office, which occupied one entire floor of the Trinity Building, one of architect Richard Upjohn's showcases. A late lunch then, at either the Astor House or the imposing Fifth Avenue Hotel with any of a dozen newly made millionaires, all looking to parlay their first fortunes, made in mining, land and cattle, shipping and railroads, into another fortune, then another. None had believed him when he denied making this trip to seize opportunity for riches. They considered him a savvy man with unerring instincts for the right deal.

Despite the terms of his bet with Suzanne, the idea tantalized him that he was in the land of opportunity. He thrived on putting together the sort of deals where money was made on a handshake over lunch and rolled over three times or more before the evening ended.

And the women... Greg stopped pacing. He mentally shut the door on thoughts of the fleeting, meaningless relationships he'd had over the years. Marriage might never be in his future. No matter that Suzanne claimed the right woman would be the making of his eternal happiness. He could not imagine having to depend upon someone else to make him happy. He certainly didn't want that responsibility for a lifetime.

What his sister should do was to speak with her circle of married friends. Many of them wouldn't agree.

Otherwise languid glances and other not-so-subtle invitations would not come his way.

If he could only put a name to this vague discontent, he could do something to correct it. His gaze fell on the washstand, in particular the water pitcher. He could do with a wash and a shave. Empty, he discovered a moment later. But what a perfect excuse to rejoin the lovely widow. He didn't understand why he was drawn to her when he wasn't even sure he liked her. She certainly held no resemblance to any woman who had attracted him in the past.

There was just that indefinable something that intrigued him.

Greg's entrance into the large, sunny kitchen was abruptly halted. The widow was bent over the open oven. Her perfectly shaped derriere was outlined by the taut pull of her trousers. Had the woman no shame? But it made for an arresting, and arousing, sight. He leaned against the door frame, water pitcher dangling from one hand, while he admired the view. His sudden lusty thoughts didn't raise a speck of guilt.

Catherine, unaware of his presence, poked the tops of the biscuits she had baking. The teakettle whistled, adding its steam to that of the boiling pot where eggshells clacked against one another as they cooked to the hard-boiled stage. She intended to serve her guest coddled eggs, but she was hungry, too, and hated runny eggs.

Mary and Sarah teased her that, no matter what troubled her, she never missed a meal. She smiled thinking about it, and how lucky she was not to resemble Caroline Arquette, a widow who owned the town's café. Caroline swore that she had an image to maintain as both the owner and cook, and as a Frenchwoman by marriage. Catherine pushed the tray back and closed the oven door.

She snitched a pinch of gingerbread Caroline had traded for two dozen eggs only this morning. Licking her lips so not to miss one crumb of the spicy cake, she caught herself wondering how Greg's lips would taste. She imagined his face, honing in on his eyes. Definitely spicy, she decided.

Suzanne's mention in one letter that her brother was refusing all effort to seriously look around for a wife popped into her mind. She didn't know why that idle bit of information or the fact that he no longer had a mistress in keeping mattered to her. She had her own problems with a few local men, especially with Hillsboro growing rapidly this year, who attempted to court her. She discouraged them all. It was far too soon to think about marrying again.

She had made a terrible mistake with Louis. She thought passion was love. It was not, and it was not enough to build upon. She had never looked beyond the whirlwind courtship to the endless days of being no more than a china doll to adorn his arm when he chose, grace his house and behave like an empty-headed doll who had no thoughts of her own, no dreams, no desires beyond pleasing him. No, there would be no marriage for some time.

And she knew from the kisses she had sampled, it would not be anytime soon. She wanted a love like the kind Mary and Rafe shared. One had only to look at them to see it.

She pinched off another corner of the gingerbread and savored it. Soft and spiced. She was sure that was how Greg would kiss a woman.

"Do you share?" Greg asked when he had tortured

himself long enough with the bewitching sight she made.

"What?" she replied absently.

"Do you share?" he repeated, his senses fully engaged. Envy for the disappearing cake made him aware of how easily she aroused him.

"What are you doing here?" Catherine spun to face him.

"I merely asked if you would share a taste of whatever put that dreamy look on your face?"

Heat flooded her cheeks. *If only you knew, you'd run as far and as fast as you could.* "Spice." Her voice squeaked. She cleared her throat. His amused expression combined with her guilty thoughts demanded a correction. "I mean, it's freshly baked gingerbread."

"Ah." He kept his disappointment hidden. A more suggestive answer would have him across the room to taste those lips. But there was no guile in her gaze. "Memories of childhood. I don't think I've tasted gingerbread since then."

"Your mother's. Suzanne and I would hang around the kitchen and pester her for the first piece. She would scold us and say it was too hot—"

"And the cake would crumble if she cut it."

"And burn our fingers."

"And Papa always got the first piece." Greg looked away as she apologized. "No. It was a good memory of them. Their deaths were an accident. I'm only sorry that I wasn't here for Suzanne. She was only sixteen, far too young to have her world ripped apart."

"Your aunt came so quickly to take her away. We wanted, that is, my father offered to have her stay with us. But your aunt thought she needed new surroundings."

Her voice trailed off to a whisper. She struggled with tears. Talking about his parents' deaths only made her remember her own father's. She, like Mary, had also lost her mother early, and later her father, and then she had Mary and Sarah to comfort her.

"Now I'm the one who is sorry this talk has saddened you." Greg thought of her loyalty and her compassion despite her young age. Her letters were a lifeline to Suzanne those first years away from the only home she had known. He had been serving out his enlistment in Europe, too far away to be a comfort. For a brief moment he held a faint image of four little girls sitting beneath the ancient oak by the back door of his home. He had been invited to their afternoon tea party with dolls and giggles and offers to share their bounty. He recalled big blue eyes and long blond braids.

He tried to hold the image, to see the memory of the lovely young woman before him in greater detail, but it disappeared. "Why wouldn't you allow Suzanne to help you when your husband died? She wanted you to come and live—"

"With her?" Catherine finished for him. "It was like your sister, kind and generous, but I couldn't accept."

He noted a slight trembling about her mouth and chin. That chin—spelling stubborn—made his spirited widow appear vulnerable. He started toward her when she lifted a hand to stop him.

"I couldn't accept because I won't live on anyone's charity. I tried to explain to her, but she didn't understand."

"Pride—"

"Yes. I have a great deal of pride. Here with Sarah I have a home where I can earn my own way. It means more to me than having some man control my purse strings."

"Men handle money better than women."

"So a man would say." A light of battle gleamed in her eyes. "I suppose you're of the opinion that marriage is a woman's only salvation. Ha! Life is unfair to females. Men are all alike. They grow toward freedom while women grow into captivity. That's my opinion of marriage."

In any other woman he wouldn't have believed she was telling him the truth. But he believed Catherine Hill. He found he admired her for making her own way when marriage offers would have poured in once her period of mourning was over, especially if she had gone to live with Suzanne. And knowing his brother-in-law as he did, there would have been no question of her paying for her keep or the fripperies so dear to a woman's heart. Dear to the women he knew, at any rate. That included his sister, if his brother-in-law's moans over her monthly bills were to be believed.

Greg ran an appreciative eye over the widow's masculine clothing. He wouldn't mind seeing that graceful, slim body dressed in the latest Paris fashions. She objected to marriage, but was she open to an offer of carte blanche?

"Was there something you wanted? I assume you didn't take your prescribed rest."

"Water?" He held up the forgotten china pitcher. "Hot?"

"Yes, as a matter of fact I am." Greg had never, ever blushed in his life, but he could feel heat rush to his face as he realized what he had said.

Catherine wisely didn't respond. But she took him at his word. "There's the pump." She waved toward the dry sink. "Help yourself. Sarah had that installed a few weeks ago. Before that we had to draw water from the well out back. If you find that too cold, there's always water heating on the stove."

Rusty, old man. Illness had robbed him of the ability to bait her into a dance of double entendre. Pity, it would liven up the days. And the nights... He left that thought.

Catherine kept her attention on the pot of cold hominy as she poured in the hot water a little at a time. Usually she fried the leftover hulled corn that served as a hearty breakfast, but Greg couldn't eat fried foods. Done for the moment, she looked over at him. He stood with a bewildered expression as he stared at the pump.

"If you pump the handle, the water comes out of the spout."

"Right."

"Mr. Mayfield, you did say you wanted water."

"Yes. I've been studying this. It would be easier hauling water from the well. I haven't used a pump."

"Never used a pump?"

"True. I've a full staff at home. Martin, my valet, usually tends to my needs."

"How does your staff get water?"

"No need for disbelief. I haven't the faintest idea. Upstairs, there are bathrooms. I imagine there is some similar arrangement for the staff below stairs. As for the kitchen, Mrs. Hill," he noted with a swift look around the large, sunny room, "I've never found the washing of dishes and pots to be of vital concern to my comfort."

She was sure that last remark was meant to put her in her place. All it did was bring a militant gleam to her eyes. "I can assure you, Mr. Mayfield, its absence would indeed be of vital concern if you found yourself without a clean dish to eat from.''

"And I assure you, Mrs. Hill, my staff is far too well trained and well paid to allow that to happen.''

Catherine gritted her teeth. Suzanne had been right. He was obstinate. "Here, we have you and me, the hand pump, the outhouse and the chamber pot.''

But her muttered words were lost as he vigorously applied himself. He pumped and water gushed out.

Unfortunately, he had forgotten to put the pitcher under the spout. Water splashed all over as he continued to pump harder while maneuvering the pitcher in place.

Catherine forced herself to remain where she was. Temptation loomed to show him the proper way, but she fought its lure, despite the mess he was making on the floor. She couldn't spoil that look of boyish delight.

She also couldn't help but wonder what other surprises he had in store for her. Obviously, she had taken a great deal for granted when she agreed to his staying. She knew she had to cook for him, do his laundry and oversee his avoidance of anything to do with business. She had never expected to show him a basic skill like pumping water. Was this the way she would help him change the way he lived?

She wasn't sure she had the patience. But her charitable nature reasserted itself. He would likely judge her inept at earning a good profit with her egg business.

He turned to look at her, dripping pitcher in hand.

Catherine boldly ran an appreciative eye over him. Her impish grin invited his in return. "You have the makings of a first-rate kitchen helper.''

Pleasure from her approval spread inside him. No matter that it was a simple, almost ridiculous thing to master. Her sculpted face with a scrubbed, clean look drew his gaze. The features were fine, and perfectly placed: soft, wide mouth, clean line of jaw, delicate ears. And those eyes, so blue, filled with a twinkle of mischief, invited him to laugh with her, even if he was the object of amusement.

His regard for her rose another degree. He could easily name a dozen women of his acquaintance who would have seized the opportunity to poke fun at his failure to do a simple thing. Not his widow. His? Where had that possessive thought come from? He couldn't forget his first glimpse of the lady's militant nature. Of the two, he preferred her this way.

He executed a small bow, and water sloshed over the rim of the pitcher, splattering his pants, already ruined boots and the floor. "I seem to have made more of a mess over this than I did putting my first business deal together."

"But this is more easily mopped up," she noted.

"Mine to do?" he asked with horror. His reputation was in shreds at this point. Thankfully, no one would ever learn what he had been reduced to.

"Afraid so." Catherine turned back to the stove. It wouldn't do to forget Suzanne's ardent instructions. *Make him aware of the simple pleasure gained by his own hand.* She wasn't sure if this qualified, but he made the mess, he'd learn to clean it up. "Yes," she repeated in a firm voice. "It's yours to do. I've a meal to finish. You'll find the mop in the pantry. Doorway to your left."

His natural authority reared its head. He was about to refuse. But she was humming as she bent over to take the tray of biscuits from the oven. A delicious aroma filled the kitchen, but Greg was beset by lusty thoughts of his hands curving over soft swells and engaging in man's oldest sport. He turned away before she could discern his thoughts.

And found himself wondering why he thought to protect her. He only knew it had nothing to do with her being his sister's friend.

The pantry, unlike his own, was not locked. He knew about the lock because Grantfeld, his butler, had been given the key by his own hand. But then, the widow had no staff to worry about stealing from her. He scanned the shelves filled with jars, crocks and some canned goods. It brought back the memory of home. The floor held sacks and larger crocks, which were tightly covered to conceal their contents. At the back he saw what he needed. Greg made a fast identification of the mop because he knew what a broom looked like. Not only looked like, but felt like, too. His mother hadn't been shy about swatting him when he got into mischief. And then, one of his housemaids was always sweeping the front granite steps of his home—a stone mansion on Madison Avenue across from the residence built by the well-known jewelry family of Tiffany—when he left for his morning ride.

Catherine stopped peeling eggs to instruct him how to swing and wring the mop. By the time he finished, she had the table set. She noted with some satisfaction that he had color in his cheeks, and his eyes had lost some of the aloofness. But she wasn't prepared for his dismay when he stood by his chair and stared at the table.

"I thought you were going to feed me."

"This isn't slop for the hogs, Mr. Mayfield."

"But it hardly constitutes what I consider a meal."

"I am following your physician's instructions, sir.

Hard-boiled eggs, hominy and plain biscuits. Milk to drink, and you have butter and jam for your bread. Plain fare to help heal your stomach disorder.'' Catherine glared at him. She gripped the back of her chair to forestall the urge to shake him. Didn't the man have sense to know that she wasn't going to ignore what was good for him?

Stubborn witch. Didn't she have the sense to know that a man needed an appetizing presentation when his diet was restricted? Greg glared right back at her.

Catherine moved to pull out her chair.

Greg scooted around the table and pulled the chair out for her. ''Allow me to seat you, Mrs. Hill.''

''Thank you, Mr. Mayfield. By all means, let us remember our manners.''

''And our roles,'' he muttered.

''Meaning?''

''Hostess and guest, my dear Mrs. Hill.'' Jailer was more like it. His lips compressed. She was worse than Suzanne.

''I agree. You should remember. Guests don't make remarks about what is served to them, unless they're going to be compliments, Mr. Mayfield, not insults.''

''Sit down, madam. I do not require a lesson in manners from you.'' The woman was insolent. Impossible. And wore a teasing, faint fragrance.

Catherine sat. She winced as she put pressure on her sore ankle just to lift herself above the seat so he wouldn't think her heavy as he pushed the chair close to the table.

Feminine vanity?

She had no answer for the needling voice. She had all she could do to bite her tongue as he made her wait to take his place. He took his time to admire the carved wooden napkin ring, and made an elaborate show of unfolding his napkin before placing it on his lap. Catherine determined to fight and win this battle over meals right now.

Greg took a deep breath and released it. He was determined to clarify the matter of his meals before this obstinate woman believed she could get away serving him food that would make his least-paid scullery maid turn up her nose. But why couldn't the widow look like a dowdy maid and not a woman who stirred his blood?

"Shall we begin?" she asked in a prim, starched voice.

He locked gazes with her and rubbed his hands together. "I cannot wait."

ing her, Miss Lily often forgot where she had hidden the eggs, and the stench was unbearable.

"Don't forget the gloves I gave you, Ramon. Miss Lily likes you, but I don't want her pecking your hands again. And don't forget to first ask your mother if you can come."

She helped him secure the mule to the back of the buckboard and waved him off.

But as Ramon disappeared from sight, another small two-seater carriage turned in the drive. Catherine shaded her eyes with one hand, moaning softly when she saw who had come to call.

Mrs. Horace Pettigrew was back visiting her daughter. She had brought along her youngest daughter. Camilla was the only unmarried one of four girls. Painfully shy, happiest when painting, miserable with her mother's blatant attempts to marry her off, the young lady also suffered from delicate health. But it was Mrs. Pettigrew's most offensive habit to boast of the successful marriages she had arranged for her other daughters that made Catherine dislike the woman.

Camilla had been left behind with her newly married sister in the hopes that she would encourage one of several single men's proposals while her mother made her monthly visits to her other daughters.

Catherine couldn't imagine why they were calling on her. She hadn't even heard that Mrs. Pettigrew had returned. The carriage was new, and the horse a spirited chestnut, which Camilla handled smartly.

The girl drew rein, nodded at Catherine, then seemed to shrink back against the carriage seat when her mother leaned forward.

Mrs. Pettigrew noticed Catherine's interest in her new spring cape and she preened at the attention. Black

Chapter Six

But wait he did.

Her candor through the meal disarmed him. Disarmed and charmed him in a way that left him thinking he had been had by a professional huckster.

At her suggestion he left her to clean up the kitchen.

Humor combined with reason. Dangerous qualities to discover in a woman who had the gumption to stand up to him.

Pointing out that plain, wholesome food was what the doctor had ordered, she assured him that his restored good health was her goal.

Hard to argue with such rationale. Even if he had been set to do just that less than an hour ago.

The climb up the stairs provided time for clearer thought.

She had tricked him into eating by the provocative way she had of closing her eyes, biting into her jam-filled biscuit with relish, and then, only to torment him, he was sure, she savored the taste—overlong, he observed.

He had been fascinated watching the tip of her tongue lick a stray crumb from the corner of her mouth—envisioning himself as the lucky recipient of such play—that he had absently finished the butter-flavored corn grits.

Her slender fingers, each move graceful, made the peeling of hard-boiled eggs an art. Only, he reminded himself, because his desire had been heightened with the thought of those clever fingers opening his shirt buttons and stroking his skin.

Greg shook his head. The woman was a danger to him.

A mere few hours and she already had him believing he would enjoy his visit in this rustic setting.

Had she known how she affected him?

The question made him stop midway up the stairs.

Images of her face came to mind. That rueful expression that didn't hide the amusement in her eyes as she licked jam from her lips. Mischievous voice...

He was bemused to find a variety of images dancing through his mind. It was her expressiveness that marked her. When she became flustered, she was quite fetching.

Certainly would entice a man to fluster her often.

When she was annoyed with him—far too frequent an occurrence since he'd arrived—her firm lips and determined chin had their own appeal.

Another temptation for a man.

And when she smiled, ah, when she smiled, her whole face brightened. Her wide, generous smile shone through her lovely skin and sparkled in her blue eyes.

Where are you going with this, old man?

Nowhere. He continued up the stairs.

Those hominy grits must addle the brain.

Addled wits. The only explanation, Catherine thought, heaving another sigh of relief.

Mr. Gregory Mayfield was going to test every bit of feminine ingenuity she possessed.

She had flirted with him. Shamelessly. Not too bad in and of itself, but the man had responded.

Trouble lay in that direction.

She had gently teased him into finally admitting that she had to follow doctor's orders or be accused of taking his money under false pretenses.

She hadn't been sure if he'd muttered "charming nurse" or "curse." It only made her think of something Mary often said. A wagonload of nursing wasn't worth a spoonful of loving. Now, there was a dangerous thought.

But not, by far, the worst one.

That had come when Greg left the kitchen.

She wanted to call him back. She didn't want their time together to end just yet. She had enjoyed sharing the hastily-put-together meal with him.

His dark green eyes fascinated her. Warrior's eyes. But when he smiled, bits of gold flecks became apparent and softened his look. Without lying to herself, she knew she had seen desire there.

And her own reaction claimed the feeling was mutual. Had he noticed the shallow breaths? Thank goodness he could not hear the quickened beat of her heart or see the warm flutters that had filled her each time he leaned closer.

But he must have noticed that she couldn't keep her gaze from lingering on his mouth.

Trouble. The man was trouble.

The challenges of past eighteen months were stimulating, but not as exciting as thinking of the next go-around with Gregory Mayfield.

She stacked the plates, then struggled to stand. Eating hominy grits twice in the same day must surely addle wits.

"You've just been alone too long," she murmured. "Have patience. You'll soon get over this initial attraction. And there's a lot to be said for patience. Given enough time, even an egg will walk. Or so Mama was fond of saying."

Which only reminded her that she had chores to do. All on an ankle that was steadily swelling within her boot.

Once the kitchen was tidy, a chore Catherine never relished—she missed having Mary there, for the kitchen had been her domain—she headed outside where she was happiest. She was limping her way across the yard when Lord Romeo streaked by on his way toward the front of the house.

"Someone's here," she muttered, changing direction.

Ramon Perez, eleven years old, and the eldest male of his family since his father had been killed in a mining accident, sat astride one of the livery's mules. His black eyes sparkled and a grin slashed his swarthy skin.

"Señor Botts say I take wagon back."

"And right he was to send you. I can't imagine what I was thinking about to leave that poor horse out here."

But as Catherine looked, the poor horse had nibbled his way across the fine shoots of grass and the flower border that Sarah planted before she left.

"How is your mother, Ramon?" Louisa took in washing by day and at night cleaned dishes at the café in return for her small family's supper. Ramon worked at the livery or wherever he found odd jobs. His sister, Clarita, did chores for Dolly and Chad Hudspeth, who owned the tailor shop in town. Even little Vicente made a contribution by sweeping up the sawdust at Ollie Walker's lumber mill.

As Ramon chatted on about what his mother thought of his schooling, Catherine had an idea. But she had to be careful about asking. Louisa Perez had pride and instilled that pride in her children. They would accept no charity, but worked for all they had. The children often wore second, third or even—if well made of good-quality cloth—fourth time hand-me-downs, but they were always clean and neatly dressed.

"Ramon, please tell your mother that I hurt my ankle. I will need help to do my chores. If Mr. Botts can spare you, would you like to work for me?"

If possible, his dark eyes sparkled all the more and his grin widened. Catherine knew the reason. She not only was generous with an hourly wage but usually sent him home with a newly hatched chick or a basket of eggs. Ramon had worked a whole day, his decision as the price of a hen, and now had three chicks, one showing signs of a rooster's fine plumage.

"When you need me, *señora?*"

"Tomorrow morning will be fine. Before dawn. We have to get Miss Lily out of the way before we gather the eggs. She's been up to her old tricks, hiding one or two eggs whenever she can get away with it."

Catherine pretended to pinch the tip of her nose with thumb and forefinger. Ramon made a face then mimicked her. Even the pigs refused to eat rotten eggs. It was the most unpleasant of chores to discover eggs days after Miss Lily, long past her prime as a laying hen, had hidden them in the hope of hatching new chicks for herself.

Unfortunately for Catherine, and whoever was helping her, Miss Lily often forgot where she had hidden the eggs, and the stench was unbearable.

"Don't forget the gloves I gave you, Ramon. Miss Lily likes you, but I don't want her pecking your hands again. And don't forget to first ask your mother if you can come."

She helped him secure the mule to the back of the buckboard and waved him off.

But as Ramon disappeared from sight, another small two-seater carriage turned in the drive. Catherine shaded her eyes with one hand, moaning softly when she saw who had come to call.

Mrs. Horace Pettigrew was back visiting her daughter. She had brought along her youngest daughter. Camilla was the only unmarried one of four girls. Painfully shy, happiest when painting, miserable with her mother's blatant attempts to marry her off, the young lady also suffered from delicate health. But it was Mrs. Pettigrew's most offensive habit to boast of the successful marriages she had arranged for her other daughters that made Catherine dislike the woman.

Camilla had been left behind with her newly married sister in the hopes that she would encourage one of several single men's proposals while her mother made her monthly visits to her other daughters.

Catherine couldn't imagine why they were calling on her. She hadn't even heard that Mrs. Pettigrew had returned. The carriage was new, and the horse a spirited chestnut, which Camilla handled smartly.

The girl drew rein, nodded at Catherine, then seemed to shrink back against the carriage seat when her mother leaned forward.

Mrs. Pettigrew noticed Catherine's interest in her new spring cape and she preened at the attention. Black braid trimmed the scalloped tiers of soft gray wool. But her hat was a tribute to the milliner's art. Black straw was burdened with sprays of lilacs, a bow of plaid ribbon, several upstanding feathers and two roses, between which nestled a small stuffed bird.

It was also a tribute to Mrs. Pettigrew's skill that the whole hat didn't slide forward into her ample lap.

"You mustn't think me vain, Catherine, for wanting to show off this lovely confection that my dearest Irene insisted she buy me. And the cape, did you ever see such fine work? I declare, the shops in New Orleans are for a woman's pleasure. You must accompany me the next time I visit my daughter, Catherine. A shopping trip will do wonders for you."

Catherine forced a smile that never reached her eyes. It wasn't the first time Mrs. Pettigrew had made remarks about her scandalous attire.

"I'm surprised to see you—"

"You must forgive this unannounced visit, dear. I had the most dreadful trip—"

"I'm so sorry to hear that, Mrs. Pettigrew. But here you are, back and safe with your family. And how are you, Camilla?"

"Well," she mumbled.

"She is not," her mother said with a disapproving look at her offspring. "I declare, I don't know what I'm to do with the girl. Adelaide informed me that she twice refused to ride out with that nice Mr. Krausse. Julian is doing so well with his butcher shop, too. That young man has big plans. He intends to open another store in Lake Valley. And this stubborn gal of mine can't see the value in having a husband who will always provide meat for her table. And he's a thrifty man, too. Has a nice piece of change put by for his future."

Catherine had no doubt this was the truth. Mrs. Pettigrew's latest son-in-law, Gerald Emmet, had opened another bank in Hillsboro. Gerald wasn't above telling anyone interested in his neighbor's business who had accounts with his bank and how much they contained. It was one reason that Catherine had kept her small account with Buck Purcell at the First National. Buck would send someone like Mrs. Pettigrew packing if she dared ask him such questions.

"Perhaps, Mrs. Pettigrew, Camilla doesn't like Julian."

The girl shot her a grateful glance.

"Nonsense. Young women don't know who will make a good husband. They have the most flighty notions. Marry a handsome face and you'll likely repent it for the rest of your life."

Catherine, aware of the chores that waited, couldn't keep a hint of impatience from her voice. "I wish I could invite you in for tea and a chat about your visit, but I have a houseguest—"

"Yes, yes," Mrs. Pettigrew interrupted with a great deal of head bobbing. "That's why I've come to call. I made Mr. Mayfield's acquaintance on the stage. Such a handsome young man. So refined in his manner. I just knew he would appreciate finding out that we do have people of culture in Hillsboro. So I've come to invite him to supper. After all we went through. I declare, I may extend my stay with Adelaide to give my poor nerves a rest. And my darling little Posie just jumped into her bed and refused to come out. Now, where is the charming Mr. Mayfield?"

"Resting. No doubt he is as exhausted as Posie."

Catherine's sarcasm was lost on the woman. *So this is what I'm going to contend with? Ladies calling to invite him to sample their brand of western hospitality.* She couldn't imagine why the idea of other women seeking him out annoyed her. Aside from her responsibility for his health, Catherine shouldn't be playing chaperon for the man.

"Resting? Well, he did appear a bit pale after he helped set the wheel. And I had so hoped to have him meet Camilla. He rushed off the moment the stage arrived."

"Then however did you know he was here?"

"Why, I sent Gerald to inquire at the livery. Do you think you might see if he is awake and up to receiving company?"

"Mama, she said the man is resting. And after hearing about your horrid journey—"

"Don't correct your mama, Camilla. Catherine will go and look for me. Won't you?"

Catherine had no desire to intrude on her boarder's rest. Not to mention the fact that climbing up and down the stairs would finish her ankle for the day. Knowing that Greg had shared the stage with Mrs. Pettigrew and Posie stirred her sympathy. She almost excused his testy behavior. Anyone cooped up with the woman for more than ten minutes would go mad.

Mrs. Pettigrew's face was set. She wasn't going to take refusal of her request. There was no help to be had from Camilla, who sat clutching her fine wool shawl and all but disappeared inside her wide-brimmed bonnet.

Catherine shrugged. Short of being rude, she didn't see a way out.

"Won't you come and wait in the parlor?"

"No, Catherine. And do hurry. If he's to come for supper, I'll need to return home immediately. Adelaide will make a muddle of supper unless I'm there to advise her."

Camilla rolled her eyes.

Catherine stifled a laugh. She had had supper with Adelaide twice while her mother was gone, and both times the food and company were most enjoyable.

Catherine tried to control her limp as she turned toward the house.

"Catherine's hurt herself," Camilla whispered to her mother.

"Nonsense. That girl's healthy as a horse."

Camilla left her seat and hurried after Catherine.

"What did you do?"

"A little sprain. Nothing to worry about." Then she faced the stairs. "On second thought, Camilla, you shall have to—"

"Don't ask me to go up there. I couldn't. I would just die. I've never been near, much less in, a gentleman's room," she declared in a dramatic whisper while clutching her shawl near her throat.

"All you need do is knock on the door. If he doesn't answer, you can tell your mother he's asleep. I promise you, Camilla, the man won't grab you and drag you inside to have his way with you like in some penny-dreadful novel.

"Please do this for me?" Catherine asked. "I don't feel comfortable refusing her invitation on his behalf. Who knows, he might have enjoyed her company."

"Oh, Catherine, do you know anyone who does? Besides, she said he hurried off. That tells me a great deal."

"You're right. But if I go up, I may not be able to

come back down. There are hungry animals waiting for me. Honestly, Camilla, he's not so bad. I mean, he won't bite.''

"Only because you haven't asked me to," Greg said in an intimately hushed voice from the top of the staircase.

Catherine, whose emotions had run the full gamut from embarrassment to anger, couldn't summon a reply. What he implied...the intimacy of it...left her speechless.

The addition of a vest over his shirt didn't add an ounce of respectability, not with such sleepy-looking eyes and his hair tousled as if someone had repeatedly run their hands through the dark thickness.

Catherine barely heard Camilla's gasp over the racing beat of her heart. She frowned, and when she did, her expression went from pixie to harpy—a look Sarah or Mary would have recognized as Catherine's temper at the boil.

But she would wait to take the impudent Mr. Mayfield to task.

"Camilla Pettigrew, this is my houseguest, Mr. Gregory Mayfield."

"Pleased to make your acquaintance, sir."

Catherine noted the young lady all but bobbed him a curtsy as if he were visiting royalty. She was ready to stop her if she did it. The real pity was that Mr. Mayfield was so far from her reach. She would like to wipe his arrogant expression from his face.

"You'll be pleased to know you left such an impression on Mrs. Pettigrew that she and her daughter have come to call on you. You might have mentioned that you had a friend in town. Won't you put on your jacket?'' she asked sweetly as a reminder that he wasn't dressed for polite company.

A small, knowing smile curled his lips. Catherine's fingers tightened over the newel post. Her ankle wasn't pleased at having her stand. As reluctant as she was to leave Camilla alone with him, she knew she had to finish her chores.

''I'll leave you to make your arrangements, Mr. Mayfield.''

''A moment, Mrs. Hill.''

''Yes?'' That couldn't have been alarm she heard from him. But if it wasn't, it was close kin.

''You can't go off and leave me.''

Not alarm. Panic. Catherine smiled.

''You'll make my excuses to Mrs. Pettigrew and her charming daughter. I've only arrived. I wouldn't think of leaving you alone my first night here. I was so looking forward to another of your culinary achievements this evening.''

Catherine gritted her teeth. So kind of him to mention the lackluster meal she had thrown together. ''Please don't refuse on my account—''

''Of course, I will. I am exhausted from my journey. However, you may convey my regrets and tell her I will call upon her in a few days' time.''

''Oh, do reconsider,'' Camilla pleaded. ''She'll be ever so cross.''

The outburst was so unlike Camilla that Catherine stared at her.

''A crossed Mrs. Pettigrew?'' Greg murmured with relish. ''The thought tempts even the most saintly among us.''

''Mr. Mayfield!'' Catherine slid her arm around the younger woman's shoulders and turned her toward the door. She was supposed to be angry with him, not offering to ease him from a situation of his own making.

"Come, Camilla. We'll tell your mother a little truth and a little white lie. We'll say he wasn't in his room. That is true. We won't mention this conversation. But I promise to tell her that I will convey her supper invitation later."

Camilla turned to Catherine, tilting her head back to see beyond the bonnet's brim. Her wide brown eyes searched Catherine's face before she looked over her shoulder and upward to where Greg still stood.

"Mrs. Hill offers wise counsel. I meant no offense, Miss Pettigrew, but three days of nonstop conversation with your mother requires solitude. And Mrs. Hill promised that I will have it here. Didn't you?"

"Yes, I did. Come along. I'll tell your mother."

Catherine hobbled back to the carriage, related the facts and thought that was the end of it.

Mrs. Pettigrew had other notions.

"I am terribly disappointed, of course. But tell me, where is Sarah?"

Catherine thought of the white lie she had told and an oft-repeated warning Sarah was fond of giving that one lie often led to another. The lie was there, on the tip of her tongue, but any one of ten women would tell Mrs. Pettigrew the truth.

"Sarah has gone to stay with Mary and her husband until their baby is born."

"Do you mean to tell me that you are here alone with Mr. Mayfield?"

Catherine straightened, ignoring the pain shooting from her ankle. The woman's reddened face warned what was coming. That she would voice one of Catherine's own concerns made little difference.

"So it seems," she acknowledged.

"Catherine Rose Hill, your reputation—"

"Is my own affair, Mrs. Pettigrew. I do appreciate your concern, but I'm not in fear of being ravished. Mr. Mayfield's sister is an old and dear friend. I assure you nothing improper is going on, nor will it. Now you must excuse me. I have work to do."

"You have not heard the last of this, young woman."

Catherine didn't answer her. She did heave a weary sigh. Mrs. Pettigrew was right. She was sure to hear a great deal more. What a thoroughly rotten, scrambled day! She couldn't afford to have Gregory offended by silly gossip. He might ask for his money back and then where would she be?

Camilla smartly turned the carriage and drove off.

"Silly, interfering old biddy," Catherine muttered as she rounded the back of the house.

"I couldn't agree with you more, Mrs. Hill."

"You! What are you doing here? Go upstairs to your room and have your solitude."

"My, my, you are in a state. I merely came down to ask if you had a horse I could ride. Now, I think you and I better have a talk. Mrs. Pettigrew, a shrewish and most unpleasant woman that it's been my misfortune to meet, has made a valid point.

"There will be gossip, Mrs. Hill. The thing is, what are *you* going to do about it?"

Chapter Seven

"Me?"

"That's what I asked."

Catherine thought how easy it would be to ruffle his calm, but innate honesty took hold.

"I must leave that choice up to you. They'll gossip about me no matter—"

"Are you saying my sister has sent me to a den of iniquity?"

"You needn't sound so pleased, Mr. Mayfield." And then the imp won out. "They don't call us the merry widows for nothing."

She made to move past him and Greg put an arm out to stop her.

"I'm serious. I am concerned about your reputation. Delightful as the thought of being with a wicked widow may be, I won't cause harm to you."

"Then kindly let me go. I have chores to do."

"Your pardon."

But Catherine didn't move on. She leaned against the corner of the house, watching the late afternoon shadows spread across the yard. The air held that very special scent of early spring. She didn't notice that

Greg wrinkled his nose as the breeze brought the barnyard odors their way.

She looked at him. He was frowning. "Don't be concerned. And I'm sure that Mrs. Pettigrew is not the first matchmaking mama who set her sights on you. She's married off her other daughters and Camilla is the last one. She'll be back with an offer for you to stay with her. And Adelaide and Gerald. Mr. Emmet has recently opened Hillsboro's second bank. You would enjoy his company. All he talks about is making money."

"I had no idea you harbored a cruel nature. You forgot Posie. And no thank you. I told you I had enough of that woman's company on the stage. As for matchmaking mothers, I avoid them. Contrary to what women believe, most men do not want to be chased. They prefer to go hunting on their own.

"As for the last, talking about making money to a banker would violate the terms that Suzanne set and I agreed to."

Catherine folded her arms over her chest. She didn't know if she should feel pleased or angry that he didn't consider her a marriage threat. Not that she wanted him to think about marriage and herself in the same thought. But it piqued female vanity—the little she believed she had—that he had discounted her from the first.

Curiosity got the best of her, and the words were out before she stopped them.

"Why haven't you married?"

"Now I feel at home. Suzanne asks me at least once a week. Can you stand a little male honesty, Mrs. Hill?"

"I prefer honesty at all times."

"Another odd trait to find," he murmured more to

himself. "I haven't found the right woman. And since we are getting into personal matters, I might ask why you haven't remarried?"

"You might ask. That doesn't mean I have to answer."

"And here I thought I had met a woman who was above using the feminine wile of creating mystery—"

"No, I'm not above using it. I simply refused to answer your question. That's a common failing among men. They can't believe a woman is capable of telling them the truth. I'm content being a widow. I do not have to follow rules society sets for single women. I do not have to answer to a man for my actions. Ah, I see by your look that you don't believe me. I told you so. Most men will not, and more than a few women, Mrs. Pettigrew among them, have told me to pray harder for proper guidance."

"Your pardon, Mrs. Hill." Greg looked into her blue eyes. Sparkling. If she wasn't inwardly laughing at him, then he was not a man. But it quickly came to mind that he faced his sister in much the same way over the very same question. He grinned at her.

"May I have your promise that you'll protect me from that woman?"

"I'll do my best. But there is another solution."

"Don't suggest that I court that child."

"No. I wouldn't want to see Camilla hurt." She glanced down at her scuffed boots. Better to find out now than later. "You could end the problem by going home."

"Out of the question." He clasped his hands behind his back and started pacing away from her. "I've got too much riding on my staying the full month."

"Oh," she whispered, disappointed. "I had forgotten the bet. Knowing your sister, she made the prize a valuable one.''

That brought him around to face her. ''She didn't write you with the details?''

''No, she didn't. Why do you think she did? Your sister wrote it was important, but she didn't want to influence me in any way.''

''Suzanne did that?''

''Your disbelief astounds me.''

''No more than what you've said astounds me,'' Greg returned. He ran his hands through his hair. ''I can't believe she didn't enlist your aid.''

''Are you,'' Catherine asked in a suddenly cool, very soft voice, ''calling me a liar?''

Distracted by thoughts that his sister intended this bet to be fair, Greg didn't answer her.

Catherine fumed. She wanted to leave him, but the idea of hobbling across the yard while he watched was intolerable. But she couldn't keep standing there.

''If you're finished questioning me, I suggest you return inside. I'm sure you're not nearly as rested as you should be.''

Her curt tone caught his attention. ''You're angry with me. Why?''

''Some things, Mr. Mayfield, are best left unsaid. Good day.''

She pushed off the side of the house, using every bit of control to walk normally. *Please let him go back into the house,* she prayed. *I don't know if I want to scream, cry or beat sense into that man!*

''How soon to supper, Mrs. Hill?''

''When I'm done with my chores.''

She was definitely angry with him. What had he said to her? Greg shrugged. They had spoken about so much in the last hour, he couldn't recall it all. But something had firmed her spine.

"Since I turned down Mrs. Pettigrew's invitation to what no doubt would be a lavish meal, you will tell me what I'll have in place?"

Catherine stopped dead. She drew in a deep breath, released it and took another. Her hands curled at her sides. She slowly turned around.

"What did you say?"

"I asked you what you planned for supper."

"Yes, I thought that's what you said." She smiled and saw that he frowned. He also took a step toward her but she lifted one hand to stop him. "Since you so kindly described the meal we had as a culinary achievement, and one you were looking forward to having again, then that is what you'll have."

"Biscuits and eggs?" he called out.

"*Cold* biscuits and *cold* hard-boiled eggs. If you like, you can have *cold* grits, too."

"You wouldn't do that to me. I'm a sick man."

Catherine derived the greatest satisfaction as she looked over her shoulder and fluttered her lashes at him. She licked her bottom lip, mentally hushing the little voice begging her not to be cruel. Pleasure bloomed. Greg was staring at her mouth. His dazed expression almost made her smile. She licked her lip again.

"Mrs. Hill...er...Catherine," he mumbled, wondering as he did what had happened to her. "Surely you wouldn't, I mean you couldn't—"

"Mr. Mayfield, watch me."

Watch her? He couldn't seem to do anything else. Wicked widow, indeed. She disappeared into the shadowed interior of the barn. He stood there, shaking his head.

Her impudent smile sent his temperature soaring, then he silently repeated her words and his temper kicked in.

"We'll see about that," he grumbled, and made a beeline for the kitchen.

Disappointment came with his first deep, inhaling breath. There were no enticing smells coming from the pots on the stove. There was the bowl of hard-boiled eggs and a basket of leftover biscuits on the table.

Rebellion seared him. He refused to eat them again. He spied the pan of gingerbread and helped himself to an overgenerous slice. The cake was delicious, sweet and light with bursts of spice melting on his tongue. He ate the first slice with relish, then helped himself to another.

When he finished, he decided that gingerbread went a long way to restoring his good humor.

He shot a last look at the table.

"She won't do it. She wouldn't dare," he stated as he left the kitchen.

"She did it. She dared to do it," Greg muttered four hours later. He was in his room, standing and staring out the window.

Darkness had descended, and with it, a quiet like the closing of a coffin.

Where were the gaslights? Or house lights? Not even a passing carriage lantern relieved the black curtain of night.

Insect noises and small rustlings were all he heard as he leaned out the window. No creak of farm wagons, no shouts of hack drivers cursing privately employed coachmen. Where were the lights? The people? Noises he could identify?

What did one do in such an isolated setting?

What specifically did the widow do to occupy her evening hours?

She had been unusually quiet. She didn't even mention the missing gingerbread. Was she angry with him over his careless remarks about her cooking?

No. Catherine had not struck him as a woman who held a grudge.

Then what was wrong? No smiles, no sparkle in her eyes. She had barely whispered good-night to him.

This was an exercise in frustration.

He was a man. How could he possibly know what went on in a woman's mind?

How many times had Suzanne, and even one or two of his mistresses, pointed that fact out to him? And why should he care what that provoking widow thought?

A wry grin teased his lips. Obviously he cared a great deal, since he couldn't stop harping on why the merry widow had withdrawn.

Disgusted for not coming to any conclusion, Greg turned away from the window. He glanced at the lamp on the bedside table and the three open books beside it. On the dresser beside his toilet articles was another stack of books. Reading was one of the quiet pastimes his doctor recommended. But not one of the three Jules Verne novels held his attention. He wasn't in a mood to journey to the center of the earth, or dive twenty thousand leagues under the sea, or travel from the earth to the moon.

He felt restless when he should be exhausted. The

closed door made the room confining. The house was so damn quiet.

At home, no matter what wee hour of the morning he returned, Martin was always waiting, someone was always on duty in the kitchen if he should want something.

But the widow was asleep. And she had reminded him more than once that they were here alone.

He didn't bother to pick up his pocket watch to see the time. But he did open his door, hoping to see a crack of light beneath the door across the hall where Catherine slept.

If he ever shared the fact that he was alone in the house with a widow as lovely as Catherine and made no attempt to seduce her to share the pleasures of the flesh, he would be banned from every private club where his friends and business acquaintances gathered.

Mad. The woman was addling his wits as badly as her grits had.

Disappointment appeared to be his lot. No light. There was a faint shadowed outline as if her door were ajar. He rubbed his freshly shaven jaw, tempted to wake her.

His stomach rumbled, loud to him in the night's stillness, and he replaced the lure of Catherine's company with thoughts of the gingerbread.

He tightened the silken tie of his robe. He decided he didn't need the lamp.

His slippers made no sound as he walked the hallway, but he crept down the stairs like a thief trying to avoid the steps that creaked.

It came as a bit of a surprise when he gained the kitchen without mishap. He gave passing thought to lighting the coal oil fixture over the table and rummaging through the pantry. She did tell him to make himself at home.

But Greg had never rummaged through his own pantry. He had no idea of what he would find or what to do with most of the canned and jarred foods on the wooden shelves.

"Better to stick with the gingerbread," he muttered.

He cautiously felt his way around the table until he reached the stove. The tray was where he remembered it. He lifted the napkin and, by feel, judged that the lovely widow had indulged herself. There was less than half of the cake left.

He wasn't about to go fumbling in the dark for a knife and so broke off a hunk.

Halfway done eating the gingerbread, he stopped.

"Where the devil would she hide the milk can? Or the tea canister?"

His mutterings didn't help. He couldn't recall where she'd put the milk and he didn't know how to brew tea. All he recalled was something about letting it steep.

He contented his thirst with water, managing to get enough on his robe to chill his skin.

Once upstairs he stripped off the robe. He threw a hasty look at the door and knew he'd better close it. He'd never worn a nightshirt and he wasn't about to start.

Greg lay awake for quite some time. His thoughts veered of their own volition back to Catherine. He didn't want to make comparisons to other women he knew. But he had discovered long ago that listing a woman's faults was better than counting sheep—a practice that never had worked for him, although many swore by it.

His widow was stubborn.

Yours?

For tonight, he decided.

Where was he? Ah, yes. Stubborn but enticing. She was simply different from other women. He couldn't name one, including Suzanne, who admitted to working without finding a way to apologize for it. His widow was a woman of pride. But, oh, that smile. And those eyes...

This is not helping you to sleep.

Leave be, he warned the devilish little voice. A man had a right to take his pleasures where he found them. *And if I want to indulge in thoughts of the woman's lust-provoking curves, I will.*

Of all the stupid things to do. From that lustful thought his body reacted with heated blood and instant arousal.

Greg couldn't summon guilt. The woman couldn't read his mind. By all that was holy, she was asleep in her bed.

His eyes drifted closed as he turned on his side and plumped the pillows. He created his own version of their first meeting.

This time, a lovely, wickedly seductive widow opened the door to his knock.

There was no horrid cat. Not one squawk marred the husky murmur of her voice making him welcome.

Her blond hair floated free over her shoulders. She wore a pale blue silk robe with a single tie—his dream, his ease of convenience. So faithfully did the thin, shimmering cloth cling to her luscious body, only the exact shading of her nipples was left to his imagination.

Greg chose a dusky rose to match her lips.

He entered the house. She offered refreshment. He

refused. He stared into blue eyes and read approval for the lust-laden thoughts reflected in his gaze. A moment or two passed, then she drew him close.

Her generous lips were his for the taking. And he took until they both shook from the blaze of desire generated by that first kiss.

Greg tossed and turned. He flopped from his back to his stomach. His hands clutched the pillow.

Nothing could have forced him from his vivid dream—which, upon later reflection, he blamed on his miserable excuse for a dinner.

There he was, looking into her eyes dark with need. Her skin flushed with passion. His breathing increased. He could almost hear her heart beat.

Her graceful fingers cleverly divested him of his clothes. She beckoned him up the stairs.

One step, two, and suddenly those blue eyes changed to green, but without the blond-tipped lashes.

Greg moaned at the change and thrashed across the bed. His legs tangled in the sheet. He couldn't breathe. The moment his hand connected with soft, silky hair, he sighed relief and then groaned with rising ardor.

She was more than willing to stop and explore, arousing him. He, in turn, tasted her silken flesh. Her slender body was sleek and supple. She pressed against him. Her heat drove him wild. The tips of her nails raked his chest. He shuddered in reaction. When the tip of her tongue—that sweet, pink tongue he envisioned himself the recipient of—played over his mouth, then circled his ear before sliding down to his chest, he swore she wove her sorcery to ensnare him.

His lovely widow became the aggressor. His hands gripped the sheet beneath his powerfully aroused body. He touched and stroked her until he heard her purr.

He wanted her. Right there on the staircase. Urged by a desperation he couldn't explain, he tried to hold her.

She eluded his arms with a graceful turn and moved up a step. His hand caressed the smooth, silken length of her hair. With a hip-swaying walk meant to bring a man to his knees, she climbed the stairs.

Greg raced after her.

He was panting by the time he reached the top of the stairway. The hall, suddenly dark with pockets of shadows, loomed before him like an endless tunnel.

No. Not endless. There, waiting at the end, floated blue silk.

With his prize so close, he ran. As he did, the walls and ceiling stretched away from him until he no longer saw them. And he was shrinking.

Danger stalked him. Panic drove him forward. He had to save his wicked widow. His breathing was the rasp of an exhausted man.

Something massive pursued him.

Greg looked back over his shoulder. A cry came from his lips.

Green eyes of monstrous size stared at him. Terror, the likes of which he had never known, struck him dumb. The feline face taking shape out of the gloom froze him in place.

He heard her seductive purr beckoning him onward.

But all he thought of now was to get away. *Move! Hurry!* his brain ordered. Finally, his body obeyed. He pounded on the doors closed to him.

No aid. No refuge.

His attempts were of a frantic nature to evade the claws trying to trap him. He felt the heat of the cat's breath. Reduced to sobbing exhaustion, he tried one more door.

It opened.

With the animal a whisker away, he had no time to shut and bolt the door. He searched for a place to hide.

The bed. Get under the bed!

Greg squirmed his way into the dark cave. His fingers pressed the wooden floor as if he would find a magic door to freedom. A dust ball tickled his nose. He almost inhaled it in an effort not to sneeze and give away his hiding place.

Prayer was beyond his capability. He lay cowering, gasping for breath.

Greg watched with horrified eyes as massive paws came into view. He cringed as the body thumped to the floor. He could see that wicked tail snapping from side to side. His eyes widened when the cat's nose was in sight, whiskers twitching. Those great green eyes settled on him.

His blood chilled the marrow of his bones. There was triumph in the creature's gaze at having cornered him. One of the large paws flashed out. His leg was caught.

Despair filled him. He was going to be this beast's midnight snack.

He punched the paws slowly dragging him forth. He knew the cat would toy with him before he crushed his puny bones between those sharp fangs.

He was to die. The victim of a cat's revenge.

Chapter Eight

Greg bolted upright in bed. He threw the pillow he had been clutching to the floor and kicked aside the sweat-soaked sheet.

A plaintive meow had him rubbing his eyes. Horror of horrors, those green eyes *were* staring at him!

For an instant he couldn't move. Slowly sanity returned as the dream-turned-nightmare faded. The weight on his leg had not been a massive claw but the cat's body.

"Hell! Double and triple hell!" Limp with relief, he slumped back against the remaining two pillows.

Breathe. In and out. Calm yourself.

He willed strength to his leg and jerked it to the side. Another meow greeted his action. How dare that cat lament his overpowering need to get rid of him?

Lord Romeo stood up. He stretched out his front paws, his head bowed between them. His haunches and tail rose in the air as the cat extended his full length.

Greg, perceiving a threat, slapped finger-spread hands over his deflated pride and joy. The cat's paws were so close to his bare thigh, he couldn't have slid a new hundred-dollar National Bank note between them.

The creature's purring did Greg in. It brought back his vivid dream where the lovely widow—due to his seductive skill—had made that same vibrating husky rumble.

"Get the hell away from me," he growled at the cat. Somewhat revived, he sat up. "Go on," he ordered. "Get lost, you savage beast."

He swatted at the animal. Lord Romeo nimbly jumped aside. Filled with righteous fury, Greg scrambled across the bed. He made a grab for the cat, muttering revenge when the animal jumped to the floor.

Greg, suffering pangs of embarrassment, went after him.

"Stalk me, will you? Not while I breathe."

Greg stubbed his toe. He went at a staggering gait toward the door. The cat sat in the hallway as if taunting him. Greg shouted. Lord Romeo hissed.

A frightened Catherine, awakened by the noise, limped into the hall with her lamp held high.

All noise ceased. All movement stopped.

Speech was beyond her for that instant. She blinked, unable to believe what she saw. The lamp's glow picked up the sheen of moisture on Gregory Mayfield's skin.

Everywhere.

Stark naked, he froze in a crouch with his arms extended to grab Lord Romeo.

He appeared oblivious to his state. Catherine wished she was. Had he taken her words to heart? Did he believe he *was* in a den of iniquity?

"Wh-what are you doing?"

Her shaken demand shredded what little control he

had left. He stooped lower, shouting up at her. "While I lay sleeping in the privacy of my room, that thing, that monster of yours, attacked me."

His growled explanation finished on the rising cries of the cat.

Catherine was too shocked for modesty. Her swift once-over found no marks on his body. There wasn't a stitch to hide his sleek body. She saw a little of his chest covered with dark, curling brown hair. Surely such an attack would leave livid marks? Her gaze fell to his thighs, where well-developed muscles rippled as she watched.

And heat bloomed inside her.

She closed her eyes and muttered, "Don't you—"

Greg lunged for the cat.

Catherine darted in front of him just as Lord Romeo darted beneath the hem of her nightgown.

They went down in a tangle of arms and legs.

Catherine cried out. Her sore ankle was twisted beneath Greg's knee. His hands grabbed her hips and his fingers sunk into her resilient flesh, sending a wave of heat through his body.

The shocking feel of his hard body pressing against her sent the lamp teetering. "The lamp!"

Greg snatched it from her hand. Not that his were any too steady. He groaned and swore. Her hips were as soft and tempting as her mouth. He had never been the kind of man to grab at what a woman wouldn't freely offer to him. But he hated letting her go.

"You broke it," Catherine moaned.

"I've got it safe in hand." His gaze was wild as he tried to find the culprit. He needed some distraction. The cat wasn't in sight, but that didn't mean he wasn't around, waiting for another chance to pounce.

"Not...the lamp. You, oh, you...my ankle. You've broken my ankle. Get up!" She looked up at his face through the blur of tears. "This isn't a bordello. You can't run around in the...the..." She motioned with one hand toward his chest. She had to force herself not to reach up and touch him. "Get away. Oh, my ankle," she wailed.

This last cry sliced through the fury that filled him. Swearing, too aroused, too frustrated to be embarrassed, Greg rose in a smooth, controlled rush and retreated into his room. He returned to her in moments wearing his robe. He set the lamp on the floor, safely away from Catherine. There was still no sign of the cat.

Catherine looked up at him. The robe should have been an improvement. A rich, dark wine color, the silken fabric gaped open across his chest and made a knee-jerking, stomach-fluttering, heart-thumping, sexy picture.

The man was going to kill her. Slowly. Heatedly. Why had she remained chaste? She wouldn't be a frustrated, trembling bundle who couldn't decide if she wanted to hit him for worsening her injury or haul him off to her bed.

Then he touched her ankle and thoughts of desire went flying.

"Take your hands off me, you...you lecher!" The word best described her own thoughts, but he couldn't know that.

Just as Catherine was unaware that her accusation came too soon after the lusty, vivid dream-turned-nightmare for him to deny the guilt that swiftly rose.

"Calm yourself. I have no designs on your body." *Liar!* He continued in a voice of innate arrogance. "Put your arms around my neck. I'll carry you into your room to assess the damage.''

So much for desire. His bald statement made her cringe inwardly. She took exception to his tone, and batted his hands away. ''Don't give me orders. Don't touch me. You've done enough. And I can walk on my own if you'd back up and give me breathing room.''

''Stop being so damn female.'' As if she could. As if he wanted her to. ''You're muttering contrary nonsense. You were screaming minutes ago that I broke your ankle. Now,'' he demanded with one brow arched in disbelief, ''you can walk on your own?''

''Breathing room,'' she moaned.

He ignored her plea and hunkered down beside her. A mistake. This close he had the faint, sweet scent of her hair. This close and the temptation to know the taste of her mouth proved too much for even his strong will. Before she knew what he was about, before she could refuse, his head bent down and his mouth claimed hers. There was a last fleeting thought that he was taking advantage of her bemused state. Another first for him.

But it was a very fleeting thought. Her soft and most generous lips parted beneath the soft pressure of his. His tongue slipped inside warmth to delve behind her teeth to fully explore the sweet, heated taste of her.

Champagne. French. Aged. Silky and heady.

She sat there in dazed delight as he slowly, gently, thoroughly kissed her. When he finally pulled back, it was only a fraction of an inch.

''This is definitely all your fault,'' he murmured, his eyes warm as he smiled down at her. ''Further payment is required,'' he added softly, thinking again of his dream. And his mouth descended again.

There wasn't anything passive about Catherine's response this time. Her mouth opened beneath his, her tongue tasting and exploring his mouth as thoroughly as he had hers. She twined her arms around his shoulders. She made a little moaning sound in the back of her throat and curled her hands tighter around him. Her fingers kneaded his tightly muscled flesh as she slowly, languorously tipped her head back against the wall. The erotic play of his searching mouth sent shivers down her spine, where they dissolved into a hot pool of need.

She felt the glide of his hand against her throat as he shifted his weight to deepen the kiss. Spicy taste, silken cloth and masculine scents plunged her into white-hot longing. Reality had no place here, but it intruded. He was kissing her as if she belonged to him, and doubts rushed forth. Her heart was pounding. Her breasts were tight and hot and she couldn't breathe. But she didn't want an end to the raw pleasure of his mouth on hers, his tongue touching hers. The faint, hungry noise she made shocked her. What was she doing?

His hand cupped her shoulder, gently drawing her against his chest. The thin cloth of her nightgown offered no protection to her sensitive nipples rubbing against his curling chest hair. His masculine groan of pleasure brought the awareness of how far she had allowed passion to take her. Catherine tried to break the kiss. She discovered Greg had a stubborn streak wider than her own.

He was devious, too. Clever fingers rubbed her nipple, his other hand slid beneath her hair. The gentle press of his thumb and forefinger on her earlobe sent a shimmering heat through her. And his mouth was never still on hers. Hard one moment, soft and coaxing the next. She felt as if she had a fever. It had been far too long since Louis had made love to her. She had never been a passive partner in their lovemaking. Her hand rose and encountered his bare thigh.

Greg jerked back as if she had burned him.

Lost in desire, Catherine could only stare at him with a dazed expression.

On Greg's part, he knew that his dream was a pale imitation of kissing Catherine. But he couldn't tell her that. Nor would he apologize. But she had surprised him.

No feminine outrage. Just a bemused expression that he had stopped. She had no idea how close he'd been to taking her here. She was Suzanne's friend.

Catherine wanted to draw herself into a tight ball and disappear. She shouldn't have tried to touch him. Obviously he was disgusted with her. She moved and cried out.

Greg glanced at her ankle. She was injured and he'd taken advantage of her. Tears sparkled in her eyes.

"Don't," he whispered, leaning closer to brush the tears from her cheeks with his fingertips.

"Catherine, you're not crying because I kissed you?"

She shook her head. She couldn't even look at him.

Guilt swamped him. But he couldn't utter that he was sorry. He wasn't sorry at all. But he was disturbed by the way her eyes closed, and in a weary gesture, she tilted her head against the wall. Her bottom lip trembled and she bit it.

Catherine wouldn't admit it, but having him near was agony and comfort at once. It made no sense. If it weren't for him, she wouldn't be in the hall in the middle of the night, praying her ankle wasn't broken and trying to will her body into forgetting a few minutes of passion.

Her body wasn't listening. She ached with need. And it was all his fault.

Greg couldn't seem to stop touching her. He brushed aside the tendrils of hair that had escaped her braid. It was forcibly brought to his attention by a guilty conscience that this was not the time or the place for sexual thoughts.

But his fingertips—the part of him touching her—sent a message to his mind and body that undreamed-of passion waited within Catherine's arms. His response was almost painful and he had to shift away from her.

It was an effort to keep his eyes on her face and not let them stray below the round neckline of her nightgown. The white garment wasn't one to entice a man's erotic thoughts. The tiny pin tucks and plain buttons without a ribbon or bit of lace shouldn't have been the least bit tempting.

But they were. He should have left when he said he was going to. Catherine Hill was a complication he didn't want in his life. Only in his bed.

"Catherine," he whispered, "you're hurt. Let me help you. Your injury's my fault."

An impulsive imp almost made her blurt out agreement. But she had promised herself to curb her impulsive nature.

"No, this isn't your fault. I twisted my ankle earlier."

"And you never said a word. Why?" Her shrug could have meant anything. "But you don't deny I made it worse?" He didn't give her a chance to answer. He rose, bent and lifted her up into his arms.

Catherine looked directly into his eyes. She shivered to see the banked passion within them. *Stop this!* How? she wanted to know. Every nerve end was alive with need. *Distract yourself.* The impulsive imp rescued her.

"You're stronger than you look," she murmured as he stepped through her doorway.

"Kind of you to notice. And I won't drop you. There has been enough of that for one night."

The distraction didn't last long enough. She was all too aware that each wore a single garment. Thin, much too thin cloth. He must be running a fever. One of them was. It was far too hot. And she had to fight the desire to rest her head on his shoulder, or touch his hair, or lift her face so her lips could graze his chin.

"Somehow I had the impression from Suzanne's letters that you worked behind a desk all day."

Greg maneuvered her to the bed beneath the window. The lamp's light didn't reach this far corner of her room. But it was none too soon. Having the lovely widow in his arms was a temptation he could do without.

"I do a great deal of business at various clubs. I do try to ride most mornings," he went on in a distracted voice as she pulled the quilt over her. "I still enjoy fencing."

"Fencing?" What was he talking about?

"One of the best things I learned in military school. The others I wouldn't mention to a lady."

Catherine's hand fell from his shoulder as he stood up. He was strong. There was a muscled hardness belied by his lithe build. She bit her lip hard as she wiggled to sit up.

Greg went to retrieve the lamp from the hall.

"Is there a doctor in town?"

''He's not dependable. At this hour, he's likely to be passed out in the storeroom of the Red Horse saloon. I'll think of something. If Mary was here, she'd know what to do.''

''Well, you've got me.'' He regretted the words the moment he spoke them. What the devil did he know about injuries and ills?

Catherine looked away for a moment. She gritted her teeth to stop from asking him to contain his humor.

As if Greg divined her thought, he said, ''I don't know how much help I'll be, but I can run up and down for you. You'll need me to fetch whatever it is you do for a sprained—''

''Possibly broken—''

''Ankle,'' he finished. Then added, ''If it was broken, you'd be screaming with pain.''

''Now you're the doctor?''

''I've seen a few broken bones from riding accidents. Believe me, you wouldn't be talking so calmly if it was broken.'' You certainly wouldn't have been kissing me with all that pent-up hunger, either. Just the thought of her mouth beneath his own was enough to send his gaze downward. Thank the heavens his tailor believed in a generous cut for loungewear or he'd embarrass himself.

Greg leaned over. He shoved aside the quilt and pushed up the hem of her nightgown. He couldn't help the way his palm grazed the soft skin of her leg. Truly, he couldn't.

''What are you doing?''

''Don't do a modesty bit on me now,'' he ordered, and removed her hand trying to push the nightgown back down. ''I need to look at your ankle.''

"I don't invite men into my bedroom in the wee hours. I certainly don't let strange men touch—"

"Am I strange, Catherine?"

He asked in all seriousness, but there was a hint of humor in his gaze. She was tempted to say yes. Something was strange or she wouldn't be reacting to him this way.

"I haven't made up my mind about you."

"There's hope then. Such a dainty foot and very puffed-up ankle."

"Ouch!"

"Sorry. From what I see, I don't think you'll be dancing anytime soon. The thing is," he said, absently caressing the smooth curve of her calf, "what are we to do about this?"

"Eggs. We need eggs."

"Charming thought. I'm hungry, too, now that you mention food. But frankly, I've no desire to look at another egg for some time."

Catherine pulled the quilt partly over her. It was the only way to get him to stop touching her. But the quilt offered little protection from his heated gaze as he straightened and stared at her.

"Do you really want eggs? I should warn you before you answer, I don't know how to cook them."

She lifted her hand. "Not to cook. If you will go into the pantry, there's a bowl with eggs in it. Bring up two. And a small bowl. You'll find that in the corner cupboard. Oh, and I'll need a fork. And if you'll stop on the way back at the linen closet, there's a pile of clean rags on the bottom shelf. I'll need two, no, three rags."

Greg leaned close to put his hand on her forehead. "No fever."

"I could have told you that."

"I'm a man who likes to have everything confirmed. Preferably by me." He'd really have to watch this touching business. It was getting out of hand. Terrible pun. But true, so true.

"You're very sure about this? Shouldn't you soak it or something?"

He sounded so doubtful that Catherine couldn't resist teasing him.

"I'm positive about the things I require. Fear not, I won't ask you to...to indulge with me."

"I should hope not. You only asked for one fork."

She stifled a giggle under his black look. He left the room muttering about eggs and nightmares and wicked thoughts that demanded sacrificial payment.

He was gone so long that Catherine grew alarmed. She glanced around her room wishing she had picked up her clothes instead of dropping them on the floor when she had undressed. There was a pile of clean laundry that she had not gotten around to putting in the drawers. She squirmed and wiggled her way to the foot of the bed and snatched a shawl from the storage chest.

She had avoided looking at her ankle, but the pain increased to such a degree that she had to look. The skin was puffy just as Greg had said. She gingerly poked the area and decided he was right about it not being broken.

But where was he? Surely it wasn't difficult to find the pantry? Or the bowl of eggs? Whatever could he be doing? She felt helpless, more so when she heard a muffled crash below.

It was a simple errand. What could he have broken? And what was she going to do about him? It was one thing for him to help her now, but what about tomorrow?

No jumping that fence until you need to.

Good advice. All she had to do was follow it.

Catherine's patience reached its limit. She swung her legs over the side of the bed, when she heard Greg coming up the stairs.

Lord Romeo chose that moment to saunter in from the hall to Catherine's bed. He jumped up on the quilt, turned around four times, lay down and closed his eyes.

"You naughty cat," she scolded in a whisper and flipped a corner of the quilt to cover him. No need to upset Greg with the sight of the cat. Who knew what the man would do.

Greg balanced a large tray. He looked around for a clear place to set it down, shrugged and found a space on the floor near the bed.

"Before you ask, I had a slight mishap in the kitchen. Here is your bowl, egg and fork. I'll be right back."

Catherine stared after him. His robe was stained with dark wet spots. What had he done? She glanced at the tray and saw he'd made tea. She leaned over the edge of the bed for a closer look. The liquid appeared almost black.

She glanced into the bowl he had handed her. There was only one egg, not the two she requested. Catherine thought of the crash she had heard. And the dark wet spots on his robe. He couldn't have dropped the large bowl of eggs. Or had he? Lord, the man did need a keeper.

He returned while she puzzled over using the one small bowl to separate the yolk from the white of the egg. He was dressed in a badly creased white shirt tucked into dark brown trousers.

He set the rags on the side of the bed and looked into the bowl. "I didn't think you'd be able to get a raw egg down without help. Vile tasting. But never fear. I have come to your rescue." He held up a silver flask. "I couldn't find any spirits in your pantry. I brought you some of my brandy."

"Sarah doesn't allow any liquor in the house. And I don't drink—"

"Well, of course not. I didn't mean to imply that you did. No lady does. But this is strictly for medicinal purpose."

"Mr. Mayfield—"

"Greg."

"Greg, then. I need your help. Please hold out your hand." She cracked the egg on the edge of the bowl and deftly caught the yolk in one of the shells. A few times of flipping the yolk back and forth in the shell halves and Catherine had enough of the egg white. She handed the yolk-filled shell to him and proceeded to whip the egg white into a froth.

Greg, staring down into the blob of yellow cradled in the palm of his hand, felt his stomach turn over. He glanced around for somewhere to put the shell and its revolting contents. He settled on wrapping it in the napkin on the tray.

He lifted up the cup of tea he had made for her and watched in fascination as she dipped the rags into the egg whites. What the devil was she going to do?

Catherine looked up at him. "How sincere were you about helping me?"

He eyed the bowl and its contents. He thought of his action causing her further injury. He swallowed.

"I'll do whatever is necessary."

"Then put the cup down, for I need you to wrap my ankle."

Greg pushed the tray out of his way and knelt on the floor. He took the bowl from Catherine. He could see how swollen the ankle was.

"I'll try not to hurt you, but you must instruct me. I've never done anything like this."

Catherine believed him. What she doubted was that he'd never knelt before a woman. He was absently stroking her calf, unaware of the shimmering warmth his touch imparted. He almost made her forget the pain throbbing as her foot hung over the bed.

"Catherine."

"Yes?" She started and found that she was leaning very close to him. Shadows and lamplight loved his face, for they played upon the curves and angles with a most flattering hand.

"You were going to instruct me?" Didn't the woman have an ounce of conscience? If she leaned any closer, he'd need to be a saint to resist the temptation of her lips.

"You don't know how to…" *Kiss.* The word almost slipped out. Flustered, she looked down at her dangling foot. "The arch. You begin wrapping around the arch."

The beaten egg white was cold. His hands were hot in comparison. Catherine blamed these sensations for the breathless quality of her voice.

"Now wrap it once around the ankle, then again over the arch and back again. Not too loose. No, no, that's much too tight."

"Make up your mind!" he snapped. Greg couldn't blame her. It was all his fault. And it had nothing to do with being present in her bedroom. He'd viewed his share. It wasn't even the sight of her dimpled knee or shapely calf or dainty toes that made him testy. It could be blamed on his unwillingness to hurt her, and the simple knowledge that touching her played havoc with his heart rate. He declined to think about other body parts that were reacting at an alarming rate.

"How this slimy mess is going to help your swelling flesh is beyond my understanding."

"It works. Mary did it all the time. The egg white hardens the cloth and somehow draws out the swelling. I need to do this once a day for a few days and then my ankle will be good as new."

Once a day? He'd have his hands on… She uttered a low cry. "Sorry," he mumbled. *Think, man. Think about what you're doing.* He neatly smoothed the edge of the cloth in place and leaned back on his heels.

"Done. Now what?"

"Now I say thank-you most kindly and bid you good-night."

"But you haven't had your tea." He offered the cup to her.

It was black. Black with an abundance of tea leaves that had settled to the bottom of the cup. Catherine looked at him with amazement. Could he have dumped the entire tea canister in one cup? She knew the cost of tea leaves was beyond his concern, but it wasn't beyond hers. About to berate him, she stopped when he smiled and nudged her hand upward.

"Go on, drink it. Suzanne's a great believer in the restorative power of hot tea. But I'll confess to you, she enjoys the brandy with it."

"Suzanne?"

"Yes. But if you don't like spirits, I do have some

laudanum. I think you could do with some sleep." He gently lifted her leg back onto the bed and rose to his feet.

Catherine took a tentative sip of the tea. It was strong enough to stand a board on end. And there wasn't a place to dump it out. It was a thoughtful gesture, one she wouldn't have expected of him. If she didn't drink it, he would be insulted, even hurt. She couldn't do that to him.

Greg returned from his room with an amber glass bottle, which he removed the cork from, and then spilled a few drops of the brandy into her cup.

"Doc Rockefeller's magic cure, obtained from the celebrated cancer specialist himself."

Catherine lowered the cup. "Cancer?"

"Is the question in your voice meant for me? I don't have cancer. Doc just made this up for me. He's an excellent pitchman. Charges twenty-five dollars a bottle for his cancer cures. I bankrolled him once and he's never forgotten."

"Does he cure—"

"Heavens no. Bunch of herbs and laudanum. Can't hurt. Certainly to anyone in pain, it's a comfort. But a cure, never."

She closed her eyes and swallowed. Bitterness coated her mouth. She took another swallow and thought of the sacrifice she was making to salve his pride. What the devil was wrong with her?

She swallowed again and handed him the cup. "I can't drink any more."

"Then you rest. I'll borrow your lamp."

"Where are you going?"

"There's a small matter in the kitchen that requires my attention."

thought of his sprint across the yard, the care he took to keep to the shadows, his heart racing. And then the near miss with the pitchfork the boy wielded with such skill. And she dared accuse him of scaring the boy?

"Well, you did scare him, didn't you?"

"He's recovered enough to find all this amusing. That grin hasn't left his mouth. I, however, Mrs. Hill, don't enjoy finding strangers lurking about before dawn."

Catherine wiggled beneath the quilt, trying to raise her upper body so she could see Greg. He had hay clinging to his hair, his shirtsleeve was torn and there was a smudge of dirt on his cheek. But he was right about Ramon. The boy was grinning.

She motioned the boy closer and whispered to him. He nodded, and with a last look for Greg ran off.

"I sent him—"

"Did I ask?"

"No, Mr. Mayfield, you didn't." Her voice was as cool as could be. It rankled that he had become thought of his sprint across the yard, the care he took to keep to the shadows, his heart racing. And then the near miss with the pitchfork the boy wielded with such skill. And she dared accuse him of scaring the boy?

"Well, you did scare him, didn't you?"

"He's recovered enough to find all this amusing. That grin hasn't left his mouth. I, however, Mrs. Hill, don't enjoy finding strangers lurking about before dawn."

Catherine wiggled beneath the quilt, trying to raise her upper body so she could see Greg. He had hay clinging to his hair, his shirtsleeve was torn and there was a smudge of dirt on his cheek. But he was right about Ramon. The boy was grinning.

She motioned the boy closer and whispered to him. He nodded, and with a last look for Greg ran off.

"I sent him—"

"Did I ask?"

"No, Mr. Mayfield, you didn't." Her voice was as cool as could be. It rankled that he had become formal again, forcing her to be the same. *How can you be formal with a man who kissed you senseless?* Her independent streak supplied the answer. Anything this man did, she could do better.

"I didn't want you to think I was whispering about you. Ramon has gone to fetch his mother. Obviously, I will not be able to do much today."

"I should have asked first. How are you feeling?"

"Cross," she snapped.

"A dead man could see that," he returned with a smug smile. "And there is no need to hire someone. I managed last night to take care of you." *Didn't do so well for myself,* he thought. *A few stolen kisses re-*

was in the potion Greg had given to her, it did help the pain.

But she had reached the conclusion that she wouldn't be running around today or anytime soon.

Lord Romeo, asleep within the folds of her shawl at the foot of the bed, suddenly lifted his head and growled. The slamming of the back door filled the house along with shouts.

She couldn't imagine what the commotion was about and swore at her helpless state.

She needn't have worried. From the tramping footsteps racing up the stairs, she would soon know what had happened.

Greg stopped short at the top of the stairs. "Are you awake?" he called out. "And decent?"

Catherine pulled the quilt up to her chin. "Come in."

Greg walked in holding Ramon by the arm.

"Ramon! What are you doing to the child?" she demanded.

"I caught him stealing into the barn before civilized people are awake!"

"I imagine so," she answered calmly. "I asked him to come help with chores."

Greg glared at the boy, who cheekily grinned at him.

"You might have warned me he would be on the premises. I might have done him harm. And he could have explained that he was here by your invitation," he stated in an aggrieved tone. "All I got was mumbling in a heathen tongue."

"Ramon's from Mexico. He's also part Apache. When he's frightened, he lapses into a mixture of both languages. Obviously, you scared him."

Greg switched his glaring green eyes to her. He

sulting in a sleepless night as if he were a youth out of knickers.

"Don't be insulted," Catherine said. "I was thinking about you."

"You were?" He was cheered by the thought. And deflated in the next moment.

"Of course. Ramon's mother will cook for you. You are my guest. I need to provide food. It will only be for a few days until I'm able to get around."

If Catherine had thought him formal before, his voice was positively glacial now.

"If you insist, then I will pay the woman. And the boy."

"Why? You've already paid for room and board."

"No argument, Mrs. Hill. It's the least I can do since I caused your injury. I will take care of all the expenses until you are well. Now, since you have no need of me, I'll—"

"I didn't say that. You're so…so male. Touchy as a ruffled hen. And stop giving me orders in my home." But there was little heat in her tone. Catherine saw that he did look exhausted. "Did you get any sleep at all?"

Greg straightened. He ran a hand through his tousled hair and came away with bits of straw, which he clutched in his hand. The straw brought fond memories of a Georgetown hayloft and one Penelope Grady's inventive experiments.

Catherine found herself annoyed that his thoughts had strayed. But she felt guilty, too. Nothing had gone right from the moment he had arrived. An olive branch was needed.

"Shall we begin once more?"

Greg glanced up at her. "If you like."

"Good morning…Greg."

His smile was worth the risk of using his first name.

"And a good-morning to you, Catherine. Can I get you anything?"

"Coffee?" she asked. Her thoughts ran to other practical needs. Hot water to wash. Clothing. A change of her bandage.

"Coffee is something I can manage."

The room seemed empty when he left. Catherine discovered that he liked to sing. She couldn't make out the words or recognize the tunes, but his baritone voice was pleasant to hear. She was humming, too, when Lord Romeo rose, shook off the folds of the shawl and hopped down to the floor. Without a backward glance, he sauntered from the room with his tail held high.

"Come back here!" Catherine yelled. She had forgotten to tell Greg the cat needed to be let outside. She squeezed her eyes shut and pulled the pillow around her ears.

Tense as a fiddle string, she waited to hear the commotion from the kitchen. And she waited. She eased the pillow away. Silence. But Greg was no longer singing.

What was going on down there?

Below, Greg was staring at the stove, which was coughing billows of smoke into the kitchen. The back door was open, and the windows. He frantically waved a towel about to dispel the cloud of thickening smoke obscuring his vision.

Lord Romeo darted out the door with Greg unaware of his nemesis's presence.

"Who the hell knew how hard it was to start a fire!" He cursed and swore and waved the towel in widening flaps. "I can manage that," he growled in mimic of himself.

Coughing, eyes tearing, he ran outside, drew in lungfuls of clean air, then returned to clear the smoke. He couldn't very well run upstairs and ask Catherine what he'd done wrong. After all, a man had his pride.

"Blast the damn thing to hell!"

Catherine heard that shout. Something was wrong. She knew it was something serious, too. When the first faint whiff of smoke entered her room, alarm spread through her.

What had he done now? Set her kitchen on fire?

The idea impelled her from bed. She managed the wardrobe on a cross between a hop and a hobble. She grabbed the first gown that came to hand and struggled into it over her nightgown. Pain shot from her bandaged ankle when she forgot and put her weight on it.

Using the same awkward gait, she traversed the hall, but the stairs loomed as a monstrous obstacle. The smell of smoke was no longer faint. If she needed a spur, that was it.

When she reached the kitchen doorway, she didn't know if she should laugh or cry.

Gregory Mayfield no longer resembled a citified gentleman. His white shirt with the sleeves rolled up was soot-spattered and clung to his body in large wet circles. He kicked the stove and cursed it to hell.

Layers of smoke hovered in the kitchen despite the back door and window being open. Catherine, eyes tearing, leaned against the door frame, trying to catch her breath from her exertion. Water dripped from the stove to the floor, where it pooled among the scattered kindling from the wood box. Her blurred gaze traveled upward to discover the cause. Just as she surmised. The damper was closed.

What had possessed the man to do such a thing then try to light the fire? Didn't he know anything?

"Open...the damper," she yelled. She coughed and had to wipe her eyes.

He spun around, a wild, glazed look in his eyes. "Damper? What the hell is that? Never mind. Tell me how you summon the fire brigade."

Panic and fury mixed in his voice. Catherine could not offer a bit of sympathy now. "Where in tarnation do you think you are? We don't have a fire brigade. Not unless you think a line of people passing buckets might help." Lord, patience. Lots of it. Please.

"I'm in the wilds of some nightmare land," he snapped.

"And you may die there if you don't open the damn damper. Up on the stovepipe. The small L-shaped piece of metal. Turn it. And hurry."

Greg spied the very piece of metal he had turned, thinking it was crooked. He twisted it back into place, feeling an utter fool as he turned to face Catherine. But he was angry, too. At her, and at his sister for putting him here.

A woman had to rescue him from another domestic crisis. Well, they were better at that. But Suzanne would pay for this. Somehow, someway.

The smoke was already beginning to clear. "How did you get down the stairs? And why, for heaven's sake? What are you doing here?"

"I might," she responded, waving a hand in front of her face, "ask you the very same thing?"

"*You* wanted coffee. And you didn't answer my questions."

"Ah, the coffee." Catherine looked at the mess.

"The beans I buy are already roasted and ready to be ground. Heat water and—"

"Don't insult me. I know that much. The coffee was not the problem, madam. Your stove is another matter." He flapped a towel in the air, but now that the stove was drawing properly, the smoke was fast disappearing.

And with it went his anger. "I apologize. I know nothing about stoves. Or the workings of a kitchen. They are the province of women. And now I know why."

There was something boyishly appealing about his admission. He swung the towel in widening circles, unaware that he sent the last lingering smoke toward her. But the room was fast filling with fresh air.

All manner of imprecations at his ignorance rose to her lips. Her impulsive imp, which would have made her speak them, was nowhere to be found. It was simpler to be kind to him than callous. He was such a handsome but pitiful sight with his perplexed expression. The sun was barely up. Perhaps she could still look forward to a quiet day of rest after all this excitement.

"Catherine, I really feel like a fool."

"You couldn't know that the…the damper sticks." She smiled at him. "I should have warned you." She wiped the last tears from her cheeks.

"Stop being so damn kind. Look at you, hobbling on your injured ankle, crying, and once again I'm at fault. I've never, to my knowledge, made a woman cry."

"You used to pull Suzanne's braids. Mine, too."

"We were children then. Now…" He came toward her, absently waving the towel.

When he was closer, she saw the look in his eyes. Catherine felt as if her blood had suddenly heated and was rushing through her. It was a dizzying, but not unpleasant, sensation. Then again, the cause could be all the smoke she inhaled.

"Don't you ever get really angry, Catherine?"

"Stop it."

"You can't keep overlooking the mess I've made of everything."

"Yes, I can get really angry. Furious. Dish-tossing and door-slamming kind of anger. But this really wasn't your fault."

"Wrong. I moved the piece of metal. Thought it was crooked."

"You didn't know. And now you do," she insisted.

Greg opened his mouth to argue, then closed it. She looked like a tousled angel risen in sultry splendor from some man's bed. And yet there was an innocent unawareness of her very feminine appeal to him.

He wanted to brush away her frown as he continued to stare at her. He wanted to be the one to brush the long, silky blond hair back from her shoulder. He thought of last night and how she'd appeared gilded by the lamp's light: creamy skin touched with the flush of passion, her lips reddened from his kiss, begging for more. The rapid rise and fall of her breasts...

He shook his head. Where had these thoughts come from? He had made the decision that he would not pursue her. No sexual contact. There was no place in his life for a woman like Catherine. He could hear his friends laughing behind his back if he were to take her east with him. She'd insist on bringing that nightmare cat, and likely her hen. No. And he had certainly proved both yesterday and this morning that he didn't belong here. If it wasn't for that damn bet with Suzanne...but the bet existed. He couldn't falter now. Too much was riding on the outcome. And it wasn't just for himself.

He touched her cheek despite his own warnings. "You never told me how you got down the stairs."

"I sort of sat and bumped my way down."

"Poor Catherine. You've made a bad bargain with my sister."

"Have I?" There wasn't the strength of a piece of straw in her words. They came out breathless and soft. This time she couldn't blame the smoke. The gleam in his eyes appeared brighter, suddenly hotter. She only knew his gaze made her feel an odd heaviness while her heart pounded.

Gracious! What was wrong with her? She had been physically attracted to a man before him. Whatever this thing was between them, she was sure it was stronger on her side. But that's all there was, this inexplicable, intangible attraction that would never be acted upon.

If only he hadn't kissed her. He awakened all the longings she thought she could live without satisfying. It was more than her missing a shared marriage bed. Louis had been a patient lover and praised the passion she brought to him. What she missed most was the special intimacy of living together with someone who shared your dreams, hopes and fears. Gregory Mayfield made her realize her life was barren without love.

Sarah would take her to task if she ever expressed such a thought. She tightened her hand buried in the folds of her gown, welcoming the feel of her nails biting into her palm. This foolishness had to stop. Right now.

"Catherine," he said, looking away for a moment. "I have something important to ask you."

"Ask."

He was oddly embarrassed to do so. Her curt tone put him off. They were both adults. And he'd been a fool twice this morning. No need to make it three times.

"I noticed," he began, then cleared his throat, "a lack of a bathroom in the house."

"Bathroom?" She felt stupid repeating it, but here she was thinking of love and he was...damn him. Once again she faced the decision of laughing or crying. "What is so important about a bathroom?"

"I need a bath," he snapped. "Smoke. Reek. And I couldn't find where you have—"

"A tub?" she finished for him with an unholy gleam in her eyes. "You have a choice. Sarah and I prefer to use the rain barrels on the side of the house. The soap-berry bushes serve as screens and if you crush the berries you have soap of a sort. Or you can use the laundry tub that is stored in the pantry. Of course, you will have to haul it out here to the kitchen, heat pots of water, and when you're done, you can begin hauling out the buckets until the tub is empty. Understand, bucketful by bucketful," she added for good measure.

"But the privacy?" he sputtered.

"Privacy? Truth to tell, I don't give much thought to that. After all, we started out three women living together. Sarah and I just mention we want a bath, and that's that."

He closed his eyes briefly. His mouth tightened, then he looked at her. "In case it has escaped your notice, Mrs. Hill, I am not a woman. I do give a great deal of thought to bathing in private. And since I am in residence here, you'd better do the same."

The temptation proved too much. After all, she was allowed a slip. Curbing an impulsive nature was most difficult with him around.

She leaned forward and kissed him. A kiss very unlike their heated exchanges of last night. But it served her purpose. Short and sweet.

"You definitely don't kiss like a woman. Enjoy your bath, Mr. Mayfield. Don't forget to lock both doors and draw the curtains. Your privacy must be protected at all cost."

"Where do you think you're going?"

"I'll try the parlor. I'm not up to tackling the stairs again."

He caught hold of her arm. "Why did you kiss me?"

"It seemed like a good idea at the time." She glanced at his hand wrapped around her arm. "Now I see it was—"

"Sweet," he finished for her. "Stay. I might need you to scrub my back."

All the mischievous sparkle disappeared from her eyes as she looked directly at him. "You don't want that. You don't really want me. And if I stayed, we both know what would happen. I won't let it."

His hand slipped from her arm. The teasing had to stop. But even with her eyes reddened, she appealed to him as no other woman had. He shifted uneasily with the silent admission. Thoughts like these would trick him into doing or saying something foolish. Like making a few promises that would be impossible to keep. Men did it all the time. Women believed them. He was tempted, but couldn't play that kind of cruel game with Catherine.

Fighting the strong need to take her into his arms
and show her how easily nature could take its course
between them, he put the distance of the room between
them. Absolving him of guilt for his part in her injury
revealed a rare, unselfish nature. He was finding it hard
to keep a level head where Catherine was concerned.

But he had to. Unless…

Ramon's breathless return ended any action on
Greg's part. He importantly announced that his mother
could not come, for the grand lady—his name for Mrs.
Pettigrew—was having a grand fiesta and needed her.
That said, he carefully opened his shirt and removed a
folded paper. He handed it to Greg and left to take care
of chores.

The note was an invitation for Greg and Catherine.
He was generous in calling it an invitation, since the
party Mrs. Pettigrew planned was in his honor.

"Will you go?" she asked when he finished reading.

"It's more like a command performance. I don't
have a choice. But it's not until next week. A lot could
happen by then."

Yes, she wanted to say, you could be gone. Catherine took two hops into the hall and found herself
where she least wanted to be. At least the sensible part
of her said she didn't. The other part, the needy Catherine she discovered last night, was perfectly content
to steal a few minutes in Greg's arms while he carried
her back up to her room.

He left her immediately. She daydreamed her way
through the morning with thoughts so erotic her body
felt fever flushed.

Catherine gave herself a good talking-to after he
brought up a brunch tray. Coffee making was not
among the man's accomplishments. It was beyond her

ability to understand how anyone could ruin coffee. Greg had managed the impossible. Not only would the spoon stand by itself, the liquid was dark, thick sludge.

She nibbled at the generous slice of gingerbread and admired the wildflowers stuck in her best china teacup. She almost admired the intricate folds of the napkin made to resemble a sailboat. An odd thing for a man to master. She took it apart and tried to make it herself, only to give up.

Thoughts of Greg had to be pushed aside. She was firm with herself. There was no room in her life for a man like him. She certainly had no place in his. Imagine her in the city, following Suzanne's routine of rising late, sipping hot chocolate in bed while her maids brought invitations and clothing for her approval.

No, it was in her best interest to forget his gender or else think of him as a brother.

She settled back to enjoy the quiet.

Her restful moments lasted just about that long, when a horrid thud, followed by a screeching, filled the house.

Chapter Ten

Catherine yanked the quilt over her head. Three seconds later she threw it aside and struggled off her bed.

Mayfield was killing her cat. From the sound of the screeching, he was succeeding, too.

The thought of attempting the stairs again made her cringe. She had expected a quiet day. What was the man doing? He was here to get better, not drive her insane.

Lord Romeo was normally well behaved. It had to be Greg's fault.

With her awkward gait she reached the doorway. There she stopped. Greg rushed up the stairs and down the hall toward her.

"Stay put!"

"But—"

"No buts. Just stay there."

She was tempted to do just that. But she couldn't cower behind a closed door while her pet was in danger. And from the look of Mayfield, Lord Romeo might not last the day.

"Just a minute, Mayfield, You can have your money back. Your sister will have to forgive me for quitting."

"No!"

"No? This is my house. And if I say—"

"The house belongs to Sarah. Or so you said. And while your cat is not long for this world, madam, you are. You will not quit." He swiped at the water that dripped from his hair, sprinkling her with droplets.

"Nothing like this has ever happened. Not until you arrived. Lord Romeo is a good cat. And don't you dare give me orders."

"Point that finger in my face again and I'll—"

"What? Bite it? Just try. You've already bitten off more than you can chew."

"What's that supposed to mean?"

His cheeks were mantled with the flush of anger. Catherine drew herself up to her full height, using the door frame for support. "It means, sir, that you lack a certain basic knowledge of the workings of ordinary things. You almost set fire to the house, you—"

He leaned close, almost nose to nose with her. "What happened to the soul of forgiving kindness I had the pleasure of meeting this morning? You're a typically fickle female."

"I'm—" Catherine closed her mouth. He was right. Things had been as topsy-turvy as one of the dolls Mary made. Forgiving kindness aside, it didn't help his cause that he nodded with satisfaction for having stopped her protest.

"Despite your lowly opinion of me, Mrs. Hill—and I know you think I'm some kind of bumbling idiot— I'm the only one who can take care of you. For your edification, I was trying to make you soup."

She gaped at him in astonishment. Her voice, when she finally spoke, sounded feeble. "Soup? You were making soup? And Lord Romeo—"

"Twined himself around my legs as I was carrying the pot of water to the stove."

Catherine started to reach out to touch him, then pulled back. "I owe you another apology. He was just showing affection. He really doesn't understand that people aren't as agile as he is." His frown didn't bode well for Lord Romeo. She touched his forearm. "If it will help, I'll ban him from the house."

"We'll see."

She didn't know what to make of that cryptic remark. His expression offered no clue. Catherine decided not to pursue the matter.

"I didn't know you knew how to cook. Suzanne wrote that—"

"In this lowly male's opinion, women have a tendency to make the most simple task into an unnecessarily complex problem. How difficult can soup be to make? A pot of water, vegetables, a piece of meat, and you have the makings for soup."

He sounded so reasonable that Catherine found herself agreeing with him. "You found the smoked bacon?"

"No."

"You used what's left of the ham?"

"No."

"Then what did you use for meat? I hadn't gone to the butcher. There's nothing—"

A smug smile creased his lips. "Did you know there are cultures that consider cat a delicacy? I've also heard of several Indian tribes that enjoy dog."

Catherine pressed her hand to her heart. She wondered if she could murder him and bury his body.

"Are you going to faint?"

"Never. And if you harm one hair of my cat's fur, I'll—"

"You leave that misbegotten creature to me. But I won't harm him."

Trust was at low ebb. But what choice did she have? "All right, you promised not to hurt him. I suppose if you're staying, you'll have to work out some way to get along."

"Do you need my help to get back into bed?"

"I do not." She turned away and hopped a few steps, when her uninjured leg buckled.

Greg caught her up from behind. "You're making it a habit to fall into my arms every chance you get. Not that I'm complaining—"

"A good thing you're not." His chest pressed against her back so tightly that she felt the wetness from his shirt seep into her gown. "And I do not make it a habit—"

"You're a woman to tempt a saint, Catherine," he whispered, and nuzzled her ear. He lifted her a bit higher and marched her to the bedside.

"I've never wanted to tempt a saint. I don't know any. I don't believe you're on speaking terms with any, either. You certainly aren't one. And I *don't* fall into your arms every chance I get. You're always underfoot."

He dumped her on the bed.

She glared up at him. "And another thing. Stop interrupting me at every turn."

"To hear is to obey, madam." He offered her a hand-waving, graceful bow, then straightened. "Now, stay put. I'll deal with this little mishap." He left an openmouthed Catherine behind and closed the door.

"Just another little mishap," he muttered over and

over on his way downstairs. He *was* going to kill that cat.

Greg stood in the kitchen doorway and surveyed the ruin of his good intention. He wasn't sure where to begin cleaning up the mess in the kitchen this time. The temptation to march back up the stairs and tell Catherine that he was leaving bloomed like the finest idea he'd had all day.

"*Señor.*"

He saw Ramon standing by the back door. There was no sign of that miserable cat.

"Ramon, how would you like to earn a twenty-dollar gold piece?"

The boy's bright smile was hard to resist. Greg's lips curved into a reluctant smile. "Here's what you have to do."

Catherine heard Greg singing. She flopped back against the pillows and gazed upward. "Lord, I know I've asked for patience, but this time, give it to me in bigger doses. Fickle female, am I? Who wouldn't be fickle dealing with a man whose moods change faster than our weather? And makes me feel like scrambled eggs?"

"*Señora?*"

Catherine's musing ended with the sound of Ramon's voice. "Come in."

He peered around the door. "The *señor,* he said I am to sit on you."

"Sit on me? I think he meant for you to sit *with* me. But, Ramon—"

"No, no, *señora.*" He stepped inside, shoulders pulled back, eyes straight ahead, standing tall. "He said I am to sit on you so you stay put."

Catherine glanced upward. "Where's that bigger dose of patience?" she muttered. Looking back at Ramon, she smiled. No point in confusing the child. "Did he say why you had to sit on me?"

"*Señora*, this thing he asks, I cannot do it."

"Never mind, Ramon. That will be our secret. You can stay and keep me company."

"This I can do."

He appeared troubled. Catherine waited until he had made himself comfortable on the corner of the bed.

"Ramon, where is the *señor*?"

"He is gone to town. Please," he said, staring at her with wide brown eyes, "you no ask me more."

His serious request kept Catherine silent for a while. She bit her bottom lip. She couldn't put Ramon in the middle. But she had her own ideas of why Mayfield had gone to town. Likely to drown his sorrows in the first saloon on Main Street. And she was supposed to keep him from drinking hard liquor.

Then again, he might be sending Suzanne a telegram telling her that all bets were off because he was not staying in a crazy house. It mattered not one whit that she was disregarding his commitment to stay. He also could communicate with his business partners. Another strike against her if he did.

There was the matter of food. He could sneak into the café and gorge himself on forbidden foods. Catherine mentally crossed that one out after a second thought. He wouldn't deliberately cause himself pain. Not after what he'd been through.

She stared at her bandaged ankle. The fresh application of egg whites had calmed the painful throbbing. Rest was what she needed. Somehow, she had to put aside thoughts of what Mayfield was up to. And a day of complete bed rest now would save her more aggravation later.

"So, Ramon," she began in a falsely cheerful voice, "tell me if Lord Romeo is still alive. And my chickens? None ended up in the *señor*'s soup pot?"

"There is no soup pot. The cat, he is in the tack room. I helped..." He stopped and offered a guilty look.

"Yes?" Catherine prompted. "What did you help him with?"

"This I cannot tell you. I promised."

"Oh." She managed a wealth of disappointment in one tiny word.

"It is a matter of honor between men, *señora*."

Leave it to Mayfield to twist the boy's thinking. And, she wanted to ask, what happened to the loyalty that came from our friendship? But she let the whole matter be.

"It's all right. Why don't you tell me about school."

While she listened, Catherine closed her eyes. She couldn't stop wondering what Greg was doing. Somewhere in the middle of Ramon's story about the new schoolmaster, she dozed off. She dreamed she was married to Greg. She saw him through a hazy cloud, sitting before the fire in the parlor. Lord Romeo and assorted barn kittens were curled close to him. He smiled at her with such tenderness that Catherine swore she had tears of joy in her eyes.

She reached for his extended hand, only to wake with a start.

Lord Romeo lay beneath her hand, his rumbling purr loud within the room.

Catherine saw no sign of Ramon. She stretched and sat up. Shadows of early evening filled the corners.

And from the darkened rectangle of the doorway came Greg's voice, heated and low, rich as thick golden honey with sensual promise.

"Disappointing to be sure. Sleeping beauty has awakened without a kiss."

Still caught in the throes of her dream of him, Catherine gave no thought to her flirtatious response, given in a voice rife with hushed intimacy.

"And are you the dashing prince come to rescue me?"

"Do you," he whispered, his half-lidded eyes raking her slender form, "require rescuing, Catherine?"

Chapter Eleven

There was an infinitesimal pause before Catherine answered. "That would depend."

"On what?"

"On what you're offering."

"Pleasure."

One word. She found he delivered it heated, soft, without promise, simply fact. Curious, and admittedly challenged, she had no choice.

"And for that I'll give—"

"The same."

"No strings?"

"Not a leading line in sight," he returned calmly, so at odds with the hot spur of need that was pushing him to step over the threshold.

"And if I wanted more..." She left it half musing, half question, wishing he would come closer, wishing this had never started.

"Whatever you'd like. I can afford to indulge you."

"Ah, yes, money."

Greg hesitated. Unable to see her expression, he had only her voice to guide him. She spoke without inflection.

"Don't you like money?"

Alarm bells held her silent. Where was this leading? She wasn't sure she wanted to know. If only she could see him.

"Catherine?"

"Yes. I like it well enough. But I like earning what I have so that it is mine."

You're stepping on cobwebs, he warned himself. *One wrong word...* "We're both adults. Free of entanglements. Sharing pleasure brings no harm. Unless..."

"Unless?" she asked.

"There is someone else."

"No. No men in my life at the present."

"I'm here, Catherine."

"Yes." She wanted to recall that breathless word, to recall its hint of invitation, its assurance that he was the only man in her life now. But the wish went begging. He walked inside her room.

And with him came the flushed heat of need that she made no attempt to fight. She felt both fragile and strong. The fragility came from how easy it would be to love him. The strength from her own feminine power to excite him. Alarm bells were silenced. All she heard was the pounding of her heart as he stood next to the bed. And just as in her dream, he extended his hand to her.

The shadows were so deep she could barely make out the form of his body. But she felt the heat of him. Just as she heard Lord Romeo's warning growl.

"No!" Hushed denial from her lips.

Greg dropped his hand to his side. "Another time, perhaps."

"But I didn't mean—"

"Oh, but I think you did."

"The cat…" she began to say.

As if in response to her words, Lord Romeo rose and stretched. If he was aware that two pairs of eyes were targets on him, he gave no sign. He jumped off the bed, skirting Greg's boots, and left them alone.

Catherine thought about explaining, but the intimate mood was broken. Perhaps it was for the best. She pushed her hair aside and swung her legs over the edge of the bed.

"Has Ramon gone home?"

"Ramon?" He sounded as distracted as he felt. Having stood in the shadows watching her sleep, his night vision—always strong—had had time to adjust to the gloom in the room. Her move to sit on the edge of the bed brought her in profile to where he stood. The woman had no idea of her provocative pose. Her hair rippled down her back. With her arms braced on the bed behind her, the curves of her breasts were lifted in offering. Below the hem of her gown he could make out the pale skin of one trim ankle and the bandage on the other.

The bandage threw a dose of cold reality in his face.

"Yes, Ramon left. I came to fetch you downstairs for supper."

What had she said? He was once again coldly formal. Just as well. All he had offered was pleasure. *I can afford to indulge you.* But could she afford to indulge herself? Wild oats could lead to a sad harvest. The words sounded like Sarah's practical advice. *Ah, Sarah, I could do with your presence. You'd keep me on the right path.*

"You are hungry, aren't you, Catherine?"

Such a simple, normal question. But he'd asked it in that heated, deep, low voice and caused a hitch in her breathing. She had to do something to regain control or she'd be racing him for the nearest bed. Her hands curled around the quilt. She'd beat him if she remained where she was.

A strong body builds a strong mind. She knew that was Mary's sage wisdom. Still, she hesitated.

"I know you are, Catherine."

"You know nothing at all about me. And yes, I am hungry. I'll be right down."

"You can't," he said with a hint of laughter, "do it alone."

"Get down the stairs?" she replied with perfect innocence.

"But of course, what else would I have been suggesting?"

"Satisfying hunger." She clapped her hand over her mouth. His laughter filled the room but did nothing to stop her from damning her impulsive nature for blurting that out.

Before she took another breath he had her snugly scooped up into his arms. "Supper, Catherine. That's all." He carefully maneuvered her through the doorway and into the hall. At the top of the stairs, he nuzzled her ear. "For now."

Then it was Catherine's turn to laugh, for he couldn't hide his reaction to the way she tunneled her fingers beneath his hair at the back of his head. His arm muscles tensed, she felt the shudder that ran through him, heard the quickening of his breath.

"Madam likes to live dangerously."

"How so?" She rested her head on his shoulder.

"I've made no secret that I want you, Catherine. Arousing me while I'm negotiating the stairs could lead—"

"To an enticing adventure?"

He closed his eyes briefly, thinking again of his dream and his amorous pursuit of the lovely widow on these very stairs.

"A serious turn of events you're not ready to—"

"Handle?" she finished for him.

"Now who is constantly interrupting whom?"

"I've never teased a man like this."

Greg stopped midway. He angled his head so his lips could touch hers. Lightly. Softly. "I said I could afford to indulge you, Catherine. I meant in all things."

"Yes, I know." And she gave in to the temptation to kiss him, gently tracing the shape of his mouth with the tip of her tongue. With a shaky sigh she withdrew. "But I can't afford to indulge myself."

Instantly, Greg went to war with himself. He knew the sexual attraction between them didn't need much to flare into flame. He sensed how close she was to yielding. He hadn't made an idle promise. He could bring her pleasure.

But there was an innocence about her that held him in check.

But a devilish voice whispered how easy it would be to arouse her past the point of refusing not only him, but herself. Incredibly responsive Catherine. Temptation slid beyond beckoning; it held aloft a prize.

So very, very easy...

"Greg?" she whispered.

"Say yes. I won't hurt you, Catherine. You do know that, don't you?"

No, she didn't know. But she had to defuse this situation right now.

"Oh, but you will." Her hand slid down to his shoulder. "We're certain to take a tumble if you keep us standing in the middle of the stairway. You did say you were taking me downstairs to feed me. Didn't you?''

''If that's all that you want.''

Catherine didn't answer him.

And that was answer enough.

The kitchen, she saw, was bathed in candlelight. He had taken pains to set the table with their best tablecloth. Each darned spot was covered with flowers that Mary had embroidered. The result was a pretty cloth. There was even a small rosebud in a glass. He set her down and pushed her chair closer to the table.

''Your supper awaits.''

''I see you've been very busy.'' Her gaze passed over the good china and the silverware she had brought with her. But how could she reprimand him when the man was accustomed to having the very finest when he dined.

She reached out to touch the rosebud. ''Where did you—''

''Mrs. Pettigrew was kind enough to cut it for you.''

''Me? No. She did it for you. And the sliced roast beef and potatoes? Baby peas, too? You didn't—''

''Ramon told you.''

''No. I knew you had left, but not the reason why.'' She blushed to remember all manner of evil things she had thought of him doing. Eyes alight, she smiled at him. ''You've gone to a great deal of trouble.''

''Catherine,'' he said, leaning over the back of her chair so that his lips brushed against her hair. ''I would do a great deal more if you—''

''Would enjoy this meal you've provided? Did you cook any of it?''

''I wish.'' He sighed and stepped around the table

to sit across from her. She looked even more lovely by candlelight. He'd be the envy of every man who saw her take tea at the Fifth Avenue Hotel. Or at the theater. Greg shook his head. What was he thinking of to imagine Catherine in New York by his side?

He saw that she watched him with a puzzled expression. Her head was tilted to one side and he was lost in watching the play of light against her blond hair.

"Go on, enjoy your dinner, Catherine. Your friend Caroline at the café supplied it all. She even included an apple pie for dessert."

"And I'll guess she made you pay a pretty price for it, too."

"Desperate men don't count cost when they need something."

"Or want it," she softly noted.

"Or want it," he agreed.

She reached for the soup ladle, only to find that he beat her to it.

"I'll serve you this evening." He caught her quick look toward the stove.

"No, I didn't make the soup. You'll have to wait to sample my try at culinary delights. Your cat effectively put an end to any thoughts I had of cooking." He shuddered expressively.

"I could almost find it in my heart to pity you."

"I hope you will. At this point, I'll take whatever I can get." He smiled that impossibly charming smile that invited hers in return.

Catherine struggled to find a safe topic of conversation. He seemed to turn everything she said into a personal reference to their attraction to each other. For her peace of mind she had to stop him. *And yourself? And myself.* She couldn't have it within herself to be insulted. Not when she wished...no, she would stop now.

She sipped at the savory vegetable broth. "Delicious. Greg, will you tell me the terms of the bet you have with Suzanne?"

"Now?"

He sounded disappointed, but she remained firm and nodded.

He set his soup spoon down and folded his arms across his chest.

"It is a safe subject," she said truthfully. "Unless there is some reason I can't know them."

"How much do you know about Suzanne's recent activities?"

"My friend, the social butterfly? She writes pages of her social life, describing this ball or theater parties. I know about her work at the orphanage. The suppers she gives, and the weekend sailing trips or visits to country estates. She loves writing about the children. I know she adores her husband. And you. But I don't think that's what you mean. Oh, and she does tell me that she shops a great deal. I can't imagine any woman needing as many gowns or accessories as she describes. I know that she requires new furs by Gunther every season. And gowns by a designer from Paris—"

"Worth," he supplied.

"Yes, that's the name. She loves jewels. I guess she has close to a queen's ransom—"

"More like an entire royal family's worth. It's true that those of us who know Suzanne are familiar with her spending habits."

"But I understand that her husband can afford to indulge her every desire. And there were those years when she couldn't have anything new, Greg. Suzanne has never forgotten that.''

"I know," he stated in a soft voice. His gaze met hers and found compassion within her blue eyes. Once again he found himself thinking how unique Catherine was of all the women he had known. Honest, sincere, loyal. And she had no idea of the thoughts she was putting into his mind.

"Greg? You are going to finish, aren't you?"

"Finish?"

"Suzanne, remember? You were telling me about the bet.''

"You were right. These things that she's written about to you are not my concern. Her joining the Ladies Liberation League is.'' Her blank stare made him thank the Lord that she didn't know anything about the league. One woman in his life involved with them was enough. *But Catherine isn't a woman in your life. Or at best, only a temporary one.*

"What's wrong? What did I say to make that black scowl appear?"

"Am I scowling?" he asked. "It's not at you. It is the mere thought of those militant women determined to see that women are given the right to vote.''

"Then I must support my friend and applaud her effort.''

"You would.''

"Pardon?''

"Your loyalty is a commendable trait, Catherine.''

"Thank you. I think. You don't sound happy to admit it. But, please, whatever has this to do with your bet?''

"I might have known that you'd be a kindred spirit.'' He expelled a deep, heartfelt sigh. "Woe to manhood if such strong-minded women have the right to direct—"

"Gregory Michael Mayfield, if you wish to survive your visit here, refrain from such remarks."

"So noted. I shall endeavor to obey. As for my sister, she took advantage of me in a weak moment. Why should I protect her? You're her loyal friend. She blackmailed me."

"Suzanne? I won't—"

"Oh, yes, you'll believe it. She cornered my doctor and used her considerable feminine charms to pry information about my health from him. I wanted to sue the man for breach of ethics, but to be fair, I know my sister when she's after something. The man didn't stand a chance against her."

Catherine smiled, but inwardly she couldn't help envying Suzanne just a little. He obviously adored his sister despite her attempt to blackmail him.

"Since you know my sister, there is no need for me to elaborate on her quick use of the doctor's prognosis."

"Are you telling me that Suzanne only had a mercenary reason for sending you here?"

"Lower that arched brow, my dear. I am trying to tell you—"

"I won't believe that of her. She loves you. She would never endanger your health over a bet for any cause."

"My dear and most lovely Mrs. Hill, am I here?"

That gave Catherine pause. She glanced down to find her soup bowl empty and Greg reaching across the table to remove it. She looked up to find his dark eyes watching her.

"Yes," she whispered, "you're here."

"Then, Catherine, I rest my case."

"I still find it difficult to believe. Suzanne wrote her concern for your deteriorating health. Her instructions to me were exacting as to the care you required to make changes."

"I am not arguing that she is not concerned. I am stating that my darling sibling is not above using any situation to achieve her own ends. As to her instructions," he said with mock severity, "her orders were so stringent that I'd balk at them and return to New York within the week."

"And lose the bet?"

"And lose the bet."

Catherine took a few moments to think about what he said. The longer she took, the more truthful his explanation appeared. Suzanne had been overly strict with her orders for his care.

She observed his strong fingers toying with the fork. A delicate shiver ran down her spine and left a wake of heat behind. She closed her eyes briefly. Warmth pooled in her breast where he had touched her. She couldn't shake the feeling.

But she had to try. "Greg, I may be dense, but I don't understand how all this fits together."

"Suzanne, with her devious mind, conceived of the idea that I needed to make lasting changes in the way I live my life. Yes, she wants me to regain my health, and if I do so, she will cease all attempts to enlist my aid to get women the right to vote.

"On the other hand, if I give up and return before the allotted time, I have promised to use my money and all political influence to help her cause."

"The woman is...I can't think of a word to commend her brilliance."

His smile was rueful. "That's one way of putting it. You'll forgive me if I can't admire her to the same degree. If I lose, I'll be lynched at any one of my clubs. Her husband will place the noose around my neck with the greatest of pleasure."

He began serving the rest of the supper but made no move to eat himself. Catherine soon put down her fork.

"You've put me in a quandary. I believe in what Suzanne is doing. Women should have a right to express their views before laws are made that rule their lives."

"Catherine, please, I never said I was against the idea. But you must see how impossible it is. Men will never stand for it. And since they have control of the money, and the political parties in this country, women will not have the right to vote in our lifetime."

"But women—"

"Women are arrested for holding demonstrations. Do you think I want to see my sister in a rat-infested prison? Anyway, it's all beside the point. I won't lose this bet. And you won't do anything to cause me to lose it. You're too honest."

She sat back, unable to decide if she should be flattered that he believed it, or insulted that he could read her so easily. And he was wrong about one thing. She was torn in her desire to help Suzanne's cause. She had never given it much thought, but it was only just that women had a say in what affected their lives.

"We won't have this become an issue between you and me," he noted. "Will you agree to that?"

Chapter Twelve

Later, lying in bed, Catherine wondered why she had so readily agreed. There was something about Greg that chased good sense out the door, across the yard, over the fence and clear to the mountains.

It wasn't fair what he did to her mind.

It most certainly wasn't fair to begin the evening in a seductive manner and leave her with a good-night kiss on the back of her hand. She lifted the offending recipient of his kiss.

Her lips had been moistened, parted and primed for his kiss. What had her hand done to deserve that pleasure?

And her knee. She couldn't forget the touch of his mouth against her knee after he had rebandaged her ankle.

She mustn't make too much of it. Flirtation meant nothing to a man like him. She couldn't remember Suzanne writing that he had escorted the same woman more than twice. Fickle male. One in a woman's life was enough.

On that thought she closed her eyes. Things would look better in the morning.

Across the hall, Greg remained awake. With his hands folded beneath his head, he stared up at the ceiling.

His bedroom door was closed, but he had no trouble imagining Catherine lying in her bed. He knew she had been waiting for him to kiss her lips. One look at her luscious mouth and his resistance took flight. But from some deep reserve well he had found the strength not to do it. He wouldn't have stopped with one kiss.

Suzanne would have a laugh if she knew the quandary she had placed him in.

And if he didn't regain control over his reaction to the lovely widow, he'd have no one but himself to blame if he made a mistake. For all her denial, Catherine was a woman made for marriage.

And he didn't want a wife.

Catherine did not find things improved come morning. A flooding downpour prevented Ramon from coming out to do chores. Her ankle was much better, so much so that she managed to get downstairs before Greg was awake.

She started the fire in the stove and made coffee.

The wood floor was cool beneath her stocking-clad feet and her toes curled upward in protest. She poured a cup of coffee and stood at the open back door, staring out at the rain. She sipped from the cup, welcoming the warmth against the chill air. The rain was a solid blanket of gray. She could barely see the barn across the yard. She leaned against the door frame, thinking of chores to be done.

She didn't move when she heard Greg come down the stairs. She even knew how he would move without having to turn to look, all fluid muscles and lean, wiry strength. He knew she was there. There was no need for words of false surprise.

She felt the warmth of his body behind her and then his arms reached around her, pulling her gently back against him. He brushed aside her hair, his lips heated against her bare neck.

Catherine closed her eyes. Doubts rushed into her mind, and denial sprang to her lips, only to be silenced as he moved his hands to rub her arms. Her head fell back against his shoulder. Through the barrier of her gown and camisole came the heat of his palm cupping her breast.

She wanted to tell herself that it was the cool morning air that hardened her nipple against the slow, circling massage of his hand, the pad of his thumb a wicked tease against the peak clearly seen through the thin material. She could even tell herself that same cool air made her lean harder against him to absorb his body heat.

But Catherine didn't lie well, and tried never to lie to herself. It wasn't cool air that made her push her soft, straining breast up against his teasing palm, it wasn't the chill that pressed her rounded buttocks against the hard rise of male flesh behind her.

At his gentle pressure she turned in his arms to stare up at him.

There was time enough to escape as he took the cup from her, sipped at it and set it on the table behind him. That impossibly charming smile was in place when he looked down at her. Mere inches apart. All she had to do was lift her arms to draw him closer...or push him away.

"Don't do it, Catherine," he whispered hoarsely. "Not yet," he added as he caught her hands within his and raised them to his shoulders. Her body flowed against his. His mouth slanted down over hers, taking possession with a gentle ruthlessness, his tongue a welcomed invader that quickly seduced her.

Instinctively her hips pressed against his in mute response, and a trembling began from deep inside, which built and spread. She could feel the tension tightening his body as she clung to him, tilting her head back beneath the sensual onslaught of his kiss.

Catherine kissed him back. She took a savage delight in arousing him as he aroused her, until a small, acquiescent moan escaped her lips.

He angled his head back, still holding her tight against him. "You know, this is the best way to greet the morning. Especially when you help." And his mouth sought hers again, only Catherine turned aside.

"We can't."

"Can't we?" he queried in a low, heated voice. His mouth traveled along her flushed cheekbone to the delicate curve of her ear. He found the rim with the tip of his tongue and teased her with a gentle tracing, then penetrated the hidden, sensitive core.

She made a startled sound as pleasure tightened her body and sent goose bumps up and down her arms. When he repeated the penetration again, she felt both restless and languid at the same time.

"Greg, don't."

"Stop?" he asked, biting her ear with a delicate touch.

She shivered helplessly and saw his male smile.

"The chores," she murmured, managing to lift her hand up between their bodies to cover his mouth. "I need to gather the eggs."

"It's raining. In case you didn't notice. And you're so warm, Catherine. Let me—"

"No. I...no," she repeated.

He was breathing hard but released her. "Stay put. I'll go."

"But you don't—" She stopped as he sprinted barefoot out into the rain. She shook her head. Miss Lily was not going to take kindly to having a stranger near the hens' nests. She debated for long moments whether she should go after him. But there was masculine pride at stake, not to mention her own part to play in Suzanne's bet. He was supposed to experience country living. If he survived gathering the eggs, she'd have to try him at milking the cow.

Despite making up her mind, Catherine repeatedly went to the door to watch for him. She was finished with the biscuits and on her third cup of coffee when he arrived at the back door. His shirtsleeve was shredded, and through the rents in the linen, she could see long, thin scratches down his arm.

"Your eggs," he said in a very controlled voice, and handed over the wooden bucket. "And don't say a word."

"You shouldn't have rushed out—"

"I needed a cold dousing. And I did not wring your hen's neck. Now, not another word."

He marched through the kitchen, pounded up the stairs, only to return in minutes.

"Is there any hot water in the kettle?"

"I was about to get it for you."

He snatched the towel from her hand, wrapped it around the handle and carried the steaming kettle out of the room.

"Wash those scratches with soap," she called out.

"And don't worry about your ruined shirt. I'll add it to the cost of your damaged suit."

A twinge of pain in her ankle forced Catherine to sit down. Greg didn't answer her but she could hear him moving around upstairs.

"The man is reckless. He truly needs a keeper." She propped her arm on the edge of the table and rested her chin on top of her fist before continuing. "I bet he didn't throw feed to the hens before he searched their nests. Men! He couldn't even wait for my instructions."

She couldn't bring herself to think that he had gotten what he deserved for being so stubborn. She glanced at the floor and saw the muddy footprints he'd left behind. Pain or no pain, she had to clean the floor. If she didn't, she'd be the one likely to take a fall. She managed to reach the table legs when Greg returned.

"What the devil do you think you're doing?"

"Do you need spectacles? It's obvious I'm washing the floor."

"From angel to shrew in minutes. I shouldn't leave you alone." With that muttered, he stepped up behind her and lifted her from the floor. He ignored her sputtering protest and her demand to know what he was doing and set her on the edge of the table. "You sit. I made the mess. I'll clean it."

"But—"

"I'm learning, lovely one. And what's a little water and mud after the experience of gathering eggs?"

Catherine bit the tip of her tongue. She couldn't argue. She was too shocked. There wasn't a man she could name who would cheerfully clean up after himself. Louis wouldn't have noticed the mess he made. And never, ever would he do what he called women's work. More surprises from Greg. She wasn't sure her heart would stand this.

But he'd soon learn that egg gathering wasn't the only daily chore. She watched him wipe the excess water from the floor, proud of not mentioning it took him longer to finish than it would have taken her.

Greg was not unaware of that fact. When he rose and tossed the last rag into the bucket, he stood before her and kissed her nose.

"What was that for?"

"A thank-you from a grateful male. You are an extraordinary woman, Catherine. I don't know another woman who would have kept silent. Most would have given me eighteen instructions on the proper way to mop up a muddy floor. But not you."

"Stop. You're embarrassing me. And I did think about it."

Greg placed his hands on either side of her hips and leaned closer. "But you didn't say it. As I said, I'm most grateful. I'm—"

"Overheated from your exertion." She bent backward as his lips drew close to hers. "Greg, you need to eat."

"My intent, exactly. Uncanny how you can read my mind."

"But I wasn't." She had to grip his shirt-clad shoulders or fall across the table. "I'm not…on the table."

"Could have fooled me. But I've always had a fondness for sweets." With a swift movement of his head, Greg captured her mouth. Her lips were parted for him and he slid his tongue between her teeth, filling her with the taste and feel of his hungry kiss. She held his mouth hard upon her own, spearing her fingers through his hair, moaning softly as the sensual heat built be-

tween them. The rhythmic motion of his tongue against
hers was echoed by the movements of her body against
his as she sought relief from the aching heaviness that
filled her breasts and condensed between her restless
legs.

Uttering a mixture of curse and prayer, Greg tore his
mouth from hers.

"What the hell is that sound?"

Catherine opened her eyes to see him turned toward
the door. It took her a few moments and a repeat of
his question before she could answer him.

"The sound you hear is the cow."

He turned to look at her in time to see her lick her
lips. Blue eyes bright with passion waited to meet his
gaze.

"What's wrong with her?"

"She needs…" Catherine paused, then smiled. "She
is in need of relief."

"One female is all I want to handle at one time."

"She won't wait. Truly. She's hurting, Greg. She
needs to be milked."

His look of bemusement forced her to swallow her
laughter. "It's not difficult. Help me down and I'll do
it."

"You're not going out there. It'll be my luck to have
you fall again." He took a deep breath, ran one hand
through his hair and stared out the back door.

"Just tell me how to…what it is I…"

Catherine tried to be matter-of-fact. It was clearly an
impossible task. Showing would be better, but he
wouldn't hear of her going out to the barn. She managed to get past the washing of Sweet Bess's udder,
but when it came to the actual milking, she thought she
lost him.

His eyes took on a glazed look. She demonstrated the motion needed. And stopped abruptly. She stared at her hands, the position of her fingers, and noticed the very defined fit of his pants. Once Louis had asked her to touch him just like this, but when she had tried to repeat it on her own, he had stopped her because it was too painful for him. Did Greg have the same problem?

But why would he be thinking of sex when she was trying to save him from having the milk bucket, stool and his legs kicked out from under him?

"Let me come with you," she pleaded. She wiggled off the table. "See? I can stand for a little while."

"Stay put. I managed the eggs. I can manage this." He paused at the door. "I'll expect a better reward when I'm finished."

"Of course," she readily agreed. "You'll have earned it."

Greg found breakfast warming on the stove, a steaming tub of water and his clean clothing laid out on a chair.

Of Catherine there was no sign.

Just as well, he thought. What man wanted a woman to see him like this?

He should have paid attention to her instructions. Instead, he had let his mind wander into the realm of the sexual delights he'd soon be sharing with his lovely widow.

Some delights. She had him so twisted in knots, his body was sure he was killing it.

Battered, bruised and filthy, he sat down with a weary sigh. Women, he decided, were the most devious creatures the Lord had created to torment men.

Amend that. Females of all kinds were the devil's own.

He leaned over to rub his shin. Even with his boots on he'd felt the cow's kick. A reproachful meow made him look up. Lord Romeo stood by the back door, stretched to his full height. His paws touched the handle.

When Greg didn't immediately respond, he meowed again.

"I don't blame you for wanting out. I'd run myself, if I could."

Once the cat was outside, he looked again at the tub, the breakfast and his clothes. Catherine was a caring woman.

The lesson was slow in coming, but he was beginning to understand how much work she did. He'd let her rest.

Besides, he was in no condition to continue an amorous pursuit.

For now.

Chapter Thirteen

At the end of the first week, Greg awoke with the knowledge that he and his lovely widow were dueling their way through the days like a fencing match. On guard, engage, parry and retreat, even a few surprise thrusts were the order of the last few days.

Not that he complained. He was learning to laugh at himself and enjoy Catherine's mischievous sense of humor as they shared inside and outside chores.

Lord Romeo was still the bane of his existence. The cat seemed to appear at the worst moments, often with what Catherine termed his show of affection. From entwining his body around Greg's legs to depositing some newly caught rodent at his feet, the cat demanded attention.

Greg stretched and saw that dawn heralded a new day. His stomach rumbled, but even the constant twinges of pain were receding.

Taking stock of himself, he realized that he had never felt better. He had never worked so hard physically, but there was satisfaction with each mastered chore. He fell into his bed each night and slept the sleep of the just.

Of course, he couldn't deny that having Catherine beside him would have made his stay complete, but he was making great strides in wearing down her considerable resistance.

He was learning to cook. There was a true challenge. He'd set fire to the frying pan, boiled potatoes into hard lumps and roasted steaks that were charred outside and raw inside.

They hadn't starved as he improved his culinary efforts. Catherine had the patience of a saint. And his pockets were deep to pay for the many meals supplied by Caroline.

At least he could look forward to being served a decent dinner this evening. They were to attend Mrs. Pettigrew's dinner party with dancing afterward. He couldn't wait to take Catherine into his arms. Her ankle was healed, so there wouldn't be excuses why she couldn't dance with him. And later... He smiled. Later he would take care of the constant ache that had him wishing his tailor had not been so precise in the cut of his pants. He arose with a prayer that no mishaps marred the day.

Apparently the Lord had been listening. He found Catherine's light, gay mood infectious. For a change Miss Lily wasn't around while they gathered eggs, and even Lord Romeo disappeared. The cow might have been a stone statue but for the flow of milk, and not one horse tried to nip him when he brought out the feed buckets.

Catherine ironed her gown and his shirt in the parlor while he bathed in the kitchen. He retreated to his room to give her privacy to bathe.

Catherine, struggling with the buttons on the back of her gown, wished Sarah or Mary were there to help her. In more ways than one. She needed to talk with someone who would understand what she wasn't sure she understood herself.

She rarely wished for finer clothes again, but tonight was an exception. The gown was her best one, worn a few months ago for Mary's wedding to Rafe McCade. But tonight she longed to impress Greg, show him that she could be every bit as beautiful as the society women who moved in his circle.

The thought upset her. Hadn't she learned her lesson with Louis? Appearances were not important. Louis lived his life around appearances. His horses had to be the showiest, his breeding bulls the priciest, his home a study in ostentatious taste. And his wife, as she had discovered a few months after their wedding, had been chosen for her looks to grace his arm when they were in public. Catherine thought with horror of all the grand parties that she had no hand in planning. And after the fighting in the beginning, she had given up. There was no way to change Louis's mind, not when every other man of his acquaintance treated his wife the same.

But she was more than her looks. She was a real person with hopes and dreams. It had taken her a long time to admit that Louis was not worthy of her love. What's more, he did not deserve her respect. He was her husband, and she had obeyed him. She never denied him whatever he demanded of her.

The day she buried him she had sworn a vow. She would not be docile. She would never allow any man to destroy the fragile sense of self-worth that had grown stronger and stronger with every day.

But Greg is not Louis. And that, too, she had come to understand. She pinned her hair back from her face with carved combs. Thick curls fell down her back. She adjusted the wide, pale blue ruffle that draped her bare shoulders. The small, delicate cameo, one of the few pieces of jewelry she had left, was pinned to the pale blue ribbon that banded her throat. She drew on long white gloves, smoothing them from fingertip to above her elbows. The loop of satin ribbon attached to her fan went over one wrist, followed by the strings of her reticule. She draped a white, lacy wool shawl over her shoulders.

A last turn before the mirror and a wish. She shrugged with a rueful smile on her lips when wishes didn't change her into a vision of shimmering white and gold. She blew out her lamp and left her room.

Greg waited at the foot of the stairway for her.

Catherine simply stared at him. He was dressed in the height of gentlemen's evening fashion in a suit of black with a snowy white, ruffled shirt front. It was not the shirt she had ironed for him. The man had hidden talents. His neckcloth and starched collar points showed in sharp contrast to the light tan he had acquired over the past week. A pearl stickpin gleamed with pale luminescence in the folds of cloth.

She started down the staircase, thinking once more of the differences between them. He didn't belong here in the territory. Married, she had been to far grander entertainments. Widowed, she found this evening a rare treat. But not for Greg. His life was filled with social events. What would he make of this evening?

"Catherine," he whispered, extending his hand as she reached the last step. "You are a lovely, lovely vision."

"And you..." Her voice broke. This close, the fine linen weave of his shirt shone like silk. Her fingers curled with her need to touch him. He looked exactly like what he was: wealthy, powerful.

She cleared her throat. "You are a handsome one." She forced a smile, wishing to banish her gloomy thoughts, and strove for a lighter tone. "I shall be the envy of every woman there tonight, having you for an escort."

He raised her gloved hand to his lips, pressing a heated kiss that lingered. His gaze held hers. "You are wrong. I'm the one to be envied. I'll have one of the elusive merry widows by my side."

"Don't listen to foolish gossip. And if Mrs. Pettigrew has anything to say about it, you'll be far from my side."

Greg didn't answer her. His gaze had strayed to the modest point that dipped in the front of her gown. The hint of a shadow between her breasts was as seductive as the lines of her gown were simple. He was reminded of his thought that he would love to dress her in silks and satin. *Better not think of it,* he warned himself. *If she can scorch your blood dressed like this, she'd burn you to cinders in more fashionable clothing.*

"Your carriage awaits." But as she moved past him, he dipped his head and pressed a kiss to her shoulder.

"Don't," she whispered with a visible shiver.

"For luck, Catherine, nothing more."

"Luck? Why would you need luck tonight?"

"It's been my experience," he said, ushering her outside to the rented livery buggy, "that I need luck to keep my wits about me to evade the wiles of women like Mrs. Pettigrew."

"And we know you have successfully evaded all wiles."

She pulled aside the folds of her gown to make room for him on the narrow seat.

Once more he took hold of her hand. "I want you to promise to protect me, Catherine. Part of your devil's bargain with my sister."

She could only nod. But the question went begging—who would protect her from him?

Mrs. Pettigrew's house was set behind the main street of town. The two-story house was ablaze with lights and the yard crowded with all manner of wagons and buggies. The cool adobe brick reflected the torchlights lit along the portico that extended around three sides of the house.

Catherine greeted Nita Mullins and introduced her to Greg.

"Lots of foolish nonsense, if you ask me," Nita muttered.

"Is that why you've worn one of your newest gowns?" Catherine teased. "You look lovely, Nita."

"Like it, do you?" She performed a slow turn for Catherine to admire the green-and-white striped silk, trimmed with layers of black lace ruffles on the lower skirt. Additional cascading ruffles created a false bustle.

"You should visit my shop, Catherine. That woman might give me pains where it ain't polite to mention in mixed company, but she keeps her word. Brought me back fashion dolls and copies of *Godey's*. The magazine ain't the same with the new owners, but with the town growing, the women are so hungry for new fashions that they'll do."

"Would you like to run away with me, Mrs. Mullins? You'd put the women attending one of the Astor's balls to shame."

"Oh, prettily said. Watch out for this one, Catherine. The smooth-talking ones have your corset strings untied before you know what they're about."

"Nita! Please..."

Nita took hold of Greg's arm as they went up the three wide steps that led to the front doors. "It's just a little intimate dinner party for twenty or so with more coming for the dancing afterward," she said in her best imitation of Mrs. Pettigrew.

"Hush, Nita, she'll hear you."

"Never mind, young woman. I've reached an age where I can indulge myself. Don't mean no harm. Your young man understands or he wouldn't be trying to swallow his laughter."

She turned to Greg. "Hortense Pettigrew gives herself some mighty fine airs as if she were born a duchess. She must want something from you to give this dinner for you. Seeing you up close, I can guess what it is. She's looking to marry off her youngest. Not that Camilla isn't a sweet girl, she is, but she ain't for the likes of you. Now, you take Catherine—"

"Nita, I insist that you stop. You're embarrassing Mr. Mayfield and me." She didn't need anyone else suggesting a pairing of her and Greg. It wasn't to be. Ever.

"No, it's quite all right," Greg hastened to assure both Nita and Catherine. "I find her insights to be true. It is refreshing to meet another honest woman."

Nita peered up at him. "And who is the other one?"

"Catherine, of course."

"You got that right. Might still be sense in those eastern men. You'd do well to remember it, too. Well, are we gonna stand out here and jaw all night or go inside? Seems like everyone else is already here.''

"And you love making an entrance, Nita."

"Goes with the age, my girl."

It appeared most of the guests had arrived. The large front parlor was filled with people milling about. Mrs. Pettigrew, gowned in royal purple, complete with a feathered turban to which was pinned an enormous pearl-encrusted brooch, stood in the arched doorway with her youngest daughter by her side.

The woman's smile of welcome was all for Greg. Catherine and Nita barely earned a nod. Nita swept by and was lost in the room, but Catherine remained as she promised, close by Greg.

She stared at the various lengths of pearls that encircled Mrs. Pettigrew's neck and wondered how the woman could breathe beneath their weight. Bracelets of blinding gems adorned her gloved wrists. The rings on several fingers were so large, Catherine wondered how she managed to wave her hands about.

By contrast, Camilla was simply gowned in a pale pink silk. A wide lace ruffle of pale cream that almost matched her skin showed off bare shoulders. A small gold locket hung from a chain around her neck.

Catherine knew Mrs. Pettigrew would not be flattered by the resulting picture they presented to her eyes. The young girl appeared a delicate, lovely flower next to her mother.

She couldn't stop watching Greg and gauging his reaction to the obvious ploy. His impossibly charming smile was in evidence. Polite, flowery phrases slipped from his lips with practiced ease. She had worried for nothing. The man was adept at handling any social situation. And it was anyone's guess as to what he really thought.

Mrs. Pettigrew, true to form, linked her arm with Greg's and swept him into the parlor, where she proceeded to introduce him to her guests.

"Mama doesn't mean to be rude," Camilla whispered as Catherine trailed along with her. "It's just her way to appear more important."

Catherine nodded greetings to most of the owners of the town's businesses. Greg, she noted, was already surrounded by the men. Peter Austin, owner of the town's newspaper, stood beside him. Mrs. Pettigrew's son-in-law Gerald Emmet had his arm thrown over Greg's shoulders as if they were old friends. She knew better than to intrude on the all-male gathering, even if it irritated her.

Buck Purcell, Gerald's competition in banking, Chad Hudspeth, owner of the tailor shop, and Ollie Walker, who owned the lumber mill, completed the inner circle. Crowding them were Marcus Jobe and Julian Krausse, owners of the grocery and butcher shops respectively, J. P. Crabtree of the Emporium, Albert Waterman, half of Waterman and Weil Assayers, and the minister, Thomas Hoffman.

Not up to Mrs. Pettigrew's idea of the social elite but the best the town had to offer. Catherine was surprised that several of the major ranch owners had not been invited for dinner.

She and Camilla continued to stroll, greeting the wives in attendance. They were like bright butterflies perched on the edge of the small chairs scattered around the room.

"Where's Adelaide?" Catherine asked.

"Overseeing the kitchen. Mama is sure something

will go wrong. She might be right this time. Trying to impress Mr. Mayfield is one of her stupid ideas.''

Catherine had been too caught up in her own thoughts before, but now she heard a note of bitterness in the young girl's voice.

''Camilla,'' she whispered, ''your mama can't force you to marry anyone. I know Mr. Mayfield intends to return east just as he arrived. A bachelor. So don't fret.''

''Oh, but I would marry anyone to escape her. Even someone as old as him. He is rich and handsome and my sister said that goes a long way when the lights are out.''

''Adelaide said that?''

''She told me only fools marry for love.''

''Well, if you and your sister believe that, then I feel sorry for you both. Marriage should be only for love. Because you want to share your life with one very special person who is both friend and lover.''

''Was your marriage like that, Catherine?''

''No. I made a terrible mistake. But I wouldn't settle for less than love if I ever married again.''

''What's that?'' Nita asked, joining them. ''Camilla, be a good girl and bring Catherine some punch. Someday I'll get your mother to give me the recipe.'' Nita steered Catherine to two empty chairs. ''Sit down and stop glaring at me. I heard you. And listen to an old fool's advice. You'll marry again, Catherine. Some women ain't meant to live alone. You're one of them.'' Nita's pointed look at Greg drew Catherine's gaze, as well.

''Oh, no. Don't get any matchmaking ideas about him. I wouldn't have him delivered with a crate full of chickens.''

"Wouldn't, huh? But that man's sneaking looks at you seven ways to Sunday, girl. Bet he'd have you without the crate of chickens. And you won't wager against that."

Catherine pondered Nita's question all through dinner. Mrs. Pettigrew had spared no expense in her effort to impress Greg. Deviled salmon, oysters on the half shell—specially shipped at her order in shaved ice—shrimp patties, soup, rabbit, lamb and roast beef, squabs roasted golden brown, squash topped with syrup and peanuts, creamed parsnips, watercress salad and sweet potatoes in a pie, mashed and baked.

The accompanying sauces and thick gravies, breads, biscuits and wines made Catherine fear the table would collapse beneath the weight. Candlelight spread from branched candelabra, and a profusion of arranged flowers prevented those on one side of the table from seeing those seated across from them.

Catherine was on the opposite side of the table from Greg, almost in the middle, while he sat at Mrs. Pettigrew's right. The woman monopolized him all through the meal without a thought to the other guests.

At long last the dinner drew to a close and the ladies retired to leave the men to their brandy and cigars. Dessert, Mrs. Pettigrew announced, would be served buffet-style in the front parlor after the gentlemen rejoined them.

Catherine longed to escape the drawing room. She had a blinding headache, something she rarely suffered. She worried about leaving, about abandoning Greg.

Several conversations whirled around her, but she paid no attention. When she saw Mrs. Pettigrew bearing down on her, Catherine edged toward the door.

"There you are, dear girl. I wanted to have a coze with you."

"Oh, I wouldn't think of taking you away from your guests," Catherine protested.

"Nonsense. They shan't miss me for a few minutes. And we have Mr. Mayfield to discuss."

Catherine offered a blank stare. "We do?"

"My dear, you must see this is the sort of social setting the man is used to. And we cannot forget the impropriety of you living in the house alone with him. You may not be aware of it, Catherine, but people are talking."

Glancing around the room, Catherine found that to be true, but she didn't see more than one or two curious gazes sent her way.

Mrs. Pettigrew went on. Catherine rubbed her temple. In a blinding flash of pain she made her decision.

"Thank you for a lovely dinner. I am sure Mr. Mayfield appreciated the trouble you went to to impress him. I can't in all honesty thank you for your unsolicited advice. Please convey my regrets and tell Greg— that is, Mr. Mayfield—that I had to leave."

"Catherine, you can't—"

She turned on her hostess. "Yes, I can. I am a widow, Mrs. Pettigrew, just like you. I have always conducted myself in a respectable manner. I will not have you, or anyone else, question my behavior. If any of your other guests hold the same narrow-minded views as you do, you are all welcome to them. Good night."

Catherine didn't stop for her shawl. She fled into the cool night. On the path leading to the street she ran into Caroline, who was arriving for the dancing.

There was just enough moonlight for her to see that

her friend was terribly upset. Caroline held on to Catherine.

"Where are you running to?"

"Home. Where I should have stayed."

"What's wrong? This isn't like you. And where is the handsome Mr. Mayfield?"

They withdrew into the shadows of the trees as others arrived. Catherine cast an anxious glance toward the open doors of the house. She couldn't imagine why she half expected to see Greg coming after her. After all, he didn't know yet that she had left. Nor could she explain why that made her want to cry.

"Why are you running away? What did that woman say to you?"

"Caroline, if you are truly my friend, please don't ask me a lot of questions I can't answer. I just want to go home."

Caroline tilted a head full of auburn curls to one side. "I've got a notion that Mrs. Pettigrew lectured you about living out there alone with him. She's been trying to stir up—"

"I don't care. She can say whatever she likes. I need to go."

Catherine pulled free and hurried to the street.

"You can't walk home!" Caroline called out.

"It's just what I need." Catherine avoided the main street. There was no point in asking for trouble with some drunken cowhand who had too much celebrating under his belt. She used the alleys behind the buildings, and once on the road outside town, kept to the middle. This way she could hear if anyone was coming in either direction and get off the road.

Running away—Caroline had been right to call it that—was the most cowardly act of her life. All she could think of, all she would allow herself to think about, was that Mrs. Pettigrew was right. Not about Greg living with her alone, but that she didn't belong in a world that judged people by their social standing, their clothes or how many ways there were to serve oysters eaten at some fancy hotel. She didn't even like oysters!

Catherine walked at a furious pace and was limping by the time she reached home. Her only pair of slippers were ruined.

She wished she had never heard of Gregory Mayfield.

Lighting the lamp on the hall table, she bent to pet Lord Romeo.

"At least you like me just as I am." She scooped up the cat, who purred with contentment and marched up the stairs to her room. In no time she was back downstairs wearing her nightgown and robe.

She fired up the stove and heated milk, then rummaged in the pantry for a bottle of brandy left over from Mary's wedding. Sarah didn't like having liquor in the house, but allowing one bottle for medicinal purposes only could do no harm.

Catherine felt in need of a great deal of medicinal brandy.

After her second cup, she abandoned the milk. The cat gave up trying to stay in her lap, since she kept getting up to peer out the window at regular intervals. With each sip she imagined Greg's smiling face as he fawned over Mrs. Pettigrew and danced his way into every woman's heart.

Between the wines with dinner and the generous dollops of brandy, she lost track of the time. But nothing impaired her hearing. She heard a carriage on the drive, the murmur of male voices, the carriage wheels on the drive again, then the front door being slammed.

As his footsteps came closer, Catherine attempted to sit up straight. She abandoned the thought as easily as she had abandoned Greg earlier.

And if it was a fight he was looking for, he had come to the right place.

Chapter Fourteen

"In the name of all that is holy, tell me why you deserted me to that woman's clutches?"

"And a very good evening to you, sir. Please, stop making noises like an irate husband."

"You would know, wouldn't you? Married to a shrew, a man must learn irritation fast." He stopped short in the doorway, where he proceeded to strip off his neckcloth.

"What do you think you're doing?" she demanded as he freed the first two studs from his shirt and tucked those, along with the neckcloth and his stickpin, into his pants' pocket. Hands on hips he glared at Catherine.

"I'm making myself comfortable."

"Well, see that you don't go farther. I have no intention of entertaining a half-naked man in my kitchen. And I'll have you know I rarely irritated my husband."

"I wish I knew his secret," he muttered. "I asked you a civil question and expect a civil answer."

"I was suddenly indisposed," she returned in a sugar-sweet, cheerful voice. "Didn't she tell you?"

"Not until I had danced once with every female and asked where you were. And the only indisposition seems to come from that brandy bottle. Pour one for me, too.''

Catherine stared into his deep green eyes. His mellow tone of voice sent out an alarm. Or maybe it was the sarcastic edge cut into each word. If she had been capable of rising from her chair, she would have made a sweeping retreat the moment he stepped into the room. As it was, her legs had the consistency of succotash. She was determined to conceal it from him.

''You can't drink hard liquor.'' She spoke softly, for her headache had returned in force, and she spoke very carefully, as the swirling effect of the brandy hit her.

''How much have you had?'' he asked.

She blinked several times in an attempt to glare at him. ''Never mind what I had. I saw you drinking wine with your dinner. That is forbidden—I mean it was forbidden. Your stomach must be upset. Have a glass of milk.'' She couldn't hold his direct gaze and looked down into the amber contents of her cup. She had seen enough of his poet's face and warrior's eyes. In her dreams. Awake. *Stop it!*

''Why did you leave, Catherine?'' he asked in a gentle voice. ''I thought you agreed to protect me?''

Her head bowed and he thought she wouldn't answer him. When she looked up he saw the sheen of unshed tears in her eyes. She pushed at her hair, losing a few pins, which sent curls tumbling over her shoulders. Why hadn't he noticed the faint shadows beneath her eyes? He had the strangest urge to kiss the tip of her upturned nose and bring a smile to the generous curve of her lips.

Catherine rubbed her eyes. He was slouched against the door frame, his arms crossed over his chest. She had a feeling he wasn't going to move. His most charming smile was firmly in place, the one that could sweeten every cake in town. The one that made her stomach think it attracted every butterfly in the territory, for the longer she stared at him, the more the fluttering sensation spread inside her.

''What are you doing?''

''Watching you, Catherine. A most pleasurable pastime, I recently discovered.''

''Yes. You do that a lot. Don't think I haven't noticed.''

He could say the same of her, but kept quiet about that. ''Does it bother you?'' he asked instead. ''You're a beautiful woman, Catherine. I'm not the first man to do it. I can't be the first man to tell you so.''

''You are the only one who bothers me.''

''Ah.''

''Ah? That's all you have to say?'' Her bare toes curled over the rungs of the chair. She made the mistake of inhaling deeply from the contents of the cup. Her gaze became unfocused as she reared back. That was another mistake. The sudden move made her head explode with pain.

''That's all I deem wise to say.'' But he moved to her side and hunkered down near her chair. ''Tell me what's wrong? Where do you hurt?''

''All over,'' she mumbled.

''Let me get you up to bed.''

''Bed?'' she repeated, shivering as he took hold of her hand.

''Yes, to bed. To rest your weary little…well, whatever it is that hurts you so.''

''Oh,'' she sniffed. ''You were being kind.''

''Have I been cruel to you, Catherine? You sound almost surprised that I would show you kindness. I'm crushed. You do little for my male ego. I've never had so many complaints from a woman before.''

She snatched her hand away and tucked it into her lap. ''The only kindness I want from you is to be left alone. As for other women, they wouldn't dare tell you the truth. They'd be cut off, pariahs all to the society that judges women so harshly.''

''Ah.''

''Stop saying that.''

He eyed the cup and the bottle and thought of the way she kept avoiding looking directly at him.

''Catherine, I don't think leaving you alone is a good idea. Something has upset you. I aim to find out what it is. Even if it takes what is left of the night.''

His threat—and she couldn't call it anything else— set off a slight buzzing in her head. She ached from all this thinking his questions forced on her.

Any intelligent woman could handle a man like him. All her life she had believed the opposite, and with widowhood had come freedom to believe differently. She was logical, practical and rational. Most of the time. Why did he have the power to upset her thought process?

She should leave if he wouldn't. But her body protested moving, especially the parts aroused by his nearness. And she didn't have the strength to fight herself.

With his fingertips he gently brushed the hair back from her face. ''Catherine,'' he whispered, ''just tell me why you left so abruptly? Did Mrs. Pettigrew upset you? Was it something someone else said to you?''

''You enjoyed yourself.''

''You make that an accusation. Wasn't I supposed to?''

''Of course, you were.'' She reached up to circle the

rim of the cup with one finger. The hour was late. She couldn't think clearly. And he, with his rich, masculine scent of some exotic blend, not only was far too close, but was sending silent messages of other ways they could be enjoying themselves.

"I don't want to talk."

"Strangely enough, sweet lady, I find myself in total agreement with you."

Greg stroked her flushed cheek. With a crooked finger beneath her chin he tilted her face toward his. She was such a warm, vibrant woman, but appeared so vulnerable at this moment that he was unsure of himself. An odd position to find himself in. He never had trouble dealing with all the vagaries of female moods. But then, as he had been reminding himself from the first moment he had seen her, he had never met a woman like Catherine.

"Sometimes..." she began, then stopped.

"Yes?"

"I do impulsive things." The words rushed out with the air of confession, a fact he didn't miss.

"Be impulsive with me, Catherine."

"Oh, no. You're the one I must be most guarded with."

"You can't know how it pains me to hear you say that."

"Don't...please, don't talk about pain."

"That's right," he noted in a silky, soft voice as he traced the delicate shape of her ear, "you hurt all over. Since we're having confession time, I'll admit I ache all over, too. So you have, among other things, Catherine, my sympathy."

"You couldn't possibly know how I feel."

"Won't you open your eyes and look at me?"

"I can't."

Greg didn't push her. "Why can't I know how you ache?"

"You're not a woman."

"At the moment," he murmured, choking back laughter, "I'm celebrating that fact."

"With milk," she reminded him in a prim little voice.

"No. There's something far sweeter, and far more healing, within my reach."

She didn't have a second to ask what he meant. His lips brushed against hers. A sigh of yearning escaped. But the corners of her mouth seemed to require a great deal of attention due to his lavishing a great many tiny kisses there, and on her chin. The heated path continued along her jaw as she tilted her head to accommodate him. She felt like an egg when one of the hens was off its feed—fragile, brittle, easily broken and all scrambled emotions inside. His touch was so delicate that she wanted to demand more, and yet so exquisite that she would do nothing to break its spell.

His lips touched her temple. Catherine's fingers curled on his shoulders, digging into the soft cashmere wool jacket. She blinked in surprise to find that she was not only holding him, but drawing him closer.

"We mustn't...you should...oh, Greg, this is a terrible mistake."

"Then tell me to stop. Now, while I can still summon the will to do so."

But once more he gave her no time to answer. His lips covered her mouth. The kiss was wet. And hot. His tongue impolite. So were his teeth. She felt their seductive pull on her bottom lip. The heady effect of the brandy disappeared under this new assault. A more powerful stimulant and far more addictive.

And Catherine wanted more.

Greg, reading her soft moan, the subtle shift of her body, the tightening grip of her hands, obliged to the very best of his ability. He wanted to comfort her.

Catherine wasn't aware of when he stood up, or when she followed. She didn't know he had turned her until she felt the edge of the table pressing against her buttocks.

It was a momentary sensation, for his hands were there to cradle her against him. Unleashed hunger prowled in kisses that left her flushed and breathless.

And still she wanted more.

A languid heat curled inside her. The taste of him swept through her as she savored the hot glide of his tongue over hers. The delicate thrust and parry brought to mind a graceful duel, but Catherine realized she was no match for his skill.

Under her hand she felt the curving muscle of his chest and the steady beat of his heart, which matched his breathing. Her own breaths had the erratic pace of Lord Romeo escaping Miss Lily. His long, slender fingers played in the wisps of hair at the side of her head and rimmed her ear, toyed with the sensitive lobe before both his hands held her head as he turned it from side to side, dragging her mouth across his.

His hands slid down her back, pressing her against him. He cupped her buttocks and lifted her slightly to the fit of his body. The cloth that separated them offered no protection at all. She tugged at his jacket. It wasn't fair that he was still dressed. Desire had her firmly in hand. Catherine heard a dim warning that this might be a mistake, but hushed that little voice. She was floating in a delicious cloud where only the senses ruled.

She softly moaned in frustration when his jacket wouldn't come off.

"Gently, Catherine, gently," he whispered. Lord, help. "There's time enough. All the time you want or need."

Time? What the devil was he mumbling about time? How could he speak of time when she was on fire with need? Her head was swimming, the room tilted and swirled. She opened her eyes to see the coal oil fixture above her. She was sprawled on the kitchen table. Time to show him she was a practical woman. She'd use whatever was at hand.

Greg didn't stand a chance. She locked her hands around his head and tugged him down toward her. Her mouth fastened to his.

He reached for his honor as a gentleman and found it had cut and run. He had never knowingly taken advantage of a woman, and swore in this that Catherine would not be the first to make that claim.

He'd only meant to comfort her. And her soft, oh, so generous mouth promised him heaven. He was no saint. One more kiss. That was it, he swore. Just one more.

Several minutes later, his swearing wasn't good-natured at all. He came up for breath and managed to get her to sit up. That's when he made his second mistake.

Greg tried to reason with her.

A more difficult task he couldn't imagine.

"I do want you," he said. He had to dodge her seductive kisses being plastered all over his face. "I want you so much I can't sleep. But you've had too much brandy, Catherine. You're tipsy. You don't know what you're doing.'' Even to his ears his words sounded foolish. If her skilled touches were any more knowing, he'd be Catherine's midnight snack. But he was damned if he'd give up. She would be filled with recriminations fired at his head in the morning.

One of them had to retain sense.

Lord, why me?

Her clever hands stripped off his jacket while he tried to retie her robe. She immediately went to work on his shirt studs.

''Catherine, stop it.'' Desperation thickened his voice. A little old-fashioned lust undercoated every word, too. His body was all for allowing complete freedom. The throw-up-your-arms-you-can't-win kind. The let's-enjoy-what's-happening-because-we-want-this-too kind.

His mind, once thought to be stronger by far, sounded an alarm that it was losing the war. He almost gave in.

Almost.

The mere idea of facing her tears in the morning kept his resolve firm. The fact that he was rock hard with tension nearly unmanned him.

''Remember, you're a lady. A respectable widow. Behave yourself.''

''I do. I have. Clever, clever, Gregory Michael Mayfield the third. You always make me smile. Tonight I throw off the shackles.''

''Try to keep them in place. For heaven's sake. For my sake, Catherine, try harder,'' he croaked.

She trailed a string of heated kisses down his throat and lavished a great deal of attention on the skin bared by the vee of his shirt. She busily fumbled with the next stud.

"Stubborn little stud." She giggled. "That could be you, too, Greg. But this little pearl doesn't know what's waiting. Pleasure, that's what. That's what the man promised us."

He couldn't take any more. He swung her up into his arms and nearly tripped over the cat. He glared at Lord Romeo. Catherine draped her arms around his shoulders and played havoc with his pulse.

"One sound out of you and I won't be responsible for what happens," he warned the cat. Lord Romeo jumped on the chair Catherine had recently vacated and began washing his front paw.

Catherine, unaware of the cat's presence, nodded eagerly. "I'll be quiet as a mouse. But do let me kiss you again. I adore the way you kiss me. You make my head whirl."

Greg was having trouble enough with his own head. Too much so to worry about hers. His blood was humming a tune of anticipation. He prayed his buttons would hold as another overly eager member of his body strained for its share of attention.

His knees threatened to give as he approached the staircase. Nothing, but nothing—not even dire consequences—could keep his dream images of the widow's welcome from forming. How could he prevent it when he felt the heated tip of her tongue licking his skin?

"Catherine, I'm warning you. You will be sorry for this in the morning."

She dragged his head down and fused her mouth to his. She teased. She tormented. She promised.

He lost.

I am only a frail male being. I can't fight her and

myself. I shall be a tender lover. I will be most gentle.
I will be shackled at the altar faster than I can say my
name.

Where had that thought come from?

Greg didn't know. But it was enough to give him
the strength to release those warm, willing, loving lips.

"More," she demanded.

"You are driving me to the brink of madness,
woman. Stop. Behave. I'm not telling you again."

"Good. I don't want to hear it." She tugged his shirt
from his pants and found warm, damp skin. "Oh my."
Heaving a delicious sigh, she stroked him, utterly lost
in the world of pleasure. "Can I confess?"

"Anything," he grunted, starting up the steps.

"I love touching you. For a man, you are very responsive, Greg."

"Thank you. I think."

"Don't you want to…well, touch me, too? Just a
little?"

"Mercy!" His most sincere plea went unanswered.
That didn't stop him from repeating it as he staggered
up the stairs and into her room.

Since his plea for mercy went unanswered, he had
none for Catherine. He intended to drop her on her bed
and, considering the state of his wildly aroused body
and shattered mind, make a quick, less-than-dignified
retreat.

Catherine had other devious ideas.

She latched onto him so tightly and nipped his earlobe as he bent to place her on the bed. He ended up
tumbling down on top of her.

He grumbled another warning.

She giggled. "We fit like peas in a pod." To make

sure, she wiggled about a little, then arched her body up to his.

Mentally, Greg had a strong constitution. But the pitiful groans that escaped him told him that was no longer true. The sweetly heated feminine scent of her filled him with every labored breath he drew. *I am a gentleman. I will not shred her clothes. I will not rip off mine. I will not kiss...*

Too late for that one.

He was weak. He kissed her with a burning frustration born of his own desire. A little mean, a whole lot wild. Raw and hungry. A scorcher of a kiss that owed nothing to the skilled finesse of a practiced lover and a whole lot to the need of a dying man going down for the count.

He was panting by the time he managed to break the kiss. He found the dregs of strength to unlatch her arms and hold them at her sides. He ignored her whispered request for more, ignored his body's demand to give her and himself what they wanted, ignored everything in his effort to remember his own name.

"Go to sleep, Catherine. You'll regret this in the morning. Likely I will, too," he muttered.

But as he rolled to his back and started to sit up, she touched his cheek.

"Stay."

As an enticement, it lacked heat. It wasn't even a seductive plea. He heard her yawn, and her sigh as she curled on her side and made more room for him.

He lay there, fighting to regain his breath, fighting for some shred of moral fiber to help him do the right thing and leave her.

Her head nestled on his shoulder and her hand came

to rest over his heart. She sighed with the contentment of a well-satisfied lover and slipped into sleep.

He could slip away and she would never know. He caught himself rubbing his chin against her hair. Why the hell was he waiting? Had he some hidden, treacherous desire to punish himself? For sure, he was going to hate himself in the morning no matter what he did.

Chapter Fifteen

Greg didn't sleep. He tried several times to slip out of bed, but Catherine was tenacious in the most tormenting ways. She was a cuddler. Not just next to him, but at times she sneaked past his guard and half sprawled on top of him.

It wasn't until the sky lightened that he finally escaped his hell. She instantly moved to fill the space he left. With a disgruntled murmur about ungrateful women, he left her to her slumber.

By the time he changed and went downstairs—no humming for him this morning—Ramon had arrived and started the coffee.

"I come early, *sí?*" the boy asked with a bright smile.

Greg, rubbing his upset stomach after last night's excess at dinner, grunted in reply.

"Where is the *señora?*"

"Sleeping, Ramon." Greg found a stale biscuit in the bread box. It suited his role as martyr and he nibbled on it while he waited for coffee. "This morning, you and I will do the chores."

Hard work, Greg discovered, rid him of most of his

dark mood. He managed to milk the cow without mishap. Miss Lily, pesky old hen that she was, drove him crazy as he helped Ramon gather the eggs. But he had a new discovery waiting for him. The old hen stole eggs and hid them.

"What is that stench?" he asked the boy.

"Miss Lily, she steals the eggs. She thinks she is still the young hen and tries to hatch them. But sometimes she forgets where she hides them. The *señora* has to search for them."

"That shouldn't be hard. We just follow our noses."

Greg ended up in the hayloft. He finally found the rotten egg, buried in the straw beneath the corner eaves. He was hot and sweating by the time he retrieved it and was awfully glad all he had in his stomach was the stale biscuit.

Not only was Catherine driving him to madness, but her pets were, too.

As he stood in the warm sunshine, first gulping fresh air, then cool well water, Greg realized that a great deal of time was wasted in searching the whole barn for eggs. What Catherine needed, if she truly intended to be independent and make her business grow, was an organized approach to housing the hens. Ramon should be a hired helper on a daily basis so that Catherine was free to expand her list of customers.

The idea of Catherine calling on strangers to sell her eggs didn't sit well with him. But he reminded himself that he had no right to tell her what to do.

The reminder didn't sit any better.

But he felt rather smug as he came up with ideas grounded in solid business practice. He could show her how to turn this into a real money-making concern.

He headed back to the barn to get feed for the guinea

hens. They tended to scatter into the woods once daylight arrived. He waved as Ramon left to deliver the eggs in town.

Town…he should send Mrs. Pettigrew a thank-you note and a suitable gift. It was the polite thing to do. Damn! He never attended to such matters, but turned them over to his man of business. And where was he to find a gift that wouldn't give that woman the wrong idea.

"Then again," he muttered as he returned to the house, "she did something to upset Catherine. Why the devil should I ignore that?"

The more he thought about it, the madder he got. Even Lord Romeo sensed something wrong, for he kept out of the way.

Greg's sense of humor returned as he set about preparing a breakfast tray for Catherine. He made the coffee extra strong, thinking of those unfortunate days when he woke with a hangover.

How much would she remember?

And how much would he tell her?

Thoughts of Catherine brought the reminder of how sexually frustrated he'd been.

And still are? queried a nagging little voice.

"No," he said aloud in a firm voice. "I'm not going to behave like a stripling military cadet with his first woman."

A cackle made him spin around. Miss Lily hovered over the threshold.

"Don't you dare come into the house," he warned the hen. "Having that mangy creature around is more than a man can stand."

She cackled again and her bright eyes seemed to be laughing at him.

Greg shook his head. "Mad. I'm going mad. She's got me talking to her hen now."

He attacked the slab of bacon, not at all concerned with the resulting slices. He tossed them into the frying pan. Prowling the pantry revealed a loaf of bread that hadn't been cut. He hacked off a few pieces, spread them with butter and jam and tried to stop thinking about Catherine as he watched the bacon sizzle.

"*Sizzle*. Now there's a word to stir a man's blood." *Just as she did last night.*

"No matter. I was a perfect gentleman. I could easily have taken advantage of her. I could have taken that sweet, deliciously responsive body right on the damn table. I could have had her on the stairs and again... No! I will not torture myself with 'might-have-beens.'"

He remained firm this time as he finished cooking and took the tray upstairs to her room.

Sunlight spilled across the bed. Sunlight that turned her tousled curls to spun gold and bathed her lovely features with a seductive innocence that threw his good intentions to the floor, stomped on them and brought back his black, frustrated mood.

"How could you sleep and leave me wrung out like some forgotten piece of laundry?"

"Did I do that?"

"You did a damn sight more, but who's complaining?" His hands shook as she stretched and yawned. Sometime during the night she had lost her robe. Catherine's nightgown wasn't the silk-and-lace-trimmed confections a woman wore to entice a man. It was perfectly respectable with its ribbon tie at her neck and its long white sleeves. The sight brought back every moment of torment he had suffered. She owed him an enormous debt.

And it didn't help her that she had a slightly husky voice in the morning. Especially not this morning.

He watched her struggle to remember. At least he thought that's what caused her to frown and sit up. She absently pulled the quilt up to her chest. As if hiding made a bit of difference now.

"You've got the most awful black scowl on your face. What in heaven's name did I do?"

"Don't bring heaven into this. Believe me, look farther south. You'd be closer to where you had me."

She offered a surprised look, then arched her brow. A slow smile of utter delight creased her lips. "Did I hear you right? Did you just say I...I had..."

"Me. In a vise. In hell. In torment. But I'll have you know—"

"Greg, stop, please. What did I do!"

"Where should I start?" He hooked one foot on the chair rung and pulled it closer to the bed. Then he set the tray down.

"Oh, you made coffee."

"Never mind the coffee. Don't you want to hear the sins you committed against me last night?"

She winced. "Ouch. Are you always so—"

"Never mind what I am. We were discussing you." There had to be some justice. He wanted his pound of flesh. Watching Catherine pour herself coffee with a steady hand made him amend that—he wanted every bit of her.

He started to pace.

She patted the bed beside where she sat sipping coffee. "Come sit. Share breakfast with me. You made enough for two. Besides, you're making me nervous."

There were many things he wanted to make her, but nervous wasn't one of them. She smiled at him. Not only with her lips but with the mischievous sparkle in her eyes.

"Whatever I did to offend you, I can only apologize," she whispered.

"Ah, you don't remember." Perhaps there was hope for justice after all.

Very carefully, Catherine set the cup down. She looked up at him. "Yes, I do. You were a perfect gentleman. I haven't kept to my promises. I didn't watch over you last night. I ran away. I—"

"And never did tell me why."

"And *won't* tell you." Catherine nibbled the jam-covered bread and chose a slice of extra-crispy bacon. She could almost feel the steam rising from him as she calmly ate. But she was far from calm. She *did* remember everything. She ducked her head, the movement sliding her hair forward so she could hide the flush rising to her cheeks. She couldn't fully blame the brandy for acting like a wanton with him.

"You were very sweet to put me to bed. You are very kind to bring me breakfast. I promise you—and this time I'll keep it—that the rest of your stay will be in accordance with Suzanne's and your doctor's wishes."

"So generous, Catherine?" Since he was fuming, he spoke softly. "I can't tell you how that reassures me. But, my dear, we still have a problem to deal with."

The dark undercurrent in his voice drew her to look at him. He stood away from the shafts of sunlight, his face in shadow. But it was the near blackness of his eyes that held her gaze. Something dangerous lurked within. Not the warning-bell kind of danger, but a gleam that sent her blood rushing through her body.

"Since you remember, Catherine, you know how much I wanted you last night. Still want you. I was reduced to begging you for mercy, Catherine. Do you have the compassion to understand what that does to a man? I have never had to beg a woman in my life."

"Oh."

"Finish your coffee, Catherine."

She thought to ask why, but reached for the cup instead. She wasn't the least bit frightened by the aura of leashed masculine ire directed at her. Truth was, she felt excitement fill her. A laugh bubbled up before she could stop it.

"So you find this all amusing?"

"I didn't mean to laugh." She set the cup down and retreated toward the headboard. "I was terrible. A wanton. I've never behaved like that with anyone else. Truly."

"I believe you. How are you feeling now, Catherine?"

"Fine. I think." She curled her hands on the soft folds of her nightgown. "If you leave, I'll get dressed and tend to chores."

"It's nearly noon. And the chores are done." He stepped closer to the bed.

"Oh."

"Yes, oh. You have turned my life upside down in a few long days. We won't even speak of the nights."

"We won't?" Wide-eyed, she watched him lift the chair with tray intact and move it across the room. The linen shirt had damp patches. He appeared hot and tired and dusty. When he turned back, her gaze roved the lean, hungry set of his features. His hair was mussed as if he had been running his hand through it. She retained the memory of doing so last night. The sleeves of his shirt were rolled up. A smudge of dirt marked the spot over his heart. Most of the buttons were open. She gulped again. He looked nothing like the man who had arrived unannounced on her doorstep.

She blinked as he came to stand beside the bed. This close, she imagined she felt the tension, frustration and desire hardening his body. Amend the last. The evidence of its cause was there before her eyes. She looked up into his eyes.

"How impulsive do you feel, Catherine?"

"Impulsive?" She gulped again.

"Last night you confessed it was a failing of yours."

"Yes. One of my goals this year is to curb it."

"Gets you into trouble, does it?"

His grin had the earmarks of a predator's. She was not sure she relished the role of tethered prey.

"So you're clearheaded this morning?"

Was the man mad? The sexual heat coming at her in intense waves would cloud the mind of the most righteous woman. And that was something Catherine never claimed to be. Never wanted to be. How could he ask that ridiculous question when her body warmed and softened with longing before he even touched her?

"Answer me, Catherine."

"Why does it matter?" she asked in a choked whisper.

"I want you to know what you're saying. Exactly what you are doing. No recriminations later. No—"

"That's all right. You needn't make a list."

"I need to know that you're sure—"

"I think I've been sure since you set the stove on fire."

She couldn't help the smile this time. A flush stained his cheeks. She held out her hand to him. Not exactly as she had dreamed, but then, reality was ever so much better.

"That's it," he murmured, reaching for her and dragging her up against him. His mouth plundered hers with all the pent-up desire the long hours had kept at a boil.

Catherine thought, in a way, that said it all. Her lips were as impatient as his, her body as tight with need and flushed with heat. She fought for breath as she melted against him.

He caught her head between his hands and dragged her head back. "I wanted to woo you. Seduce you and—"

"Later," she murmured. His eyes flashed at hers, all but scorching her.

"Later," he muttered. He took her mouth again, his blood on fire to hear the soft, welcoming sounds she made in her throat.

She fell back on the bed, taking him with her in a sprawl that covered her from lips to toes. Both greedy, they kept their lips locked in a kiss.

She dragged at his shirt as they finally broke for air. "I want you. Now. I've never said that. I've never wanted like this."

His eyes glittered as he looked down at her. In a voice all but purring with male satisfaction, he said, "I know."

"You can't. I'll show you."

Her lips imparted hunger to his. She had accused herself of being wanton, but she knew it was more than unbridled lust that drove her. She wanted one memory. Just one to store against the lonely time to come when he left her. There was greed, too, to savor it all, to capture his every groan, to hold his taste and heat, to always remember the passion to be sated.

She heard the snap of shirt buttons. The cloth went flying. Cool air touched her body as her nightgown sailed to the floor, but she was drowning in sensation. His mouth left hers to taste petal-soft skin, went down to capture one rosy-tipped breast. Her fingers dug into his shoulders, before moving to his thick, dark hair as she cradled his head against her.

His skin was heated against her hands as she explored wherever she could reach. She felt his muscles bunch with tension. She was boneless as he traced random patterns of desire over her skin. She moved to the button fly of his pants with a boldness that shocked her.

Greg had nothing but groans of approval for her.

The sheer force that exploded between them made her shudder. And this, she thought, was only the beginning. It didn't surprise her that their fingers tangled over the buttons on his pants. Only his were stronger—the buttons popped and scattered. He levered himself up, Catherine followed to her knees. She wanted to touch him everywhere, greedy as could be.

She teased him unmercifully as he struggled to kick off his boots. Oh, but it was so good to laugh with a lover. Louis never... She stopped the thought and guilt that rushed through her.

"Can't you get them off?"

"I'm trying, woman. I'm damn well trying."

She ignored the wealth of exasperation in his voice. "Well, let me try."

"I'm warning you, Catherine. Not that it does much

good. But if you put your hands on me now, I won't be responsible for the disappointing results.''

"Oh.'' She backed down on the bed.

"Stop saying that.''

"Greg,'' she called softly.

"What!''

"Hurry.''

"Oh, sweet saints in heaven.'' With a grunt and groan he untangled his leg from the pants and kicked them aside. He was half-turned away from her as she asked what the problem was.

He faced her, glaring daggers that mixed passion with his frustration.

"Oh. Oh my.'' Her wide blue eyes rose to meet his narrow-eyed gaze.

"I won't hurt you, Catherine.''

"Oh, that wasn't fear. Just sheer, unadulterated female admiration.''

Her smile beckoned his. Of course, she had no idea how much the temptress she appeared with the fall of her tangled blond hair making a game of hide-and-seek with rosy-tipped breasts. The loving expression on her face held him still. He wanted her, but what he wanted more was to claim Catherine as his own.

Somewhere, sometime, she had stolen past his guard. The welter of emotion he experienced at this moment owed nothing to sex and everything to some deeper, tender feeling.

He battled it away.

"What's wrong? Don't you…want me?''

"Want you? If I wanted you any more, Catherine, I'd die from waiting.''

He brought her raw, hungry, blatantly sexual demand in his kiss, with his touch.

She sensed there was something different, but passion made its own demands. She responded to it, and to him, joyfully, willingly, her body arching up against his.

With a low sound, he took her breast in his mouth. Each tug, each nip of his hungry mouth shot a blaze of heat through her. And she wanted more. A small part of what she had missed. The dizzying sensations that made you think you'd never survive them, and made her realize that she couldn't live without them. He feasted on her. There was no other word for it. And Catherine wondered if she could die from the pleasure.

Her hot, damp skin quivered beneath his caressing hands. He had given pleasure to women, but not like this, not with the driving need to give her more without thought to himself. Not that Catherine neglected him as he brought her up to the first peak and drove her over. She rolled on the bed with him, her greedy hands stroking his body one minute, moving with frantic haste in the next.

Mad. The woman drove him mad.

He wanted to savor. To seduce and coax. She was writhing under him. He couldn't get enough. The scent that was hers alone came with every breath, heated and heady like the finest champagne. And her eyes. Dark blue, nearly black with passion, intensely focused on his face.

No matter how he touched her, or where, the deep shudders of her body had him believing she was innocent of carnal pleasures. Her voice was a sultry plea, luring his desire to new heights. He had never felt so powerful, or needed the way he needed her.

He claimed her mouth with a wild kiss, drinking her cry and greedy for more. He rolled to his side, cupping her, a tremor passing from her flesh to his. Her fingers dug into his shoulders and she arched to his touch. Her cry for more broke whatever control he had.

"Now, Catherine. I need to be inside you." His voice was a husky demand. Some deep, primitive male force rushed him to possess. "I want to watch you take me."

Her answer came with her hands on his hips. She arched up in welcome. He drove inside her with one hard stroke. Her cry froze him.

"God. Catherine. I can't believe this." His eyes searched hers. She gloved him so tightly, his muttered "Don't move" could have been an order to himself as well as to her. He felt his muscles tremble from the strain of holding himself away from her when all he wanted to do was sink into waiting heat.

He drew breath, once, then again, as if he couldn't get enough air. She was a widow, not a virgin.

"What's wrong?"

"I don't want to hurt you."

"You can't. I want you too much."

Still he struggled for some vestige of control. She was so hot and tight, and wet. The effort was beyond him.

Catherine touched his cheek. There had been pain. It was almost two years since Louis had died. But need was stronger by far. She couldn't think what to say, all she could do was show him.

She lifted her hips. Her hands skimmed his sweat-sheened back and pressed him to her.

She felt as helpless as he did to resist the urge to mate. The room tilted and swirled before she closed her eyes. He drove her to match a frenzied pace in the race to where dark pleasure waited.

Violent shudders shook her body as peak after peak, each one higher than the last, revealed what she had known and longed for, was a pale vision to what was happening now.

The scents were thick, the breathing labored. His dark voice whispered in her ear. Her heart pounded in cadence with his. Nothing could stop the storm that hurtled them toward completion. She heard his strangled cry. Her own was lost in his kiss.

Drained, he collapsed on her. "I'm sorry, Catherine." It was a harsh whisper. He knew he should move, but he hadn't the strength to do more than breathe.

It was minutes before she understood what he had said. "Sorry," she murmured, squeezing her eyes closed. He was sorry he had made love to her? *Dear Lord, how do I...what can I say?*

"Forgive me." He managed to pull back to see her face. She was turned away as if she couldn't bear to look at him.

"Catherine, please, I never meant to hurt you."

"Hurt me?" She looked at him. The green had almost disappeared from his eyes. "Why? Why would you think you hurt me?"

"I was rough. Too hurried. I—"

Her hand covered his mouth to silence him. "Listen, I..." She tried to breathe evenly, but passion's aftermath brought tiny tremors that left her so weak she could barely speak. "No. You didn't hurt me. This was the most wonderful—"

"Wonderful, Catherine?"

It was strange to think she needed to reassure him. And a smile for the thought teased the corners of her lips.

"Yes. Wonderful. Glorious. Exciting. Fireworks and—"

"Like a Catherine wheel and—"

"Sparks. Lots of fire." His grin made her smile deepen. She lifted her arms around his neck. "Did you...I mean, was it..." Suddenly shy, she stopped.

"Wonderful." He kissed her nose. "Glorious." His lips skimmed her cheek. "Exciting and filled with fireworks and fire, and you nearly," he whispered against her lips, "killed me."

Words weren't enough. His lips cherished her mouth. And Greg discovered he was very much alive, and the desire had not abated. It was not sated. Not even close. Desire flamed anew, despite his lingering guilt that he had shown Catherine, his new lover, all the finesse of a merchant sailor on leave.

He redoubled his effort to be gentle and found, to both their delight, that going slowly brought sensual torment, tenderness brought her tears of joy, and laughter played a role in lovers' games.

As the afternoon's shadows blanketed the room, he cradled the woman who had touched his heart within his arms.

He knew that what he felt—and he didn't trust himself to name it as yet—went beyond the shattering pleasure they had shared.

He kissed the top of her head. What was she thinking? What did Catherine feel about him now?

Chapter Sixteen

Catherine mentally echoed his question. She lay there with her head nestled on his shoulder, content beyond words. She listened to the ever decreasing pounding of his heart and felt the gradual slowing of her own. Sensation drifted like fragments of clouds through her mind.

She felt the wonderful, powerful, glorious feeling of being a woman who had pleased her lover. Happiness, she decided, could be touched. Her hand caressed his still-damp chest, her fingers trailing softly through the dusting of dark brown hair. His hand rose and caught hers, stopping the lazy caress, only to offer one of his own.

She savored these quiet moments, storing all she could in memory. She was touching happiness now but didn't fool herself, it was a fleeting thing. When he left, there would be pain, and the bleak loneliness.

But she was too pleasure-drenched to allow dark thoughts to overwhelm her now.

Only the thought of his leaving her wouldn't be banished. Her life would be empty without his laughter. Even his complaints about the animals. Damn him.

This was a terrible mistake. She couldn't love him. Love him?

"Catherine, what's wrong? You are suddenly tense."

Love Greg? She couldn't. She didn't.

He shifted so that he could look down at her. Her eyes were open but didn't meet his penetrating gaze.

"You appear unhappy, Catherine," he whispered. He stroked her cheek, then brushed the hair from her shoulder.

"No. I'm not," she murmured, rallying herself not to reveal this most troubling thought. She couldn't be in love with him. It wasn't possible. She offered her lips for a brief kiss, wishing they never had to move, wishing they could lie here forever, wrapped in warmth.

With a sigh, she closed her eyes and felt him settle back down on the pillow. Catherine hoped he didn't see her hand move to cover her heart.

Long ago, when she and Sarah and Mary had been young ladies discovering young men, they had talked about the possibility of falling in love with someone so quickly and decided the idea was far-fetched. But it had happened, or so it seemed, to her.

Love, she had learned, was something that people grew into over time shared learning about each other. It simply didn't happen like this. Act in haste and repent in leisure. How many times had she told herself that? So many, she grew tired of repeating it.

She glanced at him, seeing that he slept, and smiled. What she felt was akin to love. It wasn't just his looks which made her heart rate soar, but all the kindness he showed. He was so secure in his masculine role that he had no need to shout and bluster, order and demand to prove he was a man.

Love. What would it be like to love and be loved by him? She knew he adored Suzanne's children. His sister mentioned time and again the unstinting generosity of his attentions to his nieces and nephews. Louis had wanted to wait to have children. They were too young to be saddled with them. As if she had ever thought of nurturing a child as somehow being tied down.

But what other name could she give to what she felt for Greg? She had to accept her feelings as valid. This was all part of her new life. No one could tell her what she felt, or what to do about it. And if she couldn't accept it and keep it secret from him, he would run back east and lose his bet with Suzanne. She never wanted to be the cause of him losing anything. Not even a moment of sleep.

But if she said nothing, didn't give away to him a hint of this powerful new feeling that held her in thrall, she could steal these weeks they would have together.

And afterward…

Afterward might be bittersweet, but she would be the only one hurt. She could survive that. She would survive that to have him as her lover. It was better than having nothing at all.

She leaned closer to him, her sigh whisper soft. First she fell at his feet, now she had fallen in love. Strength came from an unexpected source. Memory supplied her with the changes Louis had made once she admitted that she loved him. He had ordered her life to suit himself from that moment on. She had sworn no man would have that power over her again. The fact that

Greg was nothing like her deceased husband mattered little. Men were men when it came to their women.

Her eyes drifted closed, her breath falling into cadence with his. She could dream, and she could wish, and keep her secret safe.

In his sleep, one arm wrapped around her to draw her closer. She smiled against his shoulder, lulled to join him in the warm haven only replete lovers knew.

"What the hell is that smell?" Greg's curse as he bolted upright jarred Catherine from sleep.

"Smell?"

"It's...oh, Lord, it's that damn cat!"

"Lord Romeo?" Catherine, having been tumbled to the far side of the bed, struggled to sit up. The cat was perched on the footboard, his lovely white and orange stripes covered with bits of straw mixed with... "Oh, I know that smell."

"So," Greg declared as he lunged for the cat, "do I. I'll kill him this time."

With an agility she was forced to admire after their hours of lovemaking, Greg, unconcerned for his naked state, went running after the cat.

She was given no chance to explain that Lord Romeo, when feeling he'd been neglected, rolled in the manure pile.

Dressing quickly, she snatched up Greg's robe from his room. Really, the man had to do something about his penchant for running about the house nude. But her eyes feasted on every lithe, gracefully built inch of him.

"Go upstairs and dress," she said when she found him flat on his stomach in the parlor. His arms were lost beneath the settee, where he cursed as he tried to grab the cat. She heard the loud hissing and prayed

Lord Romeo didn't do Greg serious damage with his claws.

"Greg, please, let me get him. If you want to help, put on your robe and heat some water. I'll have to bathe him."

"You go rest. I'll tend to this."

"Go rest?" she repeated, more to herself. Was she suddenly aged? Suddenly so decrepit by a little bed sport that she had to rest?

"No." His lack of response made her repeat it. Loudly. "I said no. I won't leave. And I won't be ordered by you."

His dire mutterings were all directed at the cat. She stood and tapped her foot, arms crossed over her chest as irritation turned to anger. He paid as much attention to her as he did a piece of furniture. She could have been a ghost who spoke, but he couldn't hear.

Greg wiggled as far as he could under the settee. Lord Romeo waited for his chance, then darted out the side. Greg scrambled up and went after him towards the kitchen with Catherine following.

Lord Romeo sat on the windowsill, fur bristling, hissing for all he was worth.

"That repulsive creature belongs in the barn." He pumped furiously to fill the large kettle with water.

"Greg, cats are very good at cleaning themselves."

"But he'll remember this bath and refrain from ever rolling in a manure pile again."

From the pantry, he rolled out the tub.

Catherine, keeping out of his way, couldn't help but offer advice. "He won't get in the tub. He won't let you bathe him. I wish you'd stop being so…so male, and let me do it."

"I won't decapitate the cat. Much as I'd like to."

"That remark is unworthy of you. After all, you are a gentleman. And I love Lord Romeo. If you harm him, you might as well harm me." She skirted the table and went to stand in front of the dry sink. "Come to me, love," she crooned to the cat, breathing through her mouth as the stench of him hit her full force.

"Stop mollycoddling him, Catherine. It's no wonder that animal practically walks all over you."

She turned at that. "My, you change moods faster than Rafe McCade can draw his gun. Who whispered how perfect I was? I did hear you say it only minutes ago. Now I'm a doormat for my cat!"

He threw up one hand to stop her. The movement irked her to no end. She glared at him, while Greg offered a smug look.

"Catherine, as a lover you are perfect. One thing has nothing to do with the other. You're a woman, a soft-hearted woman. That," he announced, pointing at Lord Romeo, "is a creature bent on keeping his territory. Believe me, you don't fully understand. You're not male. There is no more to be said. He is a small animal, and I am a strong and most determined man. There will be no contest between us. He goes into the bath."

Catherine bit her tongue and marched out.

Greg watched her go with a rueful smile. But he was proven right minutes later—there was no contest.

Upstairs, Catherine stood in the hall. There had been times as a child when only learning the lesson firsthand made an impression on her. Greg, if the horrid sounds were an indication, was learning a lesson firsthand, too.

She turned and went into her room.

She had just reached for her hairbrush when Greg came rushing in. "Where is he? Are you protecting that cat? We are going to settle this once and for all."

Looking at his drenched body, then at the impotent fury of his gaze, Catherine didn't laugh. But she was only human. "You're very wet."

"Now, there's a perspicacious observation," Greg muttered, tearing the quilt from the bed, then bending down to look under it. "Do you know there is a...wait a moment." He stood holding an ecru corset. "French strip."

"Give me that." She rushed to snatch it from his hands and held it tightly to her chest. "And how did you know it was a French strip corset?"

He drew himself to his full height. "Catherine, if I answer you, I will no longer be considered a gentleman."

"Oh!"

"Stop saying that. Now, where's the cat?"

"He's not here."

"You wouldn't tell me if he was." He turned his back toward her and heard her cry out.

"You're hurt."

"What did you expect? You weren't very clear with your warning, you know. You might have mentioned that animal has twenty legs with forty razors concealed on each one. Those few scratches on my back are minor. Look what he did to my hands. And when I get my hands on that mangy carcass—"

"Stop. Let me take care of these for you. I did try to warn you. You were being very male and not listening." She poured water into the basin, then drew him closer. "This will likely sting," she said, and giving him no time started to wash his hands with soap. She was as gentle as could be, her brow knitted with concern as she washed his hands, then carefully dried them. "There's a jar of ointment in the pantry that Mary left. But you must promise to use it twice a day."

Defeated, Greg went to sit on the edge of the bed. "I can't understand it." He swiped at his dripping hair. "He let me carry him to the tub. Limp as an old rag. Then the brute howled when I dropped him in."

"Dropped him?"

"He slipped out of my hands when I grabbed the soap. He locked those damn claws wherever he could."

"You shouldn't have tried it, or let him go immediately."

"Thank you for your concern. Let him go? Let him stink up the whole house?"

"Greg…" She came to stand beside him. With one hand she pushed back his wet hair. "Did you let him out?"

"There wasn't much choice. I almost fell." He absently rubbed his hip where it had slammed into the table. "You might have come down. You had to hear all the commotion."

"Stay here. I'll be right back."

She returned quickly with a cold cloth wrung out for his hip and salve, which she applied to his scratches.

He watched her, surprised when she leaned down to kiss him.

"What was that for? I've been more hindrance than help."

"You deserve more than a kiss. You have every right to be cross."

He shook his head. Once again she kept him off balance. She had had her say and now took care of him. Her lips parted a little as she leaned over to apply the salve to his back. So he deserved a kiss…

"Catherine, I want to make love to you."

She stepped back, a trace of a smile on her lips. "You just did. Several times. At least I thought that's what we were doing. Lie down," she said, pushing against his chest. "You rest here with the cloth on that bruise. I'll take care of the evening chores and be back before you know it."

He sat up. "Why aren't you angry? Lord knows you have every right to be." He studied her as if he were fitting the pieces of an intricate business deal together. He knew what he felt for her, but just realized that he didn't know Catherine at all.

"Get dressed. I'll wait downstairs for you."

They shared the chores that evening, ate very little and shared his bed that night. The days that followed fell into an unpredictable pattern.

But there was an underlying problem that nagged at Catherine.

She ignored the possessive gleam in his eyes. She relied on patience rather than pride when he revealed his efficient plans to run her egg business with an eye toward higher profits.

If she followed his suggestions.

She agreed to think about them.

He was not satisfied with so vague an answer.

That was first on a list she compiled of grievous sins. He hired Ramon to work every day. He purchased baked goods. He conspired with Caroline or Ramon's mother to cook dinners. He charmed the ladies sewing circle, whom he met at church, his manner that of a recovering invalid, which helped put to rest Mrs. Pettigrew's gossip.

Her emotions ran the gamut from grateful to exasperated. All within the span of an hour at times.

And he spoiled her. Most mornings she woke to find

him gone. Chores would be almost finished. Coffee waited. He had learned to make a delicious brew. On the good days she relished every sip and lavished praise. On the bad ones, she reminded herself that anyone who bought the most expensive roasted beans could make an aromatic brew to savor.

The Jobe family loved to see him enter their grocery store. He shopped with the abandon of a struck-it-rich miner. J. P. Crabtree actually stepped outside to the boardwalk when he heard Greg was in town and invited him inside. He asked Greg's advice. He wasn't the only businessman to do so.

Greg thrived like Mary's garden after decomposed straw, manure and wood ash were spread on it and watered from the rain barrels.

She silently observed the changes in him, some with dismay, others with joy that he was accomplishing all that his sister and doctor wanted from this trip.

In a modest way, she knew she contributed.

He had no stomach ailments. Even after eating chili-drenched beef at a barbecue. He went back for seconds, too. She couldn't count the times her gaze strayed to him. He was tanned and fit from all his work. He never fretted about his business. Rarely did he mention the city or his associates unless it was to relate some amusing tale.

Catherine did break one rule, but it was their secret. She allowed him to read the daily paper. She knew he had lengthy discussions about the state of expansion in the western territories with Peter Austin and Ridley Beam, the newly elected and first mayor of town.

He shared her pleasures in the simplest of things: a walk in the woods, a picnic by the stream, a buggy ride in late afternoon into the mountains.

She had come to love her home and the land around it. Greg proved a willing pupil as she taught him all she knew, sharing colorful and sometimes sad stories of men who opened up the area to settlement.

They visited a few of the working mines that were not deep into Apache territory. At the Silver Bar she introduced him to Michael Cooney, once a customs inspector in New Orleans until he heard of his brother's death.

Without asking, Michael showed them the tomb he had carved in the canyon wall in memory of his brother. It was sealed with ore from the mine.

Greg was fascinated with the workings. His questions and their answers from Michael only led to more until she reminded him they'd drive home in the dark if they didn't leave now.

On the way home, at Greg's request, she told him the sad story of James Cooney's death. Both Mary and Sarah had met the charming cavalry officer who had waited out his enlistment to file his claim. He had begun the mining rush in this area five years ago. But after the death of Victorio's son-in-law at Alma, the Apache raids increased. James was going to sell off his claim and go home to marry his sweetheart, who waited all this time for him.

In that lonely canyon the Apache found and killed him.

In the encroaching darkness, his hand found hers. There was no need for words. Their touch conveyed the sadness for any unaccountable death, and joy that they were alive and together.

If the shadow of fleeting life hovered within the room as they loved each other, it only made their joining sweeter, for it was a slow taking and surrender that left them spent.

Most evenings they sat before the fire in the front parlor, where she strummed her guitar and sang to him. He had a rich, mellow voice and she often coaxed him to join her. But mostly he liked to listen to her.

Greg made her laugh with his droll wit until her sides ached. She returned the gift of laughter to him.

He loved her with all but the words.

She stored moments into memory, every happy moment she spent with him. Love gave her sharpened senses, everything was precious to her.

Even Lord Romeo had reached a truce with Greg. He only hissed when Greg chased him from whichever bedroom they were sleeping in. Catherine knew he was unaware that she knew he slipped the cat fish that he paid Ramon to catch for him.

He could deny his caring, gentle heart all he wanted. She viewed him with eyes of love.

But as the days became weeks, Catherine could no longer hide the subtle knowledge that was piling up. Dismay blossomed into full-blown fear.

Gregory Michael Mayfield the third turned into Louis Hill the second.

It was wrong to think ill of the dead. She tried not to do it. She held back as long as she could.

There was no one she could talk to. Most of the women she knew would lynch her for feeling as she did.

But a woman who had fought so hard to realize a measure of independence after twenty-two years of male dominance, first under her father then her husband, had to do what she had to do to preserve her state.

Even if it meant destroying the little time they had left together.

Love like this happens too rarely. Don't throw it away.

Catherine didn't listen to the nagging voice.

She would confront him or never live at peace with herself.

Even if it shattered her heart.

Even if it meant losing him forever.

Chapter Seventeen

It all began because of the grocery bill. Rather, it started because the bill never came. When she went into town to inquire what had become of it, Mr. Jobe—his nervousness evidence of his flustered state—said that Greg had paid it.

She wasn't alarmed then. She was perplexed.

The same happened at the butcher. Now an alarm bell rang. But not too loudly.

Mr. Botts at the livery informed her that her feed bill had been paid in full. "What's more," he added in his slow drawl and roundabout way, which required saintly patience, "he tol' me he'd be doing the ordering on account of his figuring that buying in small lots costs you more. Man's got himself a fine head for business, Mrs. Hill. You hold on to him, you hear."

She heard. She heard him so clearly and so loudly she felt the beginnings of a headache. And the alarm bell jangled.

She decided to wait before confronting Greg about his high-handed butting into her business. The next morning, she left for town to collect the moneys due her.

The first stop was the café, and there, Caroline offered another shock.

"But, Catherine, I already paid my bill. Not only what I owed you, but I paid a month in advance just as Greg suggested. I swear, woman, that man of yours has a mighty fine head for business. I saved enough to order a new pair of shoes. Oh, you should see the fine leather the Wormells have to offer. I couldn't make up my mind."

"The Wormells?"

"They just opened a shoe store. He does such nice repair work, and when I saw the boots he made for Mrs. Jobe, I just had to have a pair. You'll meet them at service on Sunday. And don't forget there's a box lunch social afterward. The money goes into the school fund."

"Caroline, I'm happy you're going to have a new pair of shoes. I know how your feet hurt standing all day. But getting back to my eggs? Who exactly did you pay the money to?"

"Why, I did what Greg suggested. I had Buck Purcell deposit it from my account to yours. This way you won't have to worry about collecting it or walking around town with too much cash. You heard about Mrs. Vaughan? She was bringing money to the bank after her husband finished the pews for the church and two men robbed her.

"Honestly, Catherine, stop looking at me so strange. Greg's idea was a good one. Buck takes the money each month and I don't have to worry about it, either."

"Just like Greg suggested?" Catherine asked in a very soft, sweet voice. Caroline nodded, then turned to wait on a customer. She never noticed the black fury bloom in Catherine's blue eyes.

As Catherine started for the door, Caroline reminded her about the box lunch social. "And don't forget to bring that handsome devil with you."

"If he's still here," Catherine muttered to herself.

The alarm bells were clanging when Nita hailed her. Catherine lifted her skirt hem and petticoats to cross the street. She had to wait while a creaking farm wagon in need of greasing passed in front of her.

There was hammering going on at the far end of the street. She stood a moment and watched as a sign was being hung. Two men stood in a wagon bed, holding the large wooden sign, while a third held the team of horses steady.

The hammering resumed once the sign was hoisted into place.

"Wormell's Finest Footwear for the Family," she read. There was other writing, smaller in size, but Nita waved for her to come inside the dress shop.

"Mighty glad I saw you, Catherine. Saved me from making a trip out to your place. Just in time, too. That shipment of trimmings arrived. Greg said he'd be bringing you by to choose—"

"Not you," Catherine cried out. "Not you, too."

"Land sakes, Catherine, what's wrong with you?" Nita hurried out from behind her counter and ushered Catherine into her private quarters in the rear of the store.

"If that woman said one word again to you—"

"No. I thankfully haven't seen Mrs. Pettigrew. It's been a trying morning."

"Your eyes are all squinted up. Bet you're getting one of your headaches. Just set yourself down on the divan and I'll get the lavender oil. Bless Mary for thinking of giving me plenty. I can't tell you how many times I've used it. Fixes you up in no time."

Catherine leaned against the thick-buttoned, tufted back of the divan. Nita returned in minutes and with a fresh hankie dabbed a few drops of oil on Catherine's forehead.

"There, close your eyes and rest. No one will bother you back here."

Catherine closed her eyes, inhaled deeply of the potent scent, but thought it would take a great deal more to rid her of this headache. She didn't think Greg would disappear if she sprinkled him with lavender oil. Of course, she was getting desperate enough to try.

She must have dozed off, for Nita woke her with a gentle shake.

"I made us tea and closed the shop. We'll sit and be quiet until you recover."

"Nita, I'm afraid my problem won't go away that easily. But I appreciate your doing this for me."

"Nonsense. Talk if you want. Or don't."

Catherine looked into her kind eyes but couldn't bring herself to tell her. She had to deal with this on her own.

When Nita removed the tea tray, Catherine rose to leave.

"Now, I've got just the thing to cure you. Never knew a woman who didn't forget her troubles when she was buying something new to wear."

"But, Nita—"

"Now, you come along and help me pick out the trimmings for your gowns."

"But I didn't order...Nita, I can't pay for—" Catherine stopped short. "Did Greg shop here?"

"You can't think I'd be telling anyone that he bought—"

"No, Nita. You won't tell anyone what he bought because he didn't buy it. I won't accept any of whatever he—"

"Where in tarnation do you think I'd find another woman with your figure? Got that cloth cut and almost sewn." Nita took hold of her arm. "I never was one to pass judgment on another. He was like a little boy in a sweet shop, wanting everything he saw for you. Then he settled down and rejected half of what I showed him.

"The man, my dear, has exquisite taste. I've lived longer than you. Take and enjoy. No one need be any the wiser about where it came from."

"Nita! He's doing this all over town!"

"Sounds to me like a man ready to cut his filly from the herd."

"No!"

"If you say so." She shrugged. "Now, come pick out the trims. I got them sent all the way from St. Louis." She removed a large box from the shelf behind her and set it on the counter. Opened, it revealed an array of braids and cords, beads and silks that dazzled the eye.

She held up a length of cream trim. "Just look at this new silk moss. The cording is woven to look like tiny roses." She took a swatch of plaid material and held it out to Catherine.

"This is for a day gown. The dark forest green plaid with its cream background goes perfectly with this trim. And this, look at the sultana mohair braid. I've never seen a prettier shade of bronze. It will look lovely

on the navy blue. Of course, if you'd rather have it in
light gray or cardinal—''

"No."

"You like the bronze, too. I thought you would.
Matter of fact, so did Greg. I have this open-worked
silk gimp that I thought—"

"Nita, you pick the trims. I've always admired your
taste. I know that Mary did, too. Whatever you choose
will be fine. Excuse me. I really do have to get home."

"But, Catherine, I need to fit—''

"Thank you for the tea, and the oil." Catherine
closed the door carefully. She was a woman, not a child
to slam doors. Besides, Greg's fingers weren't there to
get caught if she gave vent to the fury bubbling inside
her. She moved off at a sedate pace, her eyes straight
ahead.

"Catherine," Caroline called from the café's doorway. "I forgot. He said you approved of his plan.
Everyone agreed to it."

"That was all I needed." Catherine maintained her
steady pace to the livery. She climbed up on her
wagon's seat and cautioned herself to a slow ride
home.

She wanted time to simmer and burn. Greg had a lot
to answer for.

She wondered how he would feel talking to the business end of her gun.

Greg lay on the hay up in the barn's loft, unaware
he was marked for murder. When he was young, the
loft was a favorite place to dream about changing the
world.

But he had never been as content, felt as lazy as he
did today. He shifted, inhaling the fragrance of hay,

and heard the cow's stanchion rattle. He couldn't remember the last time he watched dust motes on filtering beams of sunlight. He nibbled on a long spear of hay, his hands crossed beneath his head. He closed his eyes to enjoy these moments. Soon Catherine would return.

Catherine. The thought of her brought a smile. He heard the wagon in the yard. He would stay and let her find him. The hay was thick, and soft, the afternoon theirs, and what better way to wile away the hours than loving the delectable Catherine.

The slamming of the back door jarred him. He heard Catherine calling him and she didn't sound loverlike.

In minutes she was below him. "Where are you, you mangy, conniving polecat?"

Above in the loft, Greg relished the idea of Lord Romeo getting his just desserts at long last.

"Hiding won't save you," Catherine announced. She found the tack room empty. Turning around, she saw Miss Lily come out of the far stall, cackling for all she was worth. She pecked at the wood of the ladder and Catherine looked up.

She knew he was hiding up there. If she moved the ladder, Greg would be stranded, but she burned for confrontation. She gathered her skirt and petticoats and climbed.

There he was, sprawled in the hay, all enticing shadows and sunlit male splendor. She caught her breath seeing his smile. The man had enough comfort and sweetness for every woman who baked to put in her cakes. She ignored his temptation.

"Mayfield, if you value your life, you'd better shake out your tail and get down from there."

Greg caught a brief glimpse of the upturned tip of

her nose, her eyes and a poke bonnet he longed to shred. And then she was gone.

Gone? What happened to his fantasy? Where was his lover? He winced when he heard the back door of the house slam once more. Was there no justice? The damn cat had her miffed, not him.

He roused himself to go smooth ruffled feathers. He'd better, or he would be sleeping alone tonight. There had been that kind of sound in her voice.

But as he climbed from the loft and crossed the yard, he struggled to think what he had done to upset her.

He opened the kitchen door and stepped inside. Had he used the mild word *upset?* Catherine was in a fine, blood-boiling, tear-the-hide-off-someone fury.

"You," she said, pointing a finger at him, "sit at the table. You will not speak. You will listen. You will do this, or you will pack your bags and leave."

"Just as I thought, Catherine. We're going to have an adult, sensible, rational session of 'I accuse, and you are condemned.'"

"Sit down."

Greg sat with the air of a martyr tied to the stake.

She refused to allow a bit of sympathy to surface.

He crossed his arms over his chest, leaned back and put his feet up on the seat of the opposite chair. "You don't object to my being comfortable, do you? I have a feeling we might be at this for a while. Even a condemned man has some rights."

"Do you know what you've done?"

"Nothing as offensive as you wearing that damn bonnet. Take it off. It's an offense to every man's eyes."

"Too bad. It's my bonnet. I decide when to wear it, when to take it off, and—"

"And if you think I'll sit and listen to you vent whatever made you angry while you wear that ridiculous—"

"Stop it." Catherine closed her eyes, drew a deep breath and huffily exhaled. She removed the bonnet. "I want you to know," she said, flinging the bonnet at him, "that it's off so you won't distract me from my purpose."

"Frankly, I don't care why, so long as it's gone." She paced and he watched the sway of her hips. "Tell me."

"I have never, do you hear me, never been so humiliated in my life. You interfered in my business. What's more, the whole town knows. Who the hell do you think you are?"

"Ah, now we get to the heart of it."

"As if you didn't know." She glared at him, then her gaze slid to where her holstered gun hung.

Greg thought about answering her without adding fuel to the fire. But what could he call himself? Her lover? A man who—devil take it, he didn't even know what he was defending. "Catherine, if you sat down and explained the problem calmly—"

"I don't want to sit. I'm not calm. I'm angry and I feel betrayed. I want to strangle you. Or shoot you." She gripped one of the chairs and faced him. "How dare you manage my money? Who gave you the right to pay my bills? How could you order my livestock feed? And the most grievous sin, you ordered clothing for me. Do you have any inkling of what you have done to me? No. How could you? You're a...a man!"

"I was the last time I looked."

"This isn't funny."

Greg eyed her white-knuckled grip on the chair. He nodded. "Catherine, I'll endeavor to explain—"

"Don't endeavor. Just explain."

He attempted a smile, hoping to coax one from her, but the lady was not in a cooperative mood. "It's simply a more efficient way for you to do business. I wanted to help you and you wouldn't accept—"

"If you dare say money, I won't be responsible for what I'll do to you."

"All right. I won't." He looked directly into her eyes. They were so dark that he couldn't separate the emotions. He didn't understand why she was upset. What he'd done wasn't so terrible. Everyone benefited. Mostly Catherine. "Did you speak with Buck?"

"No. I saved myself that final indignity."

"Stop speaking like a heroine in those dime novels Suzanne's always reading."

Her eyes cleared, sharpened. "I made no claim to heroic acts. And since you don't like the way I talk, I won't subject you to any more of it."

His chair fell in his hurry to go after her. He caught her in the hallway, spinning her around to face him. "You started this. Don't be a coward, Catherine. Stay and finish."

"Now I'm a coward?"

"You—"

"Be quiet." She poked her finger in his chest. "You're the coward. Sneaking around behind my back like a thief. Stealing into my affections, stealing my hard-won independence. You made yourself a bed of thorns, Mayfield. Sleep alone in it." She jerked away from him, but he wouldn't release her.

"Damn it, Catherine, I thought you had more sense. I want to take care of you. I wanted—"

"I don't care what you want. But you're right. I lost good sense the moment you arrived. But I found it now. Leave or stay, win your bet or lose it, I simply don't care. All my life I've lived with men ordering me. You took over, just like them. You couldn't wait for me to decide. And it was my decision to make."

"Catherine, look at me." He subdued her struggles until she raised wounded blue eyes to look at him. "I hated that stupid bet with my sister, but it brought me something I thought I'd never find."

"That makes two of us," she snapped. "I never thought any man would have the opportunity to betray me, to make me feel I don't have the sense of…of Miss Lily. But you did that to me. You make me feel I have cotton for brains. I don't need you to order my life. I liked it fine the way it was."

His smile died on his lips. "I never meant to hurt you. You see, I met a woman, an exceptional woman whom I admired, respected and wished to keep beside me. I wanted to buy the world and lay it at her feet. I did the only things I could. If you can't accept—"

"I don't accept. Can't you understand?" she pleaded, renewing her struggle to be free. "You humiliated me. You branded me a kept woman. A fallen angel. A soiled dove. I will never be able to hold my head up after you leave. Those are the wonderful things you did for me, Mayfield."

"No. Buck Purcell spread the word that you and I are partners."

She sagged against him, feeling faint. "Partners?" she whispered. No sooner had her head rested against his chest than she reared back to search his face for the truth. It was there in his eyes, bright as could be. She didn't want to see or admit what else shimmered in the depths of his dark green eyes.

"I had to protect you from the very gossip you feared. It's perfectly believable. My reputation didn't remain a secret. I've had more business deals offered me than I have time to sort them."

"Partners," she repeated in a stunned voice. But instead of calming her, the word, the very idea infuriated her.

Greg, thinking he'd rather sweep her into his arms and seduce his way back into her good graces, held still and silent. He had learned that Catherine would not be pushed in any direction she didn't want to go. He had become fond—no, too mild a description—he loved the way she came to him. Sometimes teasing like the veriest wanton, or with laughter in her eyes, on her lips, playful, tender, lovable Catherine. He couldn't lose what he had found with her. Wouldn't.

The thought stunned him. When had he ever wanted a woman so much that he couldn't bear the thought of losing her? And if that was true, there was a question he didn't, couldn't answer without asking one other of her. Catherine wasn't ready to hear that question. And he wasn't ready to ask it.

"Catherine, you understand now that there's been no harm done."

"No harm done."

He frowned. He couldn't identify the note in her voice. Her gaze was unfocused. He grew concerned, then dismissed it. She was simply shocked by his reasonable explanation. Women didn't think the way men did. Thank the Lord. Especially men who protected the woman they cared for at all costs.

"Will you let me go?" she asked.

"Catherine, I—"

"Please let go of me."

He released her and stepped back, ready for her to bolt. She didn't. A wry smile kicked up the corners of his mouth. Just like a woman, never doing what you expected her to do.

"Come into the parlor, no, the kitchen will suit for what I have to say, Mr. Mayfield."

Mr. Mayfield? Serious and formal? Where had he gone wrong? *Tell her you love her.* She disappeared into the kitchen. He stood stock-still in the hall. Love?

He loved a woman who goaded him beyond endurance? How could he love a woman who demanded his respect for standing up to him, while she drove him crazy with her notions of female independence? Love had nothing to do with the lust she stirred with a glance. Love, hell! He wasn't about to fall into that parson's trap.

But if it wasn't love, then why was he meekly following her into the kitchen? Did he have some mysterious need to torment himself? Did he want to be dominated by a woman?

Heaven forbid. And then he remembered that she said he could pack and leave. Those were not the words of a woman in love.

Enough about love. They would settle this unfortunate matter, go upstairs and spend the rest of the afternoon in bed. He was a man in command. But Catherine stood with her back toward him, looking out the window. She didn't turn, not even when he cleared his throat. Nor did she see his surprised expression when she spoke.

"Are you a gambling man, Mayfield?"

Less loverlike words he'd never heard. He had to

break this habit of Catherine being the first woman in far too many things. Before he replied, she spoke again.

"You are a man of business, one who thrives on challenges. You risked your health on a bet. That makes you a reckless man."

If she had cursed him he couldn't feel more insulted by her sarcastic voice. "And?" he intoned coldly.

"And I have a bet for you—partner," she added as she turned around to face him.

"Go on. I haven't had a good laugh all day."

"So you're finally angry. Good. Now you understand how I feel. And you won't be laughing when I'm through with you."

"I thought you were. Pardon me, Mrs. Hill, for the error. I judged you to be finished as finished could be."

"An expected male response."

He eyed her calm expression and the hands she placed on her hips. "Pardon me. I can't help my response. I would suggest you have your eyes examined. You require spectacles for that inane remark. Male responses to provoking female idiocy are natural when one is a man."

"I refuse to engage in a name-calling contest."

"You can't know how that reassures me. But, please, continue. Something about a bet?"

"Yes. You won't listen. You refuse to understand what you did to me. Perhaps you're not too thick-headed to be shown the error of your high-handed ways."

"No name-calling?" But he spoke without heat, for she looked so desirable at that moment, he had all he could do to stop himself from crossing the room to her. Anger flushed her cheeks and put a militant sparkle in her eyes. Her stiff bearing, even her cool, formal voice stirred his blood.

But there was an element of fear creeping inside him. He needed to halt this nonsense right now. He didn't want to risk losing Catherine on some silly, connived bet. One was enough for any man. Pride came into play.

It certainly wasn't to his rescue.

"Reckless, am I?"

The edgy tone of his voice, the flat look in his eyes pierced her anger. "You're really angry now?"

"Once more allow me to congratulate you on your keen observation of the male of the species."

"You have no right to be. You betrayed my trust."

For an instant his gaze was lethal, then it was gone. Catherine wasn't about to back down. He could take his temper all the way back to New York with him.

"I propose an arrangement—"

"No. You said a bet. A bet it will be, Catherine."

"Don't dictate terms to me."

"Do I beg your pardon again? Have I trespassed upon some feminine reserve?"

"Yes. No. Stop it. You're confusing the issue. I won't stand for it." She slapped the dry sink for emphasis. His arched brow made mockery of her resolve. She faltered, then rallied. "You said we were partners. Partners treat each other with respect. A partner treats the other as an equal. That's what I want from this bet. For you to agree to that."

"And what devilish ploy is going to gain these results?"

She smiled. "A simple bet. You and I will have a building contest. Chasing the hens all over the barn to gather eggs is not efficient. I propose—"

"No. Say bet, Catherine. That's what it is. And you can't know how glad I am to hear you agree with me on that point. I was beginning to think I was a stupid male. But do forgive me for once more interrupting you. Continue. I'm fascinated."

"You're laughing at me, Mayfield. But not for long. You will build a henhouse and I will do the same. We won't judge the results. Since you involved the whole town in our so-called partnership, they can judge. And may the best—"

"You're female. Remember?" *I do. I can't forget.*

"I was going to say may the best one win."

"That's it?"

"That's it."

"Like hell!"

Chapter Eighteen

He stalked her around the kitchen, finally bringing her to bay in the pantry, which suited his purpose. He herded her into the corner. His hands locked on the shelves on either side of her so she could not escape.

"What do you think you're doing, Mayfield?"

"I'm going to make you a counteroffer. Good, sound business practice. Never accept the first set of terms."

"You're going to make me an indecent proposal?"

He could cheerfully have throttled her. There was a definite spark of excitement in her eyes at the thought. "If I do, would you accept?"

In for a penny, in for a pound. Catherine squared her shoulders. "That would depend on your terms."

Greg called for patience and pride, and a mustering of good intentions. "Let me explain a few truths to you about men and about bets. Yours lacks a certain savoir faire. You need excitement in your terms, Catherine. You need to offer a prize worth going after. I see your point, but it's all one-sided. You need to give a man something he wants that he'll risk his reputation for. You want me to commit myself to physical work that I know nothing about. You want to expose me to ridicule without a prize worth the effort.''

She would have nodded but there was cunning in those warrior's eyes. She listened and warned herself to be careful when she did speak.

"You understand the principle of work and reward."

"What did you have in mind, Mayfield?"

"Nothing indecent." He fought a smile when she lifted her chin, a sure sign she was ready to do battle. He wasn't about to gloat over his near victory. But his militant female with her prickly notions of equality was well and truly cornered. "I'm a reasonable man. Don't you dare dispute that. Just listen. You want to be treated as my equal. That's difficult. I was raised to take care of the weaker sex. To give my protection when it's needed, to honor them, to—"

"You've made your point. I never said you had no redeeming qualities." She cast her gaze toward heaven, fighting the dizzying sensation of having him so close. He was breathing her very air. If he didn't hurry and finish so she could escape, she would shame her sex under this not-so-subtle assault to her senses.

"I'm glad you think so. I want the partnership made permanent."

"Permanent?" she parroted. Her brow knit, and she stared at him, puzzled. His expression offered no clue. "I don't understand. Why would you want a share of my egg business? It doesn't bring in your pocket change."

"That is one of the things I love about you. You always make me smile, Catherine." Amused indulgence gleamed in his eyes as he brushed his lips over hers. "Luscious," he murmured, and took another taste.

"Stop. You're taking unfair advantage."

"With you, I'll steal whatever I can get."

Catherine couldn't muster a seed's worth of doubt. She feared giving him one more advantage. She pushed against his chest, but he didn't budge. Panic replaced fear. He'd start kissing her and she'd be babbling yes to anything he said.

"Finish, Mayfield."

"I want you, Catherine Rose Hill, to be my permanent lifelong partner." He had said it. No recall allowed. No agonizing over his feelings or the question. Ready or not, he had asked.

"Goodness! You can't be…but you are. You are talking about m-m—" She couldn't say the word.

"I surprised you. Threw you off balance a little. Good. Now you know how I've felt. There is nothing devious about my offer. Just a simple question for you to answer. We will enjoy this partnership, love."

"You are mad."

"A little madness adds spice." He nuzzled her ear. "We have magic between us." Her nose required a kiss. "I was captivated from the first. You are a magnificent woman, Catherine." A touch of his lips closed her eyes.

"I adore you when you are biddable. I'll be your shelter through life's storms. If you say no, I'll be struck with an incurable malady, much worse than the one that sent me here to recover. No one makes me laugh as you do. I know I give you joy in return.

"Just keep your eyes closed and imagine the grand opportunity I offer you. You are a managing female. I freely offer you me to manage all you like. I'll give you carte blanche. Think of all the good you could do with my money. You need only say yes."

In a softer, rich, mellow voice, he added enticements. "I come with a mansion in New York, more wealth than I can use, and offer matchless devotion. Life will never be boring for us. We'll travel. I'll buy whatever strikes your fancy. I'll buy a few hundred acres and build you a summer farm on the banks of the Hudson River. A showplace, Catherine, to rival those of the robber barons.

"I need your merriment, even your mercurial moods to make my life complete. I'll add another enticement. You felt so strongly about Suzanne's effort with the league that you can join her without interference from me."

He drew a shaken breath. Was it only the press of his body against hers that held her upright? She was pale, her breathing close to panting, and he feared she would faint. But he had the advantage with her cornered, and if he didn't finish this now, he might rethink this most impulsive act. He dug deep for courage and called upon all he knew. Business taught there was always a skirmish or two to lose. What mattered was winning in the end. But Catherine wasn't business. And he'd never had a woman beguile and infuriate him at the same time.

"Catherine, say something. Argue. Discuss this. I'll even..." He couldn't say it. *Say it! Say it!* a malicious voice gleefully demanded. Growing desperation forced the words from him. "You can bring Lord Romeo and his harem with you."

He almost sagged with relief. He had her attention. If choking noises could be called that.

Catherine stared at him. Mad. The man was utterly mad. She searched his features, so dear and familiar to her. This wasn't a moonlit garden with the soft strumming of guitars and the heavy fragrance of roses surrounding her as Louis proposed marriage. This was a pantry, for heaven's sake. Not that the place mattered.

Louis had never offered himself as Greg did. Greg adored and loved things about her. But did he love her?

"Catherine?"

So impatient. He rocked her world and dared to be impatient? "Just so there is no mistake, you are not making me an indecent proposal to be your mistress?"

"Yes, mistress of my life."

"You really mean marriage?"

"I thought I said so, woman. You have the power to distract me from sensible thought. This isn't a romantic place to make a proposal. I'll get down on bended knee if you want. You see, your impulsiveness is catching."

"I didn't ask. I never said...don't you dare blame me."

"I already admitted I'll use any advantage I can. I didn't get ahead in business by waiting for perfect moments. What is important is the words I said to you. Those come from my heart."

Wonder filled her gaze. "You are serious. You'd marry me as a result of a bet?"

"Yes."

"You just admitted you're ruthless."

"That, too."

"Stop being so accommodating. You shouldn't be eager to admit your faults."

"But I want honesty between us. I know mine, you know them, and I know yours, too."

"We aren't discussing mine. And stop scattering kisses all over my face. I can't think when you do that."

"I'm ruthless." He buried his face against her shoulder, fighting laughter.

"Don't think I don't know what you're doing."

"Never." His voice was muffled.

"Look at me, Mayfield." She had to be firm with him or his madness would infect her.

He looked at her. "I'd marry you any way if I can get you to say yes. But only if you want it, too. And only if I win."

"Fairly?" She wasn't thinking clearly. His mouth hovered above hers. Temptation. She fought her need to kiss him senseless.

"Yes. Fairly." He kissed her. Briefly. Then tormented her and himself by stepping back. "It's your decision." He looked at her stunned expression and fought the sensation of having his legs give out from under him. He was sure he would not only go on bended knee but crawl to her next. The thought of not being where he could see her, touch her or hear her laugh sent blood roaring through his head. He gripped a shelf for support. She wasn't answering him.

"Greg," she pleaded, "I can't think."

"Good. Don't. Just answer me."

"You infuriating, stubborn man. Oh, dear Lord."

"I don't think he's going to help either one of us. I, on the other hand, can order building materials." He had to get out of the small confining space or he'd press his advantage. He'd take her where she stood and then, when she was truly vulnerable, and amenable to anything he suggested, he'd have the answer he sought.

That would put an end to the idiotic idea of his happiness and hers resting on the outcome of henhouses.

"We could forget this bet, Catherine. Just marry me."

"But I want to be treated as an equal. I didn't have any say in my first marriage. I won't tolerate—"

"But I'm not him."

"No, you're nothing like him." But then Louis did not reveal his dominating nature until after the wedding. She knew Greg's faults. She had had ample opportunity to witness them firsthand. She trusted Greg, but... Her spirit returned from its temporary retreat. "All right, Mayfield. I accept your challenge."

"Bet, Catherine. And no welshing. I build the better henhouse, you marry me."

"As an equal partner." *Because I love you.* But she couldn't say those words to him now.

"To the best of my ability. Agreed?"

She swallowed past the lump in her throat. *Sarah, Mary, where is your wiser counsel when I need it?* He never said he loved me. It was foolish to think of talking this over with her dearest friends. No one else but she could make this decision. Wasn't that what this was all about? Her independence? Her rights?

"Agreed, Mayfield."

"Good." He had to look away before she saw the smugness he felt. "I'll order and pay for all the building materials as repayment for the embarrassment you suffered today."

She sagged against the wooden shelves as he left her. "What have I done?" Lord Romeo padded inside and came up against her skirt, where he rubbed himself.

"Some cat you are. Where were you when I needed you? I don't want to get married again. He'll mow me down like that Gatling gun the soldiers have at the fort."

The cat's rumbling purr filled the pantry.

"Don't tell me you approve? You don't like him. And you'd have to live with him, too."

That caught the cat's attention. He stopped rubbing against her, stopped purring and began a restless prowl around the room.

"If you're looking for your nemesis, he's gone."

His reproachful meow made her lean down to scratch behind his ears. "There is only one thing to do. We have to win."

Chapter Nineteen

Catherine spent a restless, sleepless night thinking of all the things she could have said to Greg and didn't.

But she was never one to cry over spilled milk and wouldn't begin now. Someway she would make him understand that she liked the slow, steady growth of her small business. He would also understand that she resented his interference. She was going to prove to him that a woman could order her own life and do it well.

But dawn was breaking and chores waited. She dressed in a hurry, helped by the fact that she wore the more comfortable cord pants. She had banished them to the back of the wardrobe because of Greg. It was time she remembered who and what she had made of herself.

She braided her long hair into a single thick braid and even used a bit of rawhide to tie it. No ribbons, no lace. At least none that showed. She wasn't going to have any female frippery to distract her from her purpose.

She opened her bedroom door just as Greg opened his. Lord Romeo, having spent the night with Catherine, strolled out into the hall. He looked back once before, tail in the air, he padded downstairs.

"Good morning," Greg said in a cheerful voice. "I see you slept as well as I did. Really, Catherine, there's no need for us—"

"There is every need for us to maintain distance."

She started for the stairs, rankled by his remark. So her sleepless night showed, did it? His didn't. At the top of the staircase, Greg stepped aside.

"Ladies first. After you."

"Oh, no. Equal partners never do that. After you."

"I insist you go down first."

"And I insist," she said with a battle gleam in her eyes, "that you go first."

"It's not that I don't trust you to play fair, Mrs. Hill, but a slight push and I'll take a tumble. If I'm injured, I lose the bet."

"You think I'd push you down the steps!"

"I didn't say you would," he answered with a calm that he knew infuriated her. "I merely stated—"

"Don't try your fancy double-talk with me. You accused me of wishing to do you harm. Know what, Mr. Mayfield? You're right."

She pushed past him and raced down the steps. In the kitchen she stopped short. The delicious aroma of freshly brewed coffee filled the air. Damn him! He had been up before her.

"Coffee, Catherine," he whispered from behind her. "Sit down, I'll serve."

"No, thank you, I'll stand. I have a lot to get done today. Can't waste time."

"Pity," he said, and walked over to the stove. The cups were already waiting, and he poured out coffee for both of them. She was right beside him to take hers.

"What's that smell?" she demanded.

"Ah, pity you can't sit and eat with me. Ramon's mother made *empanadas de dulce.* Peach and apple fillings." He whipped off the napkin that covered the pile-high plate of turnovers.

"She only makes those for holidays."

"Or for someone who asked nicely."

"Who paid far too much—"

"Who can afford to pay for whatever he likes."

"Fine. I'll help myself."

His hand covered hers and prevented her from taking one. "You'll sit down at the table with me and have breakfast or you don't get any."

"I might have known that your true nature would come out." She slipped her hand away from his. But not before a telltale shiver revealed to him what being close to him did to her.

"And what nature is that?" He brought the plate to the table along with his coffee and sat down.

Catherine glared at his back. Her stomach rumbled. She hadn't eaten much last night. And the turnovers smelled so good.

She drew out a chair and sat across from him.

"I asked you what nature—"

"Ordering, dominating. Male."

"I keep reminding you that I am a male, Catherine. I can't help wanting to feed you, clothe you and now house your chickens."

He looked disgruntled at having to explain. She couldn't stop her smile. "House my chickens? I thought you wanted to build me a summer home?"

"That, too. Eat. You'll need your strength. We have work to do."

"There you go again, telling me—"

"Catherine, I'll give you a choice. Quiet your mouth by eating, or by kissing me."

It was stated so calmly, so softly and with such a telling glance that she had no doubt he meant it.

She ate.

When she rose to refill her cup and offered to do the same for him, Greg decided a little more needling was required. She was going to pay for his restless, sleepless night and all the doubts that plagued him.

"By the way, I like your tailor's work."

"My tailor..." She broke off and faced him, coffeepot in hand.

"It wasn't a woman who made those pants. If ever cloth was cut to reveal every feminine attribute for a male's admiration, those pants are it."

"Oh, no," she muttered more to herself. Catherine set the pot down. Hands on hips and with a walk calculated to send a man's temperature soaring, she strutted her way to his side.

"Like them, do you? Take a good look. Admire them all you like. But until I win our bet, don't touch."

Later, she told herself for the tenth time it was a miracle the cloth didn't dissolve. How could he put so much sensuality into one look? Her temper was out of sorts, and the rest of the day didn't soften it.

Catherine had just finished hitching the horse to the wagon when Greg rushed from the house.

"Where are you going?"

"Since I'm going to build the best henhouse this town has ever seen, I want to look over a few of them first."

"Without me?"

"That was my intention." She snatched her floppy felt man's hat from the wagon seat and plunked it on her head.

"Like hell you are. Besides, Ollie will be here with

the lumber soon. You need to tell him where to stack it. And we need to decide where to build."

"Later, Mayfield." She climbed up on the wagon's seat, untied the reins and flipped the brim of her hat at him.

Greg reached the wagon before she released the pole brake. "Where you go, I go. New rules for partners." He crowded her on the seat. "And take note for that list of yours that I am not insisting that I drive the wagon."

"As if I'd let you. And there's no need for you to come with me."

"Yes, there is. I'm not letting you gallivant all over the county dressed like that."

"See, that's just what I mean. Stuff your—"

"Catherine, live with this. I can't help it. It's not safe for you to be riding out alone."

"Well," she informed him, "I did it before you came and will likely do it after you're gone."

"You haven't won yet." At last he was content, for he had the last word.

And she never mentioned her loaded gun under the seat.

It was a disappointment to Greg. Chicken coop after chicken coop all looked the same. They were usually made of odds-and-ends of lumber. Catherine's flock, including Miss Lily, whom he had an understanding with since he gave her an extra ration of corn twice a day, deserved better.

"Everything we've seen is too small," he remarked as they turned out of the last ranch's road and headed back home.

"They're supposed to be small. The idea is to avoid the problem we have now of searching all over for eggs. Or did you forget that? And that keeps the var-mints out.''

"I never forget anything that's important to me." He glanced over at her. "You know, Mrs. Davis was mighty sweet to offer us lunch. You could have said yes."

"And watch Lolly fawn all over you. No, thank you. I'll eat my meal in peace."

"Mrs. Davis's daughter is a fine-looking woman."

"She is that. And that's all she is. Can't cook, which is why she isn't married."

"But, Catherine," he pointed out, "I don't need a woman who can cook."

"No, you don't. You can buy whatever you need." But not love. She guided the horse to the turn in the road that led to home. Trouble was, she couldn't get very far. Wagons of all sorts crowded the front drive.

"What have you done now?"

"Nothing, Catherine. I swear it. I didn't cause this."

This was Ollie Walker and his lumber delivery. He was waiting in the yard for them. They had abandoned the wagon and walked around the back of the house.

"Boys an' me figured you'd need help unloading it all. Figured you might need some advice to get started, too."

"Didn't do anything, huh?" she muttered to Greg.

"This isn't my fault."

"Isn't your fault? Look at what you ordered. You need a keeper. There's enough cut boards to build a house."

"You're pointing that finger at me again. Remember I warned you. And for your information, Mrs. Hill, we are building a house. Two of them."

Catherine threw up her hands. She closed her eyes.

"Praying isn't going to help."

"Thank you for your sage advice, Mayfield. I know that. I'm trying to find some patience."

"The hell with patience. Find a place to put all this lumber."

Four hours later, an exhausted Catherine stood and watched the last of the wagons leave the yard. Every last piece of lumber was stacked in two piles on either side of the barn. What should have been the simplest work was made complicated by the squabbling between the men who had come to help. The wood was raw and needed to season, so they argued over how it should be stacked. Then there was the choice of sites to build the chicken coops. Staggered piles won, as did final locations, but only after Ollie had nearly come to blows with one of the Jobe boys.

While she had been run ragged trying to hold off the next flying fist, Greg, with the jovial air of a man at a social, found something to laugh about with each back-slapping man. More than once he had caught her eye as he sneaked off toward the front of the house. Someone had a jug of whiskey. If Sarah was here, they wouldn't have dared to bring it near the house. Well, she was one woman and couldn't expect to oversee everything.

There was nothing more to do. The men had pitched in with chores. She thought longingly of a hot bath. But it would be hours before she heated enough water. She felt like an aching bundle of nerves scrubbed raw as she started for the house.

Greg came outside and met her halfway.

"You're still walking?"

"Don't sound so surprised, Catherine. Why shouldn't I be?"

"I thought you would be passed out by now from all those trips you made to the jug they had hidden."

"I'll tell you a secret. I didn't touch a sip of that whiskey. A man has to keep his word. But I had to be sociable with my neighbors."

She stopped short. "Neighbors? When did you decide to stay here? What about your mansion? Your businesses? Your sister? The nieces and nephews you adore? And your social life? All those balls and dinners and theater parties? How could you give all that up?"

"Easily." He blocked her way into the house with his arm across the doorway. "And I'll stay as long as it takes you to say yes." He gazed back at the empty yard. "I'm glad they're all gone. You had the patience of a saint to deal with them."

His praised warmed her, even eased an ache or two.

"Do you know what Ollie said about you, Catherine?"

"No. I couldn't even think with all their hollering and swearing. I never knew men could come to blows over how to place a board."

"Well, I never knew women could rip apart seams and a reputation in an hour."

Exhaustion fled. She kicked at the earth with the toe of her boot. "Mine."

"Lie?"

"No. Never lies."

"Mrs. Pettigrew tried. Nita told me. But there'll be no more. I threatened to pay Camilla's way to Paris. She wants to study painting, not get married. You'll have no more trouble from that woman."

"I could have handled her on my own."

"I know you could. I was the cause and was able to remedy the problem. Accept it as a gift with no obligation attached."

"Thank you," she whispered softly, but knew there was a debt now.

"Don't you want to know what Ollie said?" He could barely make out her nod. She wasn't looking at him. "He told me you're a gal with sand in her bottom. I almost took a swing at him for noticing your bottom, but George Vaughan explained what it meant. A woman with courage. He said I might get some sand in my craw. A compliment, I gathered, since everyone agreed. And Bill Nelson from the telegraph office said that when you sang you made everyone forget their troubles. Nice things for a man to hear about the woman he cares for."

She looked at him then. "You really like them?"

"Yes, I do. They're good, honest, hardworking men. They have accepted me, even if I won't carry a gun and haven't their skills. Ollie had to show me which end of the hammer to use when I asked him to pick up the tools I needed. He'll have them here in the morning along with the nails."

It was his sincerity that made her place her hand over his forearm. "You're a good man, Greg. Despite buying everything in sight, here—" she touched his heart "—you are good and kind."

"Catherine," he whispered, and leaned closer to kiss her.

"Oh, no. We are not going to sleep together until this is settled."

"Sweet, fair lady, who said anything about sleeping?" He didn't need the fading light to know she was blushing. "Know what else I heard today?"

"No. But I'm sure you'll tell me." She brushed the back of her hand against her flushed cheek.

"Jobe's son told me I should toss a lasso over you and hog-tie you tight or some other man was going to come along and snatch you from under my nose."

"Not likely." She threw back her head and laughed. "But you can try."

"Damn right it won't happen. Wait, was that an invitation?"

"I meant, Mayfield, that a woman doesn't get snatched from under anyone's nose unless she wants to be."

"You know, Catherine, I finally figured out that you call me Mayfield when your guard is down. Scared I'll get some advantage?"

"I'm shaking in my boots over the thought."

His hand closed over her shoulder. "You're shaking, all right, but it's not because of me. You're exhausted. Come inside."

The coal oil fixture over the table was turned down low. It took Catherine a few moments for her eyes to adjust. But the breath she drew brought the sweet scent of lavender, and then she saw the tub filled with steaming hot water. Two buckets rested on the floor. Her soap and towels were piled on a chair, and on the back of another were her nightgown and robe.

"A bath and bed for you. I'll bring a supper tray upstairs when you're done." She didn't answer. She didn't move. "Catherine, if you don't want the bath—"

"I want it."

"Then why, why are you crying?"

"You...you wouldn't understand."

"Try to tell me. I'll try to understand. This makes no sense. It's only a bath. And if this makes you cry, I'd hate to show you the Elizabethan-style bathrooms in my home. They're about the size of the kitchen, all marble and cherry wood, and half the time some guest gets lost in them."

She brushed the tears from her cheeks and laughed

as he intended her to do. "This is the nicest, best gift you could have given me."

"I'd do more. Give you more. Just say yes."

"Greg, I—" She shook her head. "I don't know that I can explain to you what I feel. But I said you were good and kind and generous, too. I meant that. But you make me forget my own name. I'm still finding what I am capable of doing on my own."

She looked up at him. His expression was guarded, then he grinned. "I can tell you what you're capable of. You make me dizzy with need. I'm about ready to crawl for a smile. And I'd kill for one of your kisses. Now," he said with a slight push at the small of her back, "go enjoy your bath. I won't take advantage when you're tired."

To her confused and very intense disappointment, he kept his word. Catherine shared her lonely supper with Lord Romeo. Finished, she sat on the bed with the cat curled at her side.

"He makes it so hard not to love him," she told the cat. He flicked an ear, a sure sign he was listening. She scratched under his chin and his purring calmed her.

"I have to try and win. I can't even fully explain to myself why it's so important to me, but it is. But, Romeo, I didn't know it would be this hard to stay away from him. I miss the closeness we shared as much as I miss making love with him."

The cat wiggled out from under her hand and rolled over to offer his stomach to be rubbed.

She laughed. "You old softie. You like him, too. And if you think petting is the way to win, you're wrong. I gave my word that it was to be a fairly won bet. No cheating allowed."

The cat stared at her with unblinking eyes as if to dispute the wisdom of that.

Catherine lay back against the pillows. She stared at the door, willing it to open.

In the hallway, Greg's hand hovered above the latch. There was no reason why he couldn't collect her supper tray. *Weak excuse.* He could see if she needed some liniment rubbed on aching muscles. Ollie's advice was the only reason he could still move. He leaned his forehead against the door. He missed her. There was no getting away from that. More than he needed to wrap her in his arms, more than the passion that exploded between them, he missed her cuddling.

He was so proud of her. Partly due to the others' admiration. He hadn't told her half of what the men said about her. He dropped his hand and clenched both of them into fists.

"Damn stubborn woman!" Couldn't she understand that he didn't want to change her? Did he expect him to crawl?

Not Catherine.

I know that.

And because he knew it, he turned away from her door. He needed to sleep. He had a bet to win. His life depended on it.

Chapter Twenty

By the time Sunday rolled around, Catherine felt she lived in an open-sided corral. Ramon, having learned his lessons well from his mentor about business, had set up a stand where he and his brothers or sisters sold lemonade or their mother's turnovers to those stopping by.

And a lot of people stopped by to check the progress of the henhouses. Greg complained that with their advice, he could tackle a whole town's buildings for his next project. Catherine's mouth hurt from smiling as men, and it was mostly the men who viewed her work, made suggestions that she had to ignore. If she followed a tenth of them, Greg would build rings around her. Or a lovely, golden cage.

But there was to be no work today. She packed her basket for the box lunch social while Greg was still upstairs getting dressed. She wrapped the basket in an old sheet so he wouldn't be able to identify it. Half the fun of the social was keeping secret which basket or cheese box was yours, so the bidding the men did had a few surprise results. Of course, some enterprising young woman who had picked out her man would cheat by finding some way to alert her chosen beau which one was hers.

Catherine knew that if he sniffed a few baskets he could easily find hers. Living in the same house prevented her from keeping the cooking aromas from wafting upstairs.

By the time he came down, she had the basket hidden beneath the buggy's seat.

It was a beautiful day. Not a wisp of a cloud marred the bright blue sky. But it was unseasonably warm for May. She shook out the folds of her blue-and-ecru summer wool skirt. She had on a diminished bustle and a corset. She wanted no comments about her appearance from the other ladies. They had quite enough to gossip about despite Greg's threat to Mrs. Pettigrew. The snugly fitted bodice had additional bones to define her waist. The soft cream percale was trimmed with small rows of ecru lace.

"I'm happy to see you're not wearing that detestable poke bonnet." He liked the black braided straw hat with its simple blue ribbon and cluster of blue forget-me-nots pinned to one side of the brim. She made a charming picture right down to the high-buttoned shoe tapping impatiently as he strolled toward her.

"Absolutely fetching, Catherine." He lifted her net-gloved hand, but instead of kissing the back, he turned it so that his lips kissed her palm, then her wrist. He smiled when she snatched it away. Too late, he wanted to say, I already felt the jump in your pulse. But he had promised himself that he would be all that she found charming, and kept silent.

Catherine wanted to return his compliment. He wore a long black frock coat, a vest with gold-and-green embroidery and one of his finely woven linen shirts that appeared to be silk. From his polished boots, tailored pants and black string tie, she knew she would have her hands full keeping women away from him.

Talk about fetching…if they put Greg up for the bidding at the social, he'd fetch enough to build and furnish the school.

Sunlight burnished his hair. She hadn't noticed the hat he held at his side until he put it on. She arched her brow. "New?"

"Don't you like it? Nita thought this flat-crowned Stetson dashing on me. And Dolly Hudspeth said no other man could wear it, since the hat seemed to be made for me."

"I wouldn't put any stock in what she said. She sold it to you."

Catherine's teasing smile faded. There was something about the way he put the hat on with the brim tilted slightly forward and off to the side that changed his appearance. A delicious shiver of awareness ran down her spine. Greg looked more like the fancy gamblers her father used to warn her about than a respectable eastern banker.

Regret for her decision that they cease being lovers darkened her eyes. She turned away and allowed him to help her climb to the seat.

"We better get going. I don't want to arrive late."

"I know," he answered, going around to the other side. "You hate walking in late, when the only available seats are down in front. Everyone stares, then whispers. The minister pauses to tip his spectacles and give you one of those condemning looks."

Since he suited his actions to fit his words, she burst out laughing.

The merry mood lasted until they reached the church grounds. Wagons and buggies of every description vied for space. Children ran wild, laughing and shouting, while mothers tried to gather their broods to usher them inside.

Greg reached over and covered Catherine's hand with his when the group of women around Mrs. Pettigrew refused to return Catherine's greeting. He deliberately turned his head when it appeared that the woman would greet him.

He found a spot beneath a stand of towering pines. There were no other wagons close by.

"Would you rather not go inside?" He caught the press of her teeth against her bottom lip. "Catherine, would you like me to take care of this once and for all?"

"I don't think there's anything you can do. I'm not a coward. They're just a group of busy gossips." She squared her shoulders. "As a matter of fact, the woman standing next to Mrs. Pettigrew is considered the worst gossip this town has. Alberta Elray will take a tiny inch of yarn and weave it into a tangled skein with the slightest encouragement. If anyone wants to listen to what she has to say, they are welcome to."

As he lifted her down from the seat, Greg held her for a brief moment. "I have felt admiration for you before this, Catherine, but never as much as this moment." He set her down and placed her hand in the crook of his arm. "I hope these vest buttons are sewn tight."

"What?"

"I'm so proud to be your escort that my chest is swelling. I just might embarrass myself and pop them."

"Don't you dare make me laugh again. Not now."

"Now is the best time. Besides, your smile is one of the things I love about you, Catherine. That is part of the trouble. Those women are long past their prime. They're jealous of you."

Thomas Hoffman, the minister, stood at the door, greeting his flock as they entered the church. Greg excused himself for a moment as Caroline arrived and came to stand by Catherine.

"I see you got your plaque hung," Greg said.

"Thanks to Mary," the minister said, "our contributions for the pews went over the required amount. We have the smaller plaques for the pews themselves, but the ladies thought it would be nice to acknowledge those families that gave a little more."

"Speaking of which, I understand that the church needs a new organ and I seem to recall there was some mention of a stained glass window."

"Once the school is completed, that will be our next fund-raising effort."

"Thomas, far be it from me to interfere, but there is a draft burning a hole in my pocket. A substantial amount, enough to buy your organ and window, and have enough left over to take care of your expenses for a few years."

"Mr. Mayfield—"

"Greg, please."

"All right. What you are offering sounds suspiciously like a bribe to me. I am a man of the cloth, above such things."

Greg eyed his enormous girth and almost smiled. A man of the cloth indeed. But he answered in a serious tone. "I meant it to be a bribe. I'd like you to change your sermon. We require a little something about casting the first stone. I seem to recall my bishop saying something about there being only two sorts of men, the just, who believe themselves sinners, and the other sinners, who believe themselves just."

Greg used a few moments to remove the draft from his pocket. "This is drawn on my account at Purcell's bank so there's no delay in your having the money. And please, Thomas, let us keep this between us. You and I are performing charitable acts this morning.''

"But I've never—"

"No one is harmed by this. Gossip shouldn't be spread, especially when it hurts a good woman. And to ease your conscience, Thomas…'' Greg leaned closer to him and whispered in his ear.

"That requires my viewing this in a different light. I admit the ladies came to me and asked that I speak to Catherine. But I shall refrain.'' He tucked the bank draft into the inside pocket of his frock coat. He flung an arm around Greg's shoulders and urged him to the doorway, where Catherine still stood with Caroline.

Greg escorted them down toward the front and chose an empty pew. To Catherine he said, "I think you'll find the minister's positively inspired this morning.''

Catherine didn't ask what he meant then, but she began to understand as Thomas's voice boomed out over the congregation on the wages of casting stones without being free of sin. There was a great deal of shifting within the pews, for he was an inspired speaker who seemed to look right at one.

By the time the collection plate reached them, she saw that Thomas had moved more than a few people to be generous this morning. The plate overflowed as she passed it behind her.

When they finally had their turn at the door, she caught the wink Thomas gave Greg and his returned nod. Before she could voice a question, he was leading her back to the buggy to get her basket. "Don't ask and I won't have to lie.''

Catherine didn't ask. They strolled back to where men had set planks on upturned barrels so the ladies could line up their baskets. The men were supposed to keep their distance, but many of them milled around.

Catherine noticed a few of the soldiers. One or two greeted her, but one possessive look from Greg and they came no closer.

The minister, sensing the mood of his flock, rapped the board with a stone to gain their attention. He was feeling pleased with himself. Several men had come to thank him for stopping the nonsense about asking Catherine to leave. They liked her, and Greg, and didn't hold with the same notions as their womenfolk. Most didn't. And Thomas patted his pocket. A little whisper here, another in someone's ear helped to quiet wagging tongues.

The married women claimed the shady spots beneath the spreading cottonwood trees. The single women and the widows stood about in groups as the rest of the men joined them. There was good-natured teasing as beaux warned other men away from this prettily decorated box or that ribbon-tied basket.

"Won't you give me a hint, Catherine?" Greg asked.

"That wouldn't be fair."

Caroline and Nita joined them just as the first box lunch was held high to start the bidding. Thomas, a young man himself, and one fond of good food, sniffed appreciatively.

"Gentlemen, whoever bids on and wins this lovely lady's offerings will find himself in earthly heaven. I smell succulent fried chicken and lemon tarts. Who is going to offer the first bid?"

Standing off to the side, Catherine saw Thomas tuck the checkered napkin back into place. He was a wonderful, kindly fraud, and as the first basket went quickly, he continued his remarks about the food contained within each lunch.

Catherine felt sad to see Camilla pushed forward by her mother when a basket decorated with flowers and bows was next.

"Poor Camilla," she whispered. "Now everyone will know that it's hers and likely cooked by someone else."

Mark Jobe started with a dollar and found himself facing competition from two soldiers who had lost the other lunches they had bid on. Camilla blushed a deep pink that matched her gown.

"There's a romance brewing," Nita commented. "One that ain't finding any favor with her mama. If she looks at Jobe's boy any harder, he'll fall where he stands."

"The boy's got more backbone than you give him credit for, Nita. He'll stay with the bidding until he wins."

"You sound very sure of that, Greg. Did you have something to do with this?" Catherine turned to look at him, and he wouldn't meet her gaze.

"Ask me no questions and I won't have to lie."

"He's a smart one, all right, Catherine. Don't you be putting him on the spot." Nita leaned forward to smile at Greg. "'Bout time that boy shook the dust off his boots and made his feelings known."

"Well, I didn't know," Caroline said. "Did you, Catherine?"

"No. She never hinted that she found any favor with him. The last I heard, she wanted to run off to Paris to study painting."

Mark offered six dollars, the highest bid so far. One of the soldiers asked if they could combine their money and share the lunch. Thomas said no. Mark, with a gleam in his dark eyes that would make any woman's heart beat faster, claimed his basket and his lady. They went off to find a spot at the edge of the crowd. Nita left them and stopped Mrs. Pettigrew from following by linking her arm with the woman's. She engaged her in conversation, a whispered one, but in the end, Mrs. Pettigrew remained with the married women close by.

Greg stood contemplating the remaining baskets. He must have been looking away when Thomas removed the sheet from Catherine's. Now he couldn't tell which one was hers. There were five left. Three belonged to ranchers' daughters judging by the sudden surge of cowhands, slicked in their Sunday best, that came to the front. Caroline's basket was there, too.

He moved to stand behind his favorite lady. "If you don't give me a hint," he murmured, "I'll have to bid on all the remaining ones. Do you have no pity in your heart for me? Do you want to see me suffer through a meal with one of those giggling young girls that look as if they stepped out of a confectioner's shop?"

"No pity, Greg."

But he heard the undercurrent of laughter in her voice and took heart. "What did I do to deserve this?"

"You respond so well to teasing that I can't help myself."

"You'll pay for that remark. Just wait."

She looked at him then with a sparkle in her eyes. "I can. I will."

"Hush, you two," Caroline warned as one of the girls squealed with delight that her chosen cowboy had her basket. "Mine is next."

"Shall I bid on it, Caroline?"

"And have my dear friend stop talking to me? No, don't. Besides, I already know who's winning my box lunch."

Before any of them could ask her who it was, the opening bid of ten dollars revealed the secret.

"Peter Austin? You and Peter?" Catherine exclaimed, squeezing her friend's hand. "When? And how? Why didn't you tell me?"

"Didn't know myself until last night. 'Sides, you have enough to deal with. Look who's stepping up front." She whispered into Catherine's ear, "That's yours, I recognize it."

But Thomas made them wait while another of the young girls' baskets went for bids. Then it was Catherine's turn.

Buck Purcell, like Peter, opened the bidding at ten dollars. Catherine wasn't all that surprised. When she had first come here to live, Buck had called on her, but she discouraged him. He was a handsome man, as tall as Greg with a heavier build. His hair was burnished shades of brown, and his eyes a rich chocolate color. What prompted him to bid was anyone's guess. But Greg soon showed his serious intent of having her and her box lunch.

"Twenty-five dollars!" he called out. Oohs and aahs followed. People crowded close.

Thomas's remarks didn't help Catherine accept being the center of all attention. She tried to stop Greg when he again topped Buck's bid by another ten dollars.

"You can't mean to pay fifty dollars. You don't even know what's in it. Maybe you won't like what I cooked."

"Then I'll have you to nibble on. There's more than one hunger, Catherine. And no one is sharing that lunch with you but me."

Buck went to seventy.

Catherine gasped. She wasn't alone. Nita came to her side.

"Girl, if you didn't want the town gossiping about you, you ain't got no more chance than a hen in a pack of coyotes to keep them quiet now."

Greg bid ninety.

Catherine grabbed his arm. "Did you hear Nita? If you continue, I'll never live this down."

"One hundred and twenty-five dollars!" he called out.

"Listen to me."

"No. You listen. Going, going and sold to me." He took hold of her hand. "Come on. I want to claim my prize."

"For goodness' sake, Greg, it's only ham in a blanket."

"That's how much you know."

Buck stopped them. He shook Greg's hand but spoke to Catherine. "I guess I waited too long, but he's a fine man. There's still one merry widow left. When is Sarah coming back?"

"Before summer's end, if all went well with Mary's confinement." She could have told him that he'd be wasting his time trying to court Sarah. She would never marry again. But then, hadn't she thought the same? Had? She still did, didn't she?

"Are you that disappointed?" Greg asked as Buck walked away and he took the basket from Thomas.

"No. No," she repeated, and smiled brightly at him.

Greg reached for his initial-embossed leather bill book and removed a few banknotes.

"Wouldn't be right to take that money after all you did."

"Thomas, that was between us. I'll pay for the basket like every other man here did."

More than a few of the married men teased them as they strolled beneath the trees, where spread blankets left little room. Catherine saw Caroline and Peter and steered Greg past them. They were so engrossed in each other, they didn't notice them.

He shook out the blanket beneath two stripling cottonwoods that barely offered enough shade. Catherine was quiet. Too quiet, he thought, watching her unpack their lunch. "Aren't you going to ask me what Thomas was talking about?"

"No."

"Just no?"

"If I ask," she said, leaning back on her heels, "you'll only tell me not to ask so you won't have to lie."

He grinned like an unrepentant sinner. "You know me so well."

"Do I? You're showing a decidedly devious streak of late."

"A man has to do what he has to do—"

"To get what he wants," she finished for him.

"Like I said, you know me so well." He rubbed his hands together. "What goodies did you make?"

"Your favorite. Hard-boiled eggs." He groaned and she laughed. "Little darlin' cookies, green coleslaw, pickles, chili popovers, ham loaf wrapped in biscuit dough and lemonade."

"A feast, Catherine." But his gaze remained locked on her lips as he leaned closer.

"Is it time to pay?" she murmured, leaning toward him to close the short distance.

"I'll need privacy for that payment."

She pulled back. Lashes fluttering, her voice at its softest, slowest drawl, she whispered, "Then hurry up and eat."

"For once, lovely lady, we are in perfect agreement."

Sensual excitement hummed between them as they drove home. Catherine couldn't pinpoint the moment she had changed her mind. She just did it. She missed his lovemaking and the closeness they had shared. Perhaps it was the sight of so many courting couples strolling around them and the kisses they exchanged out of parents' sight. And maybe she was finally admitting the intensity of her feelings for him were much more than she could deny.

Greg snapped the reins to pick up the horse's pace as they turned into the drive. "You go inside and I'll unhitch the buggy."

For once she didn't argue. Her gaze swept over the tent canvas shrouding his project, then as he halted the buggy, she looked at her own. Catherine cried out. The canvas covering was off. The walls she had labored to build had been torn down.

"I'll kill the son of a bitch who did this."

"Greg, no. At least they didn't burn it. I can rebuild the walls. It was easier than I thought. But I don't think I have a chance of winning now."

"Yes, you do. I won't work on mine until you do your repairs. Now, I want you to go inside. I'll take a look and make sure it's safe for you to work there. Who knows what the bastard might have done. But I swear to you, Catherine, I had nothing to do with this."

"I know."

"You know?"

"You gave me your word that it would be fairly won."

"And you believed me? You have that kind of faith in me? Yet you won't just forget this stupid bet and marry me?"

"Ask me no questions, Mayfield. Then I won't lie."

"Catherine, come back here."

She skipped across the yard, her mood light despite the sabotage to her project. He called her again, and she turned.

"Greg, we need to complete the bet. You gave your word that all would be equal no matter who won."

"What if I swear that now? Will you marry me?"

"But you already gave your word. I'm holding you to it."

With a mock growl he went after her, chasing her through the house and up the stairs. He caught her, too.

It was a good long while before the buggy was unhitched.

Chapter Twenty-One

With a catlike smile and a stretch that set her moaning as tiny aches sent memory rushing through the long passion-filled hours of the night, Catherine bolted up from her bed. Greg was already gone. She sensed it without having to look.

He had mentioned that he would go to town and speak to the mayor about the sabotage. She tried to warn him that without a town sheriff, there was no law. Men took care of their own. Civilized gentleman that he was, he refused to accept that.

She heard Ramon arrive, whistling some tune that Greg had taught him. She dressed hurriedly, intending to question him.

The boy denied knowing anything about the damage.

"*Señora,* I would not do this terrible thing. The *señor,* he pays me *mucho dinero.* He tells me I am a man. A man does not bring trouble to his friends."

He stood tall, barely reaching her waist, and was so serious that Catherine had to respond in kind. "I know you didn't do this, Ramon. We'll all keep a watch. This is very important to me."

"*Sí,* I know. The *señor,* he tells me you will marry

and have *niños* and *niñas*.'' He smiled with a flash of white teeth and held up five fingers.

''That many? The *señor* has grand ideas.''

''You do not want so many? *Madre,* she loves the little ones.''

She hugged him. ''I do, too. Go on, get started. I'll be out to help you in a few minutes.''

Children? Why hadn't she thought of children? Her hand slipped down to cover her flat stomach. Dear Lord, they had never discussed—how could she— ''Oh, Greg, what have I done?''

''I don't know. But you can tell me anything.''

''How did your meeting go?'' She couldn't tell him. She didn't want to admit the likelihood to herself.

''Disappointing. Your esteemed mayor expressed regret that this happened but there was nothing he could do. He is trying to get the town board to agree they need someone to uphold the law.''

Though the morning was cool, her forehead was damp with perspiration, her heart hammered against her rib cage. A child? No. She couldn't think about it. But a child? Her knees almost gave out beneath her.

''Catherine, I've been asking you what's wrong?''

Her gaze focused on Greg's concerned face.

''Nothing. Nothing at all. Sit down and I'll get you coffee.''

''I'd rather you tell me what has you looking a little green.''

''Green? I look green?''

''Sick? Like you're either going to faint or—''

She pulled away from him. ''I'm fine.'' She made a complete turn and then held on to the dry sink. ''Just fine.'' Feeling strangely exposed, as if he could see her thoughts, she fled outside. ''I need to get to work.''

Catherine threw herself into work with a frenzy. But

she couldn't stop the warm flushes that came over her every time she thought of having Greg's child. One with his charming smile. And his eyes. And… She had to stop this or she'd drive herself crazy. She certainly knew all the signs to watch for. She had none. There hadn't been enough time. Then she wondered if Mary had thought the same thing. But Mary longed for a child of her own. Always. She couldn't ever remember feeling like that. Louis had been careful. He wanted to wait. And then he was thrown from a horse he was breaking to the saddle and there was no more time.

What if she was pregnant?

Weak-kneed, she sat on an unopened keg of nails, the hammer she'd been using dangling from her hand. How long she sat there, totally unaware that people were stopping by on their way into town to see what progress had been made, she didn't know. She roused herself and stood up to see Greg deep in conversation with Ollie.

Whatever Ollie said, Greg was refusing. His hair, which hadn't been cut since he'd arrived, flew to the sides as he shook his head. Catherine went back to work. Greg would tell her soon enough.

Minutes later, he joined her. "Do you know what he wanted to do?"

"No, but you're going to tell me, right?"

"He wanted to help me build. Said a lot of men had money riding on the outcome."

"You winning."

"Yeah." He ran his hand through his untidy hair. "I refused. Told him…Catherine, are you listening to me?"

"Yes."

"You don't seem surprised."

"I guess you could say I had all the surprise knocked

out of me today." *So would you if you were shaken to the core, to the very essence of your being.*

Something about the size of a hammer slammed into Greg's throat. She appeared suddenly fragile, vulnerable. He took her into his arms, holding her head against his heart, and rocked her.

"Whatever it is, you're not handling it alone. I'm here for you. I'll always be here for you, if you let me, Catherine."

"Don't make me cry."

Lord, help! How do you stop a woman from crying when you don't know what's wrong?

"Promise, Greg."

"Word of honor." But she was crying. Her tears were soaking his shirt. His gaze lit on the half-finished wall she had been repairing. If she didn't want to cry, it was up to him to make her laugh, or get angry. With Catherine a man took his chances.

"Listen to me, lady, if anyone told me I'd pay good money for first-grade lumber and then see such shoddy work as yours—"

She jerked free of his arms. "Shoddy work? No one had to show me which end of the hammer to use." She swiped at the tears in her eyes. "What are you doing here?"

"Stealing a cuddle?"

She glowered at his grin. "Stealing is right. Likely you're looking to steal my idea. Go away. Go back to your lopsided—"

"Now, just a minute! Just a damned minute! If you are so all-fired honest, how come you know the floor is a little slanted?"

"Get spectacles, Mayfield. 'Little' isn't the word I'd use to describe that thing you call flooring."

"Oh, yeah?" He went nose to nose with her, but

when he attempted to pull her close, she evaded his hands.

"Can't you keep your pants buttoned? Stop trying to lure me into your bed at every turn."

"It wasn't my bed I got *lured* into last night."

"You—"

"This man who adores you when you're steamed as Christmas pudding."

Catherine gave him a shove, but only rocked him back on his heels. "There are times, Mayfield, when I could punch you. And I've never said that to anyone else. Never wanted to hit someone as badly as I do you. You are impossible. Go back to butchering your first-grade lumber."

He went. Whistling all the way. He'd stopped her from crying. He shot a look over his shoulder. She had a sassy, hip-swinging walk emphasized by a shrunken pair of pants. He was going to strip her wardrobe of every pair. His temperature shot up, bypassing warm and heating into hot.

He reached his spot and picked up his hammer, unable to stop himself from taking another look, but the barn blocked his vision. He thought of all the punishment he would extract from her. Just like last night. And proceeded to work.

Still thinking about her walk, he held the nail in place and aimed a mighty blow.

Catherine almost jumped out of her skin when she heard him yell. She leapt over the small stack of lumber and ran around the barn calling his name.

"What happened? Where are you?"

"I'm fine. Go back to work." He didn't want her to see him cradling his hand against his chest. His thumb felt four sizes too big with all the blood throbbing.

"Are you hurt? Let me see you."

He got to his knees and looked over the nail kegs. "I said I'm fine. Just taking a break."

"If you're so fine, why are you talking through gritted teeth?"

"'Cause I got a woman pesky as a bluebottle fly buzzing around asking foolish questions."

"Fine. Suffer in silence." She started back, then turned. "Soaking it in a bucket of water from the well will help." Men and their pride. But she veered off and returned a few minutes later with the bucket for him.

"Thank you."

"You're welcome."

That night, Catherine pulled out the tub and had a hot bath waiting for Greg. There had been more swearing and a few crashes from his side during the day. As he limped inside the kitchen, she assumed he had taken a tumble or two. He wore such a forbidding black scowl that she didn't say a word.

Two days later, Catherine couldn't find her saw. Greg lent her his. Then it rained for a whole day. He went into town, she baked off her frustration.

He hadn't returned by the time she dragged herself off to bed. A wicked headache began her monthly cycle. Why that should have made her cry herself to sleep, she didn't know.

Morning found her staring into her mirror. The headache was gone, the cramps bearable, but she could do nothing to hide her red-rimmed eyes. The lids were puffy. All she wanted to do was cry again.

Greg knocked on her bedroom door.

"Go away."

"Stop sulking, Catherine, and come out. There's something I want to show you."

"I'm not sulking. And I don't want to see anything you have."

"That's not what you said the other night."

"Don't remind me of my foolishness. And stop sounding so amused. I'm not indulging in some female whim, Mayfield."

"Then why is your door locked? Are you sick? Why won't you let me help you, thickheaded as you are?"

"Don't use that arrogant know-it-all male tone with me. Go back to town. Find someone else to amuse you." She glared at her reflection, then turned away.

"Fine. Maybe I will. I just want you to know that there will be no more sabotage to your henhouse. I—"

"What did you do, buy an army detail to stand watch?" She jumped when the door handle rattled from the force of his attempt to open it. Then there was silence. She walked to the door and put her ear against the wood. Nothing. She should apologize for snapping at him. But how could she tell him why? Until she came to live with Sarah and Mary, a woman's monthly problems were her own.

The creak of the floorboard in front of her door made her step back. She opened her mouth to send him away, when her gaze landed on the slip of paper sliding under the door.

She snatched it up and walked over by the window, where she unfolded it.

Like me the coffee's waiting, chores are, too, the sun is shining, but all I see is blue, there is no one to share with, everything, Catherine, waits for you.

"It's not the Song of Solomon, Catherine," he said against the door. "I'm afraid that writing poetry is beyond my skill. You did read it? Catherine? Answer me. Did you read it!''

"Stop shouting. Even through the door I can hear you just fine. Yes, I read it. And I never said I admired Solomon's song. This is—''

"Damn you! Open this door or I'll break it down. I know you're crying. Don't cry, please, don't.''

She twisted the key and yanked opened the door. "Do you know what your trouble is, Mayfield? You think every woman wants to fall at your feet.''

He saw the ravages of tears and nothing else. But he heard her. "I don't want you to fall at my feet. Fall in bed, yes. But as for the rest of time, by my side is where I want you.''

"No, you don't. Do you know why I'm crying?'' She sniffed, but didn't wipe her tears away. "I had the most miserable night you could imagine. On second thought, you couldn't. You're a man.''

"You know, Catherine, I'm getting very tired of your throwing my gender in my face every time you can't think of telling me the truth. Try me. I had a sister. I've had—''

"Go on, say it. You've had women. Lots and lots of women. But I'll bet you that not one ever thought she was having your baby.''

"Baby?'' He had a blank look that was replaced by panic. His gaze fell to her stomach. His hand lifted from his side toward her, then fell back. "Are you—''

"No. I'm not. And yes, I'm sure.''

Knowledge dawned in his gaze. "Is that why you're crying? Hell, sweetheart, if you want a baby, I'm your man.''

"You want children?''

"With you, lots of them. All little girls with bright blue eyes and sunshine hair.''

She swayed toward him and planted a kiss on his chin. "Thank you. But not yet. I still have a bet to win." She stepped back before he could take her into his arms and closed the door.

He stared in disbelief as he heard the lock click.

"Woman, if you don't marry me soon, my sister won't send me away to cure my health. It's my mind that she'll be worried about."

"Greg," she crooned against the door, "you woo me with an ardor that simply takes my breath away. I don't know another woman who hears such lovely, loverlike sweet nothings whispered to her. My heart is beating so fast, I feel faint."

He shoved his hands into his pant pockets and rocked back on his heels. She didn't sound as if she were still crying. Truth was, unless the door distorted her voice that badly, she sounded amused. Joyful, more like his Catherine. That woman and her mercurial moods!

"So you like sweet nothings whispered in your ear?"

"Love hearing every word."

"I'll promise to say nothing else but loverlike utterances for the rest of our lives if you'll forget this bet and marry me."

"You will?"

He grinned. She'd be opening the door and flying into his arms. She'd be kissing him and hugging him and likely drag him off to bed to celebrate. He rocked. He waited. He listened to the growing silence.

"Catherine?" He put all the aggrieved male frustration he could into her name. It gained him nothing. He could hear her moving about in the room. He barely kept a lid on his temper. "Aren't you going to answer me?"

"What did you want to know again?"

He growled and heard an echo. A quick look showed him Lord Romeo sitting at the top of the steps. The cat stared at him with that intense curiosity peculiar to him.

"The morning wasn't bad enough. It only wanted you to show up."

"What's that you're mumbling, Mayfield?"

"I wasn't talking to you. I said that to the cat. I want an answer. If I promise—"

"Oh, yes. You promise sweet nothings. I marry you. I forget the bet. You know, Mayfield, your mind might be showing early signs of dementia. I add that up and come out with two minuses for me and only one for you. Equality, remember?"

He was suffering from dementia? She dared say that! If anyone's moods indicated mental illness... Greg froze. The whole conversation replayed in his mind. Crying. Baby. No baby. More crying. Teasing. Calling him Mayfield. He hit his temple with the heel of his hand. And he had bragged that between his sister and the women he'd known, there was little she could keep secret.

Whistling, he walked away.

She heard him go and was tempted to open the door. Had she driven him off with this latest refusal? But if she gave in now...no, she wasn't even going to think about doing that.

She finished dressing, made her bed and generally delayed as long as she could.

When Catherine opened her door, it was to find a few boxes from Nita's dress shop stacked there. Perched on top, like the decoration on a towering cake, was her best teacup. A sip of the still-warm liquid told her it was chamomile. How could he have known?

The man was weakening her resolve with his kindness. All without embarrassing her. She wanted to fight off the memory of the first time she had told Louis. It was painful to remember his disgusted reaction. He hadn't wanted to know. She developed a week-long series of headaches, and to provide her with comfort, he slept in one of the guest rooms. No one, from his father to the multitude of servants they employed, thought anything wrong with the arrangement.

She had a feeing that Greg wouldn't be like that. He'd comfort and cuddle and spoil her. He wouldn't shun her. No wonder he walked away whistling. He had it all figured out. She did, too. All that stood in her way was pride. Still in a thoughtful mood, she went down to the kitchen. She could hear Greg hammering with his usual audience, judging from the horses hitched to the corral fence. She could no longer see him or his henhouse. The tent canvas had been nailed to poles to prevent each other from seeing the almost completed work.

Mary had opened the door to a stranger and his child in need and found love. Had she done the very same thing?

Chapter Twenty-Two

From the kitchen window, Catherine watched with dismay as additional poles and canvas were erected on Greg's side of the barn.

What was he building? A two-story addition to the barn?

She couldn't ask. After their last squabble over their respective projects, they had agreed not to talk about them to maintain some peace.

But she worried about him. He worked up on ladders most of the time.

And she had other, more pressing problems to think about. They were building chicken coops, but the hens were off their feed and the egg count was down.

And Miss Lily was missing.

The first problem was easily solved. She had to get rid of all the company they had had these past few weeks. People constantly milling about, walking in and out of the barn, disturbed her flock. She had tried to put a stop to it and ended up with a group of irate males. Almost every man had bet money that Greg would win. They came out at all hours to check his progress. They no longer offered well-meaning advice.

A few had come to blows over the right and wrong way to build a henhouse.

Greg, true to his contrary and most honest nature, had his own vision in mind.

Catherine's hand faltered on the pot she was scrubbing.

He would never forgive her for what she had done.

She simply had to know, and last night, after making sure he was asleep, she had gone outside to sneak a peek at what he had built.

It truly was a brief look. But she was certain that in all the history of mankind, no chickens had ever been housed in so grand a creation. If the man added one more embellishment, the structure would collapse.

There was no doubt in her mind that she would win the bet.

It was what she had worked hard toward, what she really wanted.

Wasn't it?

Nita, bless her interfering soul, had told her repeatedly it was not. What did she know?

What Catherine knew was that Nita had become an unsuspected problem. She also had her own suspicions that Nita was behind the sabotage that had slowed her progress. The woman meant well. Catherine believed her when she claimed that she only wanted her happiness.

But singing Greg's praises within his presence was calculated to get her back up.

Catherine shrugged. She couldn't explain the contradicting feelings to herself. She finished washing the lunch dishes.

When the last plate had been dried and put away in the cupboard, she went outside and reminded everyone that Caroline's engagement party started at seven.

There was an argument in progress, but she retreated into the house.

She could be thankful that Caroline, too busy with plans, hadn't joined forces with Nita. The brief times she had seen her friend, she had marveled at the changes in her. Peter had proposed to her after the box lunch social. He didn't want a short courting period and quiet wedding. Caroline, so in love with him, willingly put aside her wishes for his.

Catherine knew she had more backbone than that.

Later, staring into her mirror, she wondered where her backbone had gone. She gave in without a squeak of protest and wore one of Greg's gifts.

His impeccable taste and Nita's talented hands made her appear a new woman. She felt new from the skin out, for all the underpinnings had accompanied the gown.

She ran her hand over the bronze grosgrain silk panel below the pointed bodice. The side panels were trimmed with six bands of bronze gimp. Beading edged the cuffs and the oval neckline. It was elegant, and in the very height of fashion with its satin ribbon bow perched on the bustle.

She pinned a smaller bronze satin bow with a few French rosebuds attached to her upswept hair. A shawl of black silk Spanish guipure lace rested on her almost bare shoulders.

"Backbone, Catherine?" she asked her reflection, and then answered, "Sometimes a woman makes small sacrifices."

She lifted her hem, smiling at the kid slippers. Greg had provided them, too. She opened her bedroom door just as he opened his.

Greg lost his breath somewhere for a few seconds. Had he been out of his mind in truth? What had possessed him to ask her to wear that particular gown tonight? That damn neckline dipped low enough to reveal the soft rise of her breasts! He wasn't going to be the only man to notice, either! His heart beat fast, and heat filled him as he drew in one ragged breath after the other.

Catherine was frozen in place on the threshold of her bedroom. She had to moisten her lips before she could ask him what was wrong.

"You look positively green, Greg."

"Green?" Wasn't that the color of jealousy? Jealous? He didn't have a jealous bone in his body. He'd never objected to another man's admiration of his latest lady love. But this was Catherine, for the love of all saints! His Catherine! He was overcome with the force of a possessive male need to wrap her in a blanket and lock her in her room.

Preferably with him.

"Greg, please, don't torment me. Didn't I button and tie everything in its place? Is the color all wrong? The hem sagging? What is wrong? Are you having second thoughts? Don't you want to be seen with me?"

"Not seen, there's a thought, but no..." He shook his head. "I love the way you look. A spun-sugar creation to tempt the most jaded appetite. Just like something my French chef would create to entice my dinner guests into bursts of rapture. Beautiful. Lovely. Did I buy that flimsy excuse for a shawl? Don't you have something warmer? Heavier?"

Catherine's fear that he *had* lost his mind gave way to confusion, and then slow dawning of what was truly wrong. A cat-licking-the-cream smile creased her lips.

"There is an old horse-blanket jacket hanging on the back door. Is that more what you had in mind? Or I could," she couldn't resist adding, for his eyes had this strange unfocused glazing, "snatch the quilt from my bed. That would cover me from neck to feet."

"Yes."

The word came from between gritted teeth with a choked, growling sound.

"Having a fit, are we?" She had no mercy in her eyes, less in her voice.

"Tell me, sweet Catherine, do you bother to use a knife when you dine, or is your tongue sharp enough without?"

She stepped across the hall and took hold of his arm. "Poor love. That would depend on what's being served."

"Meaning?"

"Food or you." She turned and offered an arched, innocent look and was thoroughly kissed for her sass.

She tasted that kiss for most of the evening. The fiddlers were in fine form, helped no doubt by a few trips out the back door of Caroline's house, where a jug was stashed in nearly every wagon.

Most of the parlor furniture had been cleared from the room, and couples crowded the floor to dance.

Caroline had never looked lovelier. She simply glowed every time she held out her hand to show off the emerald-and-diamond ring that Peter had given her. It had been his mother's, and Caroline had shown her where she had wrapped string around the band to make it fit her smaller finger.

Catherine thought her glow was catching. Each time she was apart from Greg, her gaze sought him out and found that he was looking at her.

There was a great deal of laughter, especially when toasts were made to the engaged couple.

"Peter, you remember that the best way to get married is with ignorance and confidence," Marcus Jobe said.

"Never mind," Ollie said. "You treat her well. Take good care of that gal. I'm a mite fond of her pies."

Caroline's cheeks flamed hot when Ollie finished. She opened her mouth to answer him, but Nita beat her.

"Ollie, ain't you heard that if women are foolish, it's 'cause the good Lord made them a match for a man?"

There was a great deal of laughter and clapping from the women.

And so it went around the room, with most people offering good wishes for their happiness. It was Greg's turn next, and he tried to do the same, but a few men wanted more from him.

"Tell us what those eastern dudes say," someone called out to him.

"About the same advice."

But no one was satisfied with his evasive answer.

"All right. All right, be quiet. Peter, Caroline," Greg said, lifting his punch glass. "Try not to make his ring around your finger feel like a rope around his neck, Caroline, for we all know that a man is incomplete until he falls in love, and then he's simply finished."

Hoots and catcalls followed, while he offered more sincere and appropriate felicitations to the happy couple. Shouts for Catherine to make a toast brought quiet to the room.

Some enterprising soul shouted for her to go Greg one better. She doubted she could, but a wink from Caroline told her she had better try.

"Peter, if Caroline can't make you miserable, she can't make you happy. Caroline, if you can't tease him, he isn't in love with you, for a day without a laugh shared makes for a sorry marriage.''

"Got you there, boy," Ollie said, slapping Greg's back. "Go get her, son. We're all countin' on you."

Greg's gaze found Catherine's. He lifted his near empty glass. "You know you're in love when there are only two places in the world...where she is and where she isn't.''

He earned boos from his male cohorts, but sighs from the women. Catherine, being urged to respond, felt as if she were in the middle of town without a stitch on as all eyes focused on her.

She couldn't respond in kind. The message she saw in his eyes was too intimate, too private to be shared.

In the end, her sense of humor rescued her.

"As every married woman knows, there are two very important things a man must do to keep his wife happy. First, he must let her think she's getting her way. And second—" she paused and smiled "—he's got to let her have it.''

"Gotcha, boy." Nita hooted. "You best remember that when a woman's had her say, you'd be plum loco to start it up again.''

"I'll drink to that." Greg drained his glass, set it down and came to fetch Catherine for the next dance, a waltz.

"Have I told you how beautiful you are, Catherine?''

"Tonight?''

"I don't think I've said it enough times. I don't believe I'll ever tire of telling you that." His hand tightened its hold on hers. "When can we safely leave? I want very much to make love to you.''

She gazed into his eyes, already dark with need, and felt an immediate response echo within her. "Soon.

But first they expect us to announce when the grand unveiling will be."

"Tomorrow?"

"Yes, that's fine." She was floating in his arms, but drowning in the hot, silent promise of his eyes.

"Late afternoon, Catherine?"

"Very late."

He swirled her to the space where the laden tables were. "That's good that we agree. I love a biddable woman."

"As much as I love a biddable man."

His lips grazed her bare shoulder as the last note of music died away. "I always wondered if satin had a taste all its own. Now I know." He raised her hand to his lips, but turned it over so his lips kissed her wrist. He lingered just long enough to know her pulse raced as madly as his own.

They waited until the fiddlers retired for their liquid refreshments before they made the announcement. It was almost an hour before Greg made good their escape.

Chapter Twenty-Three

They drove home slowly, content with each other's company and comfortable with the silence between them.

He surprised her when he finished unhitching the buggy and turned the horse into the corral.

"Will you dance with me?"

"Here?"

"Anywhere, Catherine."

She floated within his arms in the yard beneath the moon's glow, the music of rustling cottonwood leaves provided by a cool breeze. The waltzing circle grew smaller and smaller, until they stood swaying together.

Catherine averted her gaze from the shrouded hen-houses. She wanted nothing to break this almost magical spell.

From far off came the cry of a coyote and the horses moved restlessly within the corral.

He stole a kiss and whispered it was time to go inside. "And, Catherine, tonight, only one rule applies."

With her hand in his as he led the way, he opened the back door. "Aren't you going to ask what it is?"

"You'll tell me. You always do." She heard the dreamy tone of her voice and smiled.

"No rules at all." He stole her hair ornament and shawl halfway through the kitchen.

She stole his tie.

Greg pocketed her hairpins in the hallway.

Catherine unbuttoned his vest.

On the first step he launched a tender assault on her mouth. He lifted her high and swirled her slowly around and she lost her slippers.

"I love the way your skin looked in the moonlight." He paid homage to every bit his lips could find.

She teased him with kisses scattered everywhere but his lips and slid his jacket from his shoulders.

Halfway up the stairs, he told her about his dream.

She did her best to inspire him, reward him and make his fantasy come true. Never had her hands been as quick or clever. His shirt and studs fell to the floor below. Her stockings and bodice soon followed.

"No fair," she whispered. "I'm wearing far more than you."

"No rules, remember, but I'll soon remedy your pressing problem." His lips briefly caressed hers, before moving to her throat, her ear, where he delicately feathered his breath over the shapely shell. He nibbled her lobe, patient, sweetly seductive as he sat with her across his lap.

But the snap of her skirt buttons, the rip of the petticoat ties told her his need was as heated as her own.

Yet he continued to kiss her with unhurried leisure, his hand courting the flare of her hip, the indentation of her waist, the unfettered rise of her breast. The small needy sound she made drove him crazy. His fingers deftly untied her corset strings as his own fantasy came to life.

Her luscious mouth promised heaven with kisses that were tinted with wine-flavored punch. Her touches on his bare skin sent small claws of desire to heighten his pleasure. He gathered her loose hair in a gentle fist, drawing her head back against his shoulder. Every slow, plunging thrust of his tongue lured her to lose herself in the dark magic of passion's dance.

Under the warm caress of his hand, the ribbon tie of her camisole opened. He deserted her mouth to taste this newly revealed treasure. His thumb and forefinger stroked one crest into pouting hardness.

Catherine couldn't draw a breath as blood rushed to fill sensitive skin. Her hand clasped his neck and she moaned.

"More, Catherine?" he inquired, his voice deep and rich with the desire that thickened it as he gently rubbed the tip of her breast.

"Please," she whispered, her eyes closed. Her body arched into his with erotic grace.

"I'll share another pleasure with you," he murmured. He nestled her breast's softness within his palm, rolling his lips over the nipple, tenderly stroking it with his tongue.

"Better?"

"Yes. Yes." Her fingers found that the strength of his body was all she had to anchor her dizzy descent into his pleasure-rich world of passion. Her body was no longer her own to govern, but his. She felt full, swollen with a lush heaviness that drew her blood to the peak suckled within his mouth.

He coaxed and teased her to new heights, feeling the

strain of controlling his desire to be buried deep within her.

She whispered in a fretful voice that her clothes were in the way. His rich laughter filled the hallway.

Her hand tunneled through his hair. She stroked his shoulders, his upper arms, then touched his throat with her lips. She drew back and whispered her words against his mouth.

"You said I would never doubt that you wanted me. Can you have any doubts that I want you as much?" Her voice was husky with want, her gaze imploring.

"Now, Catherine?"

"Now."

Their lips met in greedy, sharp-set passion.

She was a fire in his blood. He lifted her free of her silken cloth and brought her down to straddle his thighs. His mouth closed over hers possessively, fueling his need to lose himself in the sweetly heated scent of her.

"Mine," he whispered. "Tell me you're mine."

Catherine heard his demand. She clung tighter to him, answering his hard and hungry kisses. Feelings rose to the surface. She desired him, yet desire was not the force that made her answer the rawness of his passion.

It was the power of the need in his voice that made her admit that she loved him. Loved him beyond reason.

"Do you want me?" The words were harshly uttered; he had no softness left.

She gripped his shoulders, shuddering. "All I want is you."

He pressed her closer, lifting her up and into him, rubbing her over the hardened swell of his sex, and both of them shuddered. Her mouth opened under the force of his, his tongue taking her into the deep-heavy rhythm that she instinctively responded to.

She felt the new callus on the hands that slid up the length of her thighs. His lips closed over one erect nipple, suckling so strongly that her back arched and she cried out. There was a quickening inside her that gloried in the wildness of his mouth, the surge of his body, hot and hard against hers. The sleek skin of his back bore the crescent nail marks she left as she hotly sheathed him.

His groan came from deep inside his throat. He lifted her with deliberate slowness, then lowered her once more. With his hands on her hips, he rose to meet her peaking ardor, and she cried out again as violently intense sensations flooded her body.

Greg clamped his teeth together, a savage need washing over him. Feverishly he drove upward, plunging her over the edge. One of his hands caught her hair, dragging her mouth to his. He crushed her lips as she melted against him, and with a last violent thrust, he joined her.

The intensity diminished slowly between them. Catherine lay against him, tiny tremors still racking her body. The soft caress of his hands on her bare back lulled her into a quiescent state. Their heartbeats slowed in unison, as did their ragged breathing. She toyed with his hair, her lips nuzzling his neck.

"Sweetheart, I need to get you upstairs to bed."

"Must we move at all?" He was still hard within her, and she gently shifted her hips, increasing the tremors to a heated trembling inside her.

"That is one of the things I adore about you, Catherine. You're as hungry as I am. But no more for you."

His words lacked conviction. He swelled inside her, his passion rekindled as if he hadn't made love to her.

"Are you still hungry? Show me."

He smiled at the provocative invitation. The slow, gliding rotation of her hips enforced her demand. She nipped his earlobe.

"I should take you up to bed." But his hands came to rest on the flare of her hips as his mouth sought hers.

"Yes. Yes, take me."

His kisses coaxed, giving and then taking when her mouth softened with a sigh. Against him, her body yielded. And all he wanted to do was cherish her.

His tender, slow touches, the patient, fluid dance of love tempered the wild need running through her. He lingered where he knew it pleased her most, softly, ever sensitive to her need. She floated in that darkened space, rich with the scents they created, his voice a dark murmur of lover's promise, a music that captured and held her heart. She wrapped her arms around him as he slowly built the pace, letting the desire sweep her up, only to begin all over again.

She was lost in him, and knew he felt it, too. He told her with his groan, his whispers and sighs. She answered with the catch of her breath, a moan, a plea, until passion poured through them like heated wine.

He had shown her hunger and tenderness, and now a loving storm. She went with him willingly, her mouth desperate on his, her body surrendering to each shattering climb and fall. And begged him for more.

Her fingertip touched the taut line of his lips, the edge of his teeth gently caught and held it. She was lost in pleasure. Her head fell back. She cried out as he held himself still, and then she clutched him tight and he was dragged over the edge with her.

She didn't remember the climb into bed or dozing off safe in his arms. But when she woke in the darkness, she knew what she had to do.

Chapter Twenty-Four

Exhausted, Catherine stood by the kitchen window. She offered fervent prayers that it wouldn't rain today. Thick clouds rolled in from the north, filling the dawn sky.

She went back to stirring the grits she had cooking, then turned the ham steaks to brown on the other side. Greg was still sleeping, which was just as well. She had enough to worry about, without thinking of how to greet him.

Lord Romeo, like Miss Lily, was missing.

She had extended her search beyond the barn and the small outbuildings. She went with a lantern into the woods, calling them. All she heard was the rustling of small animals. Not one cackle, not one meow offered any hope they were close by.

She was startled by Greg wrapping his arms around her waist. He nuzzled her neck, made mock growling sounds and whispered of waking alone with a ferocious appetite.

"I was making breakfast."

"I know. I smelled the ham cooking." He turned

her within the circle of his arms and shared the first kiss of the day with her.

He lifted his head, searching each feature of her face, now as familiar as his own to him. "Today's the big day. But I want you to know that I won't hold you to marrying me, Catherine, if I win."

"You won't?"

"No. I made a decision last night. I can't force you over a bet. I want you to marry me because you love me."

She felt his arms free her as he turned to get coffee, so calm while she stood swaying. He slipped one hand into his pants' pocket, bunching the tail of his white, unbuttoned shirt over his hip, and sipped from his cup.

The decision she had made and acted upon had been a most difficult one. She had spent the long hours of the night examining her reasons to be sure it wasn't the impulsive act of a gratified lover. She had acted as a woman in love, and now he dared to tell her this!

And where was his declaration of love?

"The ham's burning, Catherine."

There was a smug smile on his lips, quickly hidden as he raised the cup again.

"So it is. The grits are burning, too."

"You're not very loverlike in the morning, sweetheart. Good thing I employ a chef to cook."

"And a maid?"

"Several. A housekeeper and butler, too."

"I'm surprised you don't have a boy to shine your shoes, and another to pick up after you. You must have at least three women just to wash and iron your white shirts."

"Only two. My valet supervises."

"Do you see how wrong we are for each other?"

Before he could summon an answer, she fled.

He ran as far as the back door. "Where are you going?"

"To look for my hen. It's a darn sight better than watching you crow."

He turned back and rescued his breakfast. She wouldn't run far. But at least he had erased that cloud of doubt from her eyes. And that's all that really mattered to him...Catherine's happiness.

Lord Romeo strolled inside and headed for his favorite perch on the windowsill. He eyed the dish Greg filled.

"I suppose you expect me to share my food as well as my love with you?"

The cat's meow could have been agreement. Greg took it as such. He broke a small piece of ham from his slice and blew on it to cool the meat before he offered it to the cat.

"Go on. Eat it. I've seen her spoil you. And you are going to get used to sharing with me. I intend to be around for a long time."

Lord Romeo snatched the meat from his palm but made no move to eat it.

Greg shook his head and sat down. He was halfway through his slice of ham when he looked up at the cat. He sat washing his paw. There was no sign of the ham.

"Don't think I'm bribing you or anything, but have some more." This time the cat didn't hesitate. Greg almost attempted to pet him, but thought better of it. One set of scars was enough for any man. Then the cat surprised him, actually shocked him. He left his perch and padded over to the table, where he jumped into Greg's lap.

Greg was thankful he was alone. He was sure there

was a ridiculous expression on his face. He didn't know what to do with his hands. He held them out at his sides. The cat did a half turn, then curled in his lap. Lord Romeo wasn't purring, but he wasn't growling, either.

And that's how Catherine found them.

She had returned from another futile search when thoughts of how unfair she'd been to Greg haunted her.

Greg watched her. Now he knew what he must have looked like. Her expression truly defied description. Shock, surprise, relief and laughter all crossed her features in seconds.

"Where did you find him?"

"I didn't. He found me."

"Whatever did you do to him? I can't believe I see him in your lap, Greg."

"It just goes to show you that I can win the affections of the most stubborn heart."

She looked to see him grinning. "Sure of yourself, Mayfield?"

"Desperate is more like it."

There was no smugness left in his eyes. Only the truth of what he said. Why that should make her smile, she didn't know, but it did.

"Don't get too cozy, wagons are turning in the drive. The men won't care what you look like, but I don't need swooning women on my hands."

"Did you find Miss Lily?"

"No. And I've got to accept that she's gone. I keep telling myself that—"

"Blaming yourself is more like it. Help me get him off my lap. Friendly as this appears, I don't trust him."

She tilted her head to the side, giving him a wary look. "Can I trust you?"

"Always. I would never betray your trust, Catherine. Unlike your friend here," he added to lighten the mood. He saw her back up a step when he answered, and heard the little sigh she released at the end. She skittered away from him like a banker after he'd heard your deal went bust. He didn't even know what he'd done to cause her to feel this way.

He heard the first wagons arrive and Ramon calling his name. "Catherine, take him." If his demand was sharp, who could blame him? He hadn't the privacy of the barn cat with her litter of kittens. A few hours more. He could wait. He had a lifetime ahead that was worth waiting for.

The yard took on the aspect of a party or a traveling circus, Catherine thought. Her friends and neighbors had brought covered dishes. The men had set out planks on the sawhorses to accommodate all the food. The three fiddlers from Caroline's engagement party—looking as hungover as she felt—were tuning up, ready to play. It was bedlam. Children ran around the yard, climbed on the corral fence and took turns swinging from the window in the barn loft where the pulley rope hung.

And there was Greg, moving among them with a smile firmly planted on his mouth, laughing and talking as if he had known these people all his life.

She wiped her damp palms down the sides of her pants. *Admit it. You're scared.*

What if he didn't understand what she'd done?

What if she had to explain it to him in front of everyone?

"Catherine?" Nita called, then came into the

kitchen. "Why are you hiding in here? We're all waiting for you."

"I'm going to be sick."

"You look a little green. Expectin', are you?"

"No! I'm just—"

"Nervous as any bride on her wedding day. Come on. Delaying ain't gonna cure what ails you." Nita took hold of her arm and led her outside. "Do you love him?"

Caroline stepped up to the other side.

Catherine looked from one to the other. "Do I require an escort?"

"Several women have placed bets, too, Catherine," said Caroline. "They were afraid you'd bolt. After all, it isn't every day that a woman's marriage hinges on how well she builds a henhouse." Caroline looked to Nita for support.

"Gal's got the right of it. But you ain't answered my question. Do you love him?"

"No, of course not. I'm making myself the laughingstock of the town because I despise the man and everything he stands for."

She nearly stumbled when Nita slapped her back with approval.

"Gal's got gumption just like Ollie said. You'll be happy to know that Mrs. Pettigrew took the stage this morning. Gone off to visit her daughter Irene in New Orleans. Adelaide finally showed some backbone and told her to stop interfering in her marriage. Kept Camilla here with her, too. See—" she pointed "—they're waiting on you, too."

Catherine felt her stomach churn. She faced a sea of faces but really wasn't seeing any of them. Only one face had the power to move her. And when she saw Greg, saw his wink, she squared her shoulders.

"You might have gussied up a bit, Catherine. Wore one of my gowns like you did at Caroline's party."

"Nita, you're all lucky I'm still here. Come on, I want to get this over with before that jug gets passed around. This is worse than any hanging in Santa Fe."

"She's got a bad case of the all-overs, ain't she?" Nita showed her teeth with her smile. "Gonna be hog-tied and brought to the altar before she takes a full breath."

Catherine didn't answer. She stood in front of Greg and the press of people around her made it hard to breathe.

"I think you should unveil yours first," she said, surprised she sounded calm. Once again she rubbed damp palms against her pants and felt against the pocket for the match safe.

"Are you sure, Catherine?" He gazed directly into her eyes, ignoring the hoots and calls to get on with it. He saw her bottom lip tremble. He was that close and that sensitive to every facial expression that was burned into his memory.

She nodded and forced a smile. "Good luck."

"And you." He wanted to say more. He needed to tell her he loved her. But people pushed and crowded them toward the canvas.

Nita shoved Catherine forward. She elbowed a few men aside to make room. "Go on, get up there next to him. That's where you belong. That's where your heart is telling you to be."

"Nita, I—"

A loud collective gasp cut Catherine off.

Greg ripped aside the canvas to reveal his idea of a

hen...house. Catherine swallowed. Hard. "House" didn't quite describe what he had built. Everyone, she saw, was at a loss for words. He had, with one stroke, effectively silenced them all.

But her love's pride was at stake.

"Greg," she cried out, "it's magnificent! Oh, to think I wasted my labor. My chickens would never even look at my poor effort when they can roost in such...such splendor!"

She turned to look at Nita, silently crying for help.

"Have you ever seen anything so grand, Nita?"

"Gal, I swear to you all, never have these poor old tired eyes of mine beheld such a sight." Her hand pressed her heart.

Catherine wasn't sure if it was an indication that she told the truth or that she was about to faint.

"Catherine?"

She faced Greg. "I meant every word. It's a glory. A wonder. A perfect...I'm running out of words." She faltered at the strange looks she received. But it was what Greg thought and felt that concerned her.

He watched her every breath. She smiled. Brightly. She nodded. She put her heart into her gaze. She knew what the others saw. A leaning towered creation that would likely collapse with the first strong wind. It partly resembled a castle. There was a walkway and a window. The front was narrower than the back. He'd even put double doors on the side. True, none of the hinges lined up, but they worked. She knew, because she had tried them. There wasn't a perch inside for the hens to roost on. A minor inconvenience. One had only to look at the tiers of roofs he had created. They rose two and three stories high. A few were flat, some were arched, others pitched. None of the joinings matched. So, what was a little rain for the hens?

"I love it." She had nothing to lose at this moment and everything to gain. Each word, each look and move had been calculated to sustain his pride, to win his love.

"Love it? You love it?" His heart was in his gaze. He lifted a hand toward her.

"I declare you the winner, Greg." She would never mention the slight tremble of the hand she grasped with her own.

She was compelled to fling her arms around his neck and kiss him with the pent-up emotions that had kept her awake most of the night.

"You can't declare him the winner, Catherine. It's for the rest to us to judge."

There was an angry murmur at the protest that Buck Purcell raised.

"Sore loser, Buck? Bet on Catherine, did you?" Ollie taunted.

"He's got a right to have his say," Caroline said. "Catherine would want this to be fair. Right?" she asked her friend.

"Yes. It is to be fairly judged. Just give me a minute and then you all come over to the other side."

She slipped from Greg's arms, ignoring his bewildered expression. She never saw the fist he planted in Buck's face. Nor the skinned knuckles he raised to his lips.

No one uttered a protest. Not even Caroline.

Catherine took a deep breath and went forward to the canvas around her henhouse. It was big enough for twenty laying hens. Plain as could be. She heard Greg shout her name. She dropped to her knees. Her hand shook. She couldn't breathe now, for the stench of the kerosene she had poured earlier to soak every bit of wood was overpowering.

"For his love," she whispered, and with a cry, she struck the match, flung it at the canvas and jumped back. With a loud whooshing sound the flames erupted.

She ran back around the barn. Smack into Greg.

He gripped her arms and held her away from him. "What the hell have you done?"

"Given you a wife," she answered, then dropped the match safe to the ground.

"Are you mad?" he demanded to know, shaking her. "You've burned your henhouse."

"I know."

"Answer me, Catherine. Are you mad?"

"Yes, answer him, Catherine!" the crowd shouted in chorus.

She flushed to the roots of her hair, and Greg glared at all who closed in on them.

"Mad? I suppose I am. I need to travel for my health. I understand that New York is lovely in the spring. I have it on good authority that the Paris countryside must not be missed in summer. And then—"

He kissed her. Quick and hard. Then he lifted his head to look down into her eyes.

Her chin rose, her gaze as direct as his. Smoke stung her eyes, but the tears came from the love that filled her heart.

"I love you, Catherine Rose." He tightened his arms around her and lifted her up with his lips sealed to hers. Slowly then, he turned them in a circle to everyone's enjoyment. He heard nothing of comments or cheers, only the roar of his blood.

"Mine. Truly won, and mine," he whispered against her lips.

"Do you love me, Gregory Mayfield?"

"I fell in love with a dream and found the dream was real."

Catherine clasped her hands on the back of his neck. Her head fell back and she demanded that he spin them faster. "Now, while I'm dizzy, ask me to marry you."

"Why, for heaven's sake?"

"I need an excuse to fall back on when we fight."

He fought not to laugh. "Planning to do lots of fighting, are we? But you'll need more than one excuse."

"Ask me, Mayfield."

He slowed, then stopped and lowered her to stand, but kept her caged within his embrace. "Will you be my love? The keeper of my dreams? Live with me? And laugh with me? Be mother to my children? Guardian of my heart? My wife, my wanton, my sweet enchantress? Obedient until death do us part?"

With her eyes closed, she had been murmuring yes to all his questions. Her eyes opened wide on hearing the last. "I can't promise that, Greg. No more than you could, or would."

"That's my Catherine, contrary to the end. Kiss me."

She offered her lips, cherishing the tenderness that flowed between them as much as she did the passion that flared to life.

"You two planning on burning the ground where you stand or helping us fight a real fire?" Nita pushed a bucket at Greg. "Right smart of you, Catherine, to soak the ground with water and clear the wood away. Pity, though. It was a real fine chicken house." She gave Greg a head-to-toe look and smiled. "Guess I can't blame you none. He's a prize, all right."

"Yes," Catherine answered softly, holding Greg's arm. "And he's all mine."

After the fire was out, they danced, for no one wanted to go home. It was then that Greg made his confession.

"I knew you were up to something, Catherine. Between us you won the bet, but I had a few more ready. And Nita was right. You built the better henhouse."

"You cheated? You—you—"

"Now, Catherine, don't make a scene." He held her tighter. "I've had enough of feeling like one of my sister's parrots with everyone gawking at us."

"Suzanne has parrots?"

"Six at last count. I wouldn't be surprised to find my brother-in-law living at his club. She has them in the drawing room, her dressing room, even the back parlor. There might be one on the upstairs sunporch."

"Greg?"

"What?" he asked, but wouldn't look at her.

"You're trying to distract me."

His gaze locked on hers. "It works every time, doesn't it? And as you have repeatedly pointed out to me, I'm a man. I use whatever means are at hand. Especially with such a prize at stake. I even had another bet all set for offering if this one hadn't worked."

"Another bet?" She knew by the tantalizing, charming smile he wore that she had fallen right in with whatever he had planned. It didn't seem to matter. "No doubts, Greg?" She had never searched so deeply for the truth as she gazed into her beloved's face.

"A few. Will I be a good husband? A good father? Will you always love me? And you?"

"About the same." She snuggled against him. No sense in upsetting him with her thoughts. She didn't want to tell him now that having a husband who was inept at a few things made her more his equal. Greg was very good at making money, and making her laugh, and kissing—she couldn't, wouldn't ever forget that—but most of all, he loved her just as she was.

Her head fell back. "About that other bet?"

"Later, after everyone's gone."

He drew Catherine to his side as the last wagon rumbled down the drive. "Want to bet I can find Miss Lily?"

"Is that find or already found?"

"Must you, to quote Ollie, split hairs over a word? In the joyous spirit that prevails in my heart at this moment in time, just say yes or no."

"Yes, but first I want to know what I win."

"You're pushing, Mrs. Soon-to-be Mayfield."

"I know. It seems to be one of the things you love about me."

"Such a smug woman. We have a bet, and the prize...let me think what I want." He cupped her shoulders and turned her to face him. Moonlight shimmered in her eyes. "My prize is that you never change, Catherine. No matter what, never change the woman you are."

She threw her arms around his neck, burying her face against his chest.

For once he needed no words. He accepted her nod and the slight dampening of his shirt. He took her hand after a few minutes and led her into the barn, passing the stalls to the tack room, where he'd left a lantern lit.

He moved from Catherine's side to lift an old crate aside. "There's where she's been hiding."

On old sacking, the hen had made a nest of straw.

Peeking beneath her feathers was a tiny beak. The hen's eyes were bright as she watched them. A muffled cheep left no doubt that Miss Lily had finally hatched one of her stolen eggs.

Greg took his love in his arms and gazed into her eyes. "New life, Catherine. I guess I'll order more lumber. She deserves a henhouse all her own." He pecked at her nose. And smiled. "But this time, love, you do the building."

Her laughter rang out, sweet and joyous, joined by his deeper, masculine sound.

And in her heart, she echoed his words...a new life was just beginning for them.

Epilogue

Between wedding and travel arrangements, the time of waiting for Sarah to return passed quickly. And now Catherine faced her wedding day. She had a telegram, her first, from Suzanne, who was already planning a ball in their honor. She knew Greg understood without her explaining the need that she had to be married here, surrounded by friends, before she began her journey with him.

And Lord Romeo.

Greg had established a truce of sorts with the cat. Never once did he complain about the hairs he had to brush from almost every article of clothing he owned. Of course, contrary cat that Lord Romeo was, he never went near the clothing while Greg was wearing it. He would wait and then sneak into the wardrobe.

Catherine swore to Greg that this was a hopeful sign that the cat felt affection for him.

Greg still had his doubts.

She turned from her window as Sarah came into the room. "It's time?"

"Yes. You've a very impatient groom. I wish that Mary could be here. Greg is so in love with you, Catherine, just like Rafe adores Mary and their new son. You look lovelier than I've ever seen you.''

They hugged each other, Sarah making her wishes for her friend's happiness, and Catherine feeling the bittersweetness of having to leave Sarah behind.

''I'm wrinkling your gown. I still don't understand why you chose to wear this old one.''

''Greg understands. I leave this behind and with it the memories of a first marriage.''

Sarah smiled at her. ''I shall miss you. You brought laughter back into my life, Catherine.''

''You'll come and visit. Promise?'' Catherine asked as she picked up the bouquet of roses that Camilla had clipped from her mother's garden.

''We'll see. Rafe and Mary have promised to visit when the baby's a little older. I think he has her convinced to travel with him this time. Now, before Greg comes looking for you, which is bad luck, let's go down.''

But at the door, Catherine stopped her. ''Sarah, do you realize that both Mary and I opened the door to strangers that we fell in love with?''

Sarah shook her head. ''Ah, Catherine, you'll never change. Such fanciful thoughts.''

''Well, it could happen. One dark night, some man will come knocking, and before you know it, you'll marry again, too.''

''But who would be the merry widow of Sierra County then? Not that it matters for you to answer. I won't be getting married a second time. And no more talk. You have love waiting...go on.''

Catherine took a breath and started down the steps. She didn't turn, but had to have the last word. ''Just think about the possibility, Sarah. That's all I ask. If a man that's not old enough to be your father walks through that front door, you'll give him every chance.''

But Catherine had reached the bottom of the steps and found Greg waiting. His gaze narrowed her world to only him. Hand in hand, they walked to stand before the minister in the parlor. And there, love's promises were made.

When the rainstorms came, Sarah had reason to recall Catherine's words. It didn't quite happen as she had thought. It wasn't a door but a window that brought a man into her life. And he wasn't old at all...

* * * * *

Four Bright New Stars!
Harlequin Historical™ launches its *March Madness* celebration with these four exciting historical romance debuts:

THE MAIDEN AND THE WARRIOR
By Jacqueline Navin
A fierce warrior is saved by the love of a spirited
maiden bride.

LAST CHANCE BRIDE
By Jillian Hart
A lonely spinster finds hope in the arms of an embittered
widower.

GABRIEL'S HEART
By Madeline George
An ex-sheriff must choose between revenge or the feisty
socialite who has stolen his heart.

A DUKE DECEIVED
By Cheryl Bolen
A handsome duke falls for a penniless noblewoman
whom he must marry in haste.

Look for all four books from four fabulous new authors
wherever Harlequin Historicals are sold.

Coming in August 1997!

THE BETTY NEELS RUBY COLLECTION

August 1997—Stars Through the Mist
September 1997—The Doubtful Marriage
October 1997—The End of the Rainbow
November 1997—Three for a Wedding
December 1997—Roses for Christmas
January 1998—The Hasty Marriage

COLLECTOR'S EDITION

This August start assembling the
Betty Neels Ruby Collection. Six of the
most requested and best-loved titles have
been especially chosen for this collection.
From August 1997 until January 1998,
one title per month will be available to avid
fans. Spot the collection by the lush ruby red
cover with the gold Collector's Edition banner
and your favorite author's name—Betty Neels!

Available in August at your favorite retail outlet.

◆ HARLEQUIN®

DEBBIE MACOMBER

invites you to the

★ ♥ HEART OF TEXAS ★

Join Debbie Macomber as she brings you the lives
and loves of the folks in the ranching community
of Promise, Texas.

If you loved Midnight Sons—don't miss
Heart of Texas! A brand-new six-book series
from Debbie Macomber.

Available in February 1998
at your favorite retail store.

Heart of Texas by Debbie Macomber

Lonesome Cowboy	February '98
Texas Two-Step	March '98
Caroline's Child	April '98
Dr. Texas	May '98
Nell's Cowboy	June '98
Lone Star Baby	July '98

HARLEQUIN®

HPHRT1

KEY TO MY HEART

Unlock the secrets of romance just in time for the most romantic day of the year—Valentine's Day!

Key to My Heart
features three of your favorite authors,

Kasey Michaels,
Rebecca York
and Muriel Jensen,

to bring you wonderful tales of romance and Valentine's Day dreams come true.

As an added bonus you can receive Harlequin's special Valentine's Day necklace. FREE with the purchase of every *Key to My Heart* collection.

Available in January,
wherever Harlequin books are sold.

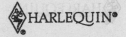

**Make a Valentine's date
for the premiere of**

HARLEQUIN® **Movies**

starting February 14, 1998 with

Debbie Macomber's

This Matter of

Marriage

on **the movie channel**

Just tune in to **The Movie Channel** the **second Saturday night** of every month at 9:00 p.m. EST to join us, and be swept away by the sheer thrill of romance brought to life. Watch for details of upcoming movies—in books, in your television viewing guide and in stores.

If you are not currently a subscriber to The Movie Channel, simply call your local cable or satellite provider for more details. Call today, and don't miss out on the romance!

the movie channel
*100% pure movies.
100% pure fun.*

HARLEQUIN™
Makes any time special.™

An Alliance Production

HMBPA298